A Perp by Any Other Name

"We have a lead in our search for the elusive Charles de Gaulle," Clouseau announced, marching up to his superior's desk.

"Yes, get on with it," the chief inspector replied.

"Although no one bearing that illustrious name boarded a flight out of Paris on the day of Bellafonte's murder, a passenger with the name and passport of one—" Clouseau opened his Louis Vuitton notebook and turned a page. "Yes, here it is. One Paul Gauguin *was* aboard Flight 1069 bound for John F. Kennedy Airport."

Charles Dreyfus stared. "And?"

Clouseau handed him a piece of paper. "Gauguin's passport photo."

"This man looks exactly like Napoleon Bonaparte."

"Indeed!" Clouseau closed his designer notebook with a snap. "I suspect this 'Paul Gauguin,' who resembles Napoleon Bonaparte, is not, in fact, the late painter Gauguin, father of modern art, but the very same man who pretended to be Charles de Gaulle! He is the serial murderer we seek!"

"You suspect that, do you?" Dreyfus replied. "Well, I should hope so. It's a fairly tiny leap of reason, even for a moron such as yourself."

"Why thank you, sir!"

Pink Panther Books
From HarperEntertainment

THE PINK PANTHER'S JUST DESSERTS
by Marc Cerasini and Alice Alfonsi

THE PINK PANTHER GETS LUCKY
by Marc Cerasini and Alice Alfonsi

and

THE PINK PANTHER
by Max Allan Collins

The
Pink Panther's
Just Desserts

MARC CERASINI and ALICE ALFONSI

HarperEntertainment
An Imprint of HarperCollinsPublishers

This is a work of fiction. Names, characters, places, and incidents are products of the author's imagination or are used fictitiously and are not to be construed as real. Any resemblance to actual events, locales, organizations, or persons, living or dead, is entirely coincidental.

🏛
HARPERENTERTAINMENT
An Imprint of HarperCollins*Publishers*
10 East 53rd Street
New York, New York 10022-5299

ISBN-13: 978-0-06-079331-9
ISBN-10: 0-06-079331-7

First HarperEntertainment paperback printing: November 2006

Printed in the United States of America

Visit HarperEntertainment on the World Wide Web at
www.harpercollins.com

10 9 8 7 6 5 4 3 2 1

To the beloved Pink Panther director
Blake Edwards
*because, as medical science has recently confirmed,
laughter makes our hearts last longer.*

ARS GRATIA ARTIS

Assigning Jacques Clouseau to a brand-new case involved the efforts of a number of people, which is why the authors would like to pause for a moment and shout out a big *"Merci!"* to the following individuals:

Sarah Durand, Senior Editor, HarperCollins, for her cheerful support, great suggestions, and shared appreciation of the Iron Chef's secret ingredient;

Hope Innelli, Associate Publisher, HarperCollins, for the all-important start and shared appreciation of a really good plate of pasta;

Jon Rosenberg, Executive Director, Publishing, MGM Consumer Products, and everyone at MGM who participated in making this book happen, as well as all of the grand people at the MGM Grand in Las Vegas, especially ...

Angelo Giancola, Front Services Manager; Barry Rushakoff, Bell Desk Supervisor; Jim McDaniel, Executive Director of Security; William R. Frishkorn, Assistant Concierge Manager, Skylofts.

Personal thanks also to our family and friends for their great good humor and unflagging support, especially: (Dad) Antonio A. Alfonsi; Ethel DeIuliis; Grace Alfonsi, M.D.; George Capaldo, M.D; Alex and Andrew Capaldo; Vance, Debbie, and Tia Cerasini; our financial advisor Roy A. Snyder; and our literary agent John Talbot.

(Okay, all done! So start the book already!)

CONTENTS

Contents

I will decide what is ridiculous!

—Inspector Jacques Clouseau,
A Shot in the Dark

The
Pink Panther's
Just Desserts

Prologue

In a cool, quiet forest northwest of Bordeaux, Claude Bellafonte hiked briskly along a leaf-strewn path. "Ah, Brigitte," he murmured, "the morning is magnificent, is it not?"

Bellafonte had been with his beloved Brigitte for so many years, he knew her every mood, her every expression. At present, he took delight in the pink bloom on her fair cheeks; the ardent gleam in her soft, dark eyes; the spry, coltish energy in her shapely legs as they hastened to keep up with him—an obvious sign of her keen anticipation of their impending ritual. That thought alone sent a shiver of delight through the Frenchman's compact form.

"I tell you, my love," Claude cooed, "it thrills my heart to see you so eager, so ready!"

Spying a cluster of oak and wild walnut trees bordering a

grassy knoll, he gently touched Brigitte's waist. "Here, my sweet. This spot is perfect."

Well into his fifties, Bellafonte knew another man might be tired after such a breathless trek. Instead, he felt as alive and vital as a man half his age!

"I will make myself ready, my love," he said. "In but a moment."

After shrugging the heavy pack off his narrow shoulders, Bellafonte set the canvas bag on the ground. He yanked off his jacket, shivering a bit as the autumn air penetrated his thin shirt, chilling his lean, pale frame.

Brigitte shifted her feet and uttered an impatient sound.

"Just another moment," Bellafonte promised.

Fearing she would lose the mood, he hastily fumbled through his canvas bag and drew out the leather apron. With practiced movements, he slipped it over his head, tied the cords behind his back, then reached into the bag again and removed his leather gloves.

"Almost . . ." he said as he slipped them on.

Brigitte brushed her quivering flanks against his legs in a sensuous, almost catlike gesture. Bellafonte's senses were heightened, and the blood sang in his ears. Now came the critical moment. Would his Brigitte willingly comply with his wishes—or resist?

Once more, he dipped his hand into the bag. Brigitte squealed when she saw the muzzle. As she took one step backward and looked away, he sighed with relief. He understood his love well enough to know when she was truly resisting and when she was simply being coy.

"Come, come, Brigitte! You are familiar with this part of our little game! You know what must be done."

With a gentle but firm hand, he steadied her. She submitted. Her naked belly rubbed against the soft loam as she lowered her head until her eyes saw only dark soil, yellow grass. Efficiently, the Frenchman slipped the hard leather muzzle over her long snout, linked the buckle across the bristling fur on the back of Brigitte's stout neck.

"That is not so bad, is it?"

The bristling pig snorted, the sound slightly muffled by the jaw-locking muzzle.

"And now, the hunt begins, eh!"

Chef Claude Bellafonte slapped Brigitte's flanks and watched her short legs scurry to the tree line, where her snout began digging up the topsoil, searching for culinary gems.

Bellafonte was, of course, one of the greatest truffle farmers in all of France. Since he'd been a boy, learning the art of the *trufficulteur* on his grandfather's knee, he had marveled that one of the most expensive, most elusive and precious foods in the world was best located by the lowly pig. Of course, carefully trained dogs could also find the savory fungus, a highly prized delicacy that grew at the base of walnut, oak, and chestnut trees, but their noses were far less keen that the swine's.

The only drawback to the pig was the animal's proclivity to gobble up the black diamond—understandable in the face of such a delicacy. Fortunately, the problem was solved through the use of the muzzle.

"Wheeee! Wheeee!" Brigitte squawked, her snout nuzzling the ground near the base of a century-old oak tree. The limbs were twisted, the bark dull and weathered.

"Brigitte! You have the scent already?"

Pushing aside some brush, Bellafonte observed the pig as it dug with its front hooves. Producing a tether, he roped the squirming swine to the stout bole of the oak, pulling her back before she could damage the prize.

The Pink Panther's Just Desserts

In the shade of the spreading branches, Bellafonte fell to his knees. Truffles lurked between three and twelve inches under the surface, near the root of the tree and never beyond the range of its branches. With his gloved hands, he carefully moved the soil and gasped.

"Mon dieu . . ."

He had unearthed a black truffle—one of the largest he had ever seen! Since the time of the ancient Greeks and Romans, the black truffle had been treasured, and, when harvested at the peak of ripeness, could fetch two or three times its own weight in gold. This one was a veritable fortune. Its irregularly shaped dome was larger than a soccer ball, its thick, coarse exterior craggy as the surface of some mysterious, undiscovered planet.

The pungent flesh of truffles, mingled with the odor of newly turned soil, made Chef Bellafonte dizzy and delirious. He marveled at variegated shades the black diamond's wrinkled flesh. Hues ran from ruddy brown to darkest ebony, and the fungi could not be riper or more perfect. One touch of human flesh against the fungus would cause the truffle to rot, which is why Claude always wore gloves and a leather apron—and also why he held it safely away from his face as he deeply inhaled its rustic fragrance.

Bellafonte's revelry was interrupted by Brigitte's grunt as she strained at her leash a few feet away. "What is it, my love? Your stomach?" Bellafonte asked, his eyes still feasting on the massive truffle.

The French chef heard another sound. An animal rumble—distressing, but still piglike.

"Sacré bleu, Brigitte!" Bellafonte cried. "Is it the truffle you want? Are you not full enough from that third helping of crêpes I made you for breakfast?!"

4

Prologue

But the low growl did not come from his beloved pig. It emerged from a tangle of brush just beyond the range of the oak tree's branches. Sensing the danger, Brigitte snapped her tether and dashed into the forest. Bellafonte, however, remained rooted to the spot as the slavering beast stalked into view.

The horror of claws and tusks and ivory horns finally galvanized the man. Bellafonte rose to flee, but with a wet snarl, the creature lurched forward and sank its fangs into the calf of the terrified human, bringing him down in a nightmare of slashing claws and gnashing teeth.

Chef Claude Bellafonte, still gripping his prize truffle, watched the world fade blacker than the perfect dark diamond in his dying hands.

ONE

The Stench of Murder

A noisy armada of emergency vehicles invaded the serene forests of the Périgord Vert region. Lights flashing and sirens howling, the police cars and ambulances crisscrossed rutted ground, spewing exhaust fumes into the spreading branches of walnut, oak, and chestnut trees.

Tromping through a once-tranquil grove, a veritable army of blue-coated policemen shared the damp grass beside a host of white-coated forensics specialists flown in by helicopter from the Sûreté's crime lab in Paris.

The circle of human chaos extended beyond this remote farmer's field to a rural road a half-kilometer away. There the national press gathered, awaiting a statement from the authorities on the bizarre and mysterious death of Claude Bellafonte, France's greatest *trufficulteur* and one of the most celebrated pastry chefs in the world—his lobster in puffed pastry with truffle hollandaise literally made gourmands swoon.

In the eye of the storm, among the forensic investigators, Chief Inspector Dreyfus surveyed the corpse of the victim. At his side stood Monsieur Pierre Marmiche, trade minister for the French government.

Marmiche had the look of many similarly polished EU politicians. In his middle years, he sported a thick head of dark hair, graying at the temples, regular features, and a beautifully tailored wardrobe. Today's suit was blue silk pinstripes. Unfortunately, like all politicians, the man didn't know when to stop talking. His headache-inducing tirade had begun an hour before, over the screaming sirens of the police cars, and hadn't stopped since.

"The nation is in crisis! National prestige is at stake!" Marmiche now cried. "This is the third murder in six months and still the police have no suspect. Not even a solid *lead*!"

Chief Inspector Dreyfus did not reply. Instead he wondered how Marmiche dared to speak—or even take a breath—with the air so foul. The man's corpse had been disemboweled, and the remains had not been well served by lying exposed to the elements for the past twenty-four hours.

Dreyfus withdrew the Egyptian cotton handkerchief he'd kept clutched tightly to his nose and mouth.

"We don't know if this *is* murder, Minister Marmiche. Surely no human being did this. Bellafonte's death might well be accidental—"

"Preposterous!" Marmiche interrupted. "This was no accident, Chief Inspector. Like the others, Chef Bellafonte was to represent France next week in a world-class culinary competition. And like the others, Bellafonte is dead—*assassinated*."

"True, there have been other murders, but in this case—"

Minister Marmiche cut him off. "I've heard claims of accidental death before, Chief Inspector Dreyfus. The Sûreté was wrong then, too."

Dreyfus was forced to concede that Trade Minister Marmiche had a valid point. The murder of the culinary team leader five weeks ago had been investigated by an inexperienced member of the Police *Nationale*'s detective division in Bourg-en-Bresse, the poultry capital of France—a country bumpkin, in the chief inspector's estimation.

The facts were well known. Chef Marcel Dubois, owner and master chef of the restaurant Zanadu on Paris's Left Bank, had apparently drowned in a barrel of lard in the basement of his familial villa in the Rhône Valley. The culinary master was putting up cooked duck parts in vats of goose fat, a medieval French delicacy and the chef's specialty.

Police investigating the death noted that the area where Chef Dubois worked was very cluttered, the ladder the man was using slippery with fat. Since there were no apparent signs of foul play, the police concluded that the chef had fallen into his own vat and could not get out. An accident, pure and simple.

Except that it had not been so pure, or so simple. "The man who investigated that first death was a novice. Totally out of his league," Dreyfus replied. "I'm told he's been reassigned, that he is reading parking meters in Algeria even as we speak."

"I'll have *you* reading parking meters if I do not see results soon, Chief Inspector."

Dreyfus purpled. He'd had enough of this insufferable little man, and more than enough of the foul odor of rotting flesh! Even more infuriating, this case did not technically belong to the chief inspector. Dreyfus had been ordered to stand aside by the prime minister of France himself, turn over the running of the investigation to a man "more capable."

"These are high-profile crimes," the prime minister had told the chief inspector. "Therefore, we need a Frenchman of recognized genius to solve them. The people of France require the services of a Star of Valor winner, the man the press calls Europe's greatest living detective . . ."

Scowling at the memory, Dreyfus whirled to face his lieutenant. "Lamothe! Have you made radio contact with Inspector Clouseau? Where is that fool? Why is he not here?"

"He's coming now, sir," said the uniformed officer, pointing across the clearing.

"So he is."

Dreyfus instantly recognized the imbecile. Who else would be wearing that Scotland Yard-aspirational trench coat; that ridiculous, wrinkled Trilby; that stupid moustache under that prominent nose? Who else would have that arrogant, self-important stride? Those pompous, insufferable mannerisms—

Dreyfus clutched his chest and closed his eyes. Sweat blossomed on his brow, trickled down his back as he tried to steady his pounding heart.

Long a student of modern psychology, he had searched for a reason for his violent reaction to Inspector Jacques Clouseau. He had settled on the simplest answer: an instinctive primeval loathing that emerged from the reptilian antecedents of his human brain. Why else would mere proximity with Clouseau drive Dreyfus nearly mad with rage and frustration? Even now, he felt his sanity slipping as the man approached him with a silly smile plastered across his moronic face.

"Ah, Chief Inspector," Clouseau began, "what brings you to this region? The scenery is pleasant enough, but I smell something rotten in the air."

Of course, you do! There's a dead body ten feet away! Dreyfus winced at the very idea of conversing with the half-wit. But he knew the trade minister was watching. So, steeling himself, Dreyfus forced a civil reply. "Clouseau. You've arrived, I see. And with your partner. Yes, very good."

Detective Second-Class Gilbert Ponton respectfully saluted his commander. Dreyfus ignored the gesture.

Although Ponton possessed the height and solidity of a tree trunk, his vigorous physique was belied by a perpetually blank expression and hooded, basset-hound eyes that gave one the impression he was about to nod off at any moment. Nevertheless, Ponton was a capable policeman as well as an accomplished martial artist. Why such a man would risk a promising career in the Sûreté by hooking his star to a complete idiot like Clouseau was more of a mystery to Chief Inspector Dreyfus than this absurd spate of culinary murders!

Dreyfus leveled a jaundiced gaze on Clouseau. "You ask what brings me to this region? Claude Bellafonte is dead, that's what."

Clouseau displayed astonishment. "And I just recently dined at his Left Bank establishment, Le Champignon. You know, of course, Chef Bellafonte created his own version of coquille Saint-Jacques."

Dreyfus gritted his teeth. "Is that so?"

"Oh, yes! He is well known for this dish. I am surprised, Chief Inspector, that you are ignorant of a cuisine so famous in our capital city. But I am happy to enlighten you."

"That won't be necess—"

The Stench of Murder

"You see, he cooks the seafood in a rich cream sauce, but he uses black truffles in place of ordinary mushrooms! Genius!"

"I see—"

"And that's not all!"

"Not all?"

"Oh, no. He eschews the traditional seashell presentation and instead showcases his magnificent pastry-making skills, serving it in the lightest, flakiest shell imaginable!"

"Is that right?"

"Oh, yes! The dish was absolute ambrosia! The filling was so rich yet so earthy with the truffles lending that distinctive yet elusive hint of woodsy nuts—"

"Woodsy nuts, you say? Hum. Very interesting."

By now, Dreyfus's stoic composure was enduring more cracks than a painting in the Louvre's Renaissance wing. He was just about ready to throttle Clouseau when an interruption brought him back from the brink.

"Have your forgotten your manners, Chief Inspector?" Minister Marmiche asked. "You must introduce me to France's greatest detective!"

Dreyfus clenched his fists. *Greatest detective? Greatest imbecile, you mean! Yes, by all means, this pair of fools must meet.* "Clouseau, this is Pierre Marmiche, Minister of Trade."

"Such a delight, to meet the famed Pink Panther detective," Marmiche exclaimed, pumping Clouseau's hand. "I am so happy you are taking over this case. It is a matter of national prestige . . ."

"Coming aboard?" Dreyfus cried. "My good man, Inspector Clouseau has been at the *forefront* of this investigation since the second murder."

Marmiche's eyes widened. "You are speaking of the death of the baker, Jean Miguel?"

"The very same," Clouseau declared. "If I may be so bold in stating it was I who determined the baker's death was the result of foul play."

"Just how did you accomplish that miracle?" Marmiche replied. "I am *all ears*, Inspector Clouseau."

Clouseau did not speak. Instead, he carefully examined the trade minister's cranium. "All ears? *Non!* You have hair—" Clouseau tugged it, eliciting a yelp from Marmiche "—Yes, hair. Not a toupee! I also see you have a scalp, a forehead, and a pair of eyes." Clouseau paused and met the trade minister's gaze. "You are hardly 'all ears,' Monsieur Marmiche!"

The minister's expression changed from keen interest to appalled perplexity.

"There, now you see!" Dreyfus threw up his hands. "Now you understand. Clouseau is a fool. A nincompoop. An absolute moron!"

Oblivious to the chief inspector's outburst, Clouseau continued to expound. "As to your question, it was really quite simple to determine the famed baker was a victim of foul play, even though the murderer wished the authorities to believe otherwise."

Marmiche nodded. "Please elaborate, Inspector Clouseau."

Clutching his hands behind his back, the inspector began to pace the dewy grass. "Chef Miguel choked to death alone, in his pastry shop, in the wee hours of the morning as he was baking croissants. Indeed, during the autopsy, the remains of several *consumed* croissants were found in the chef's stomach."

"*Oui*, this is true," said Ponton, whipping out his notebook. He leafed through the pages, squinted as he read. "There were three croissants in the deceased's stomach at the time of the autopsy. They were all well masticated, and partially digested."

Dreyfus moaned as he felt his gorge rise. The grisly details of the autopsy, coupled with the pervasive stench of death, had sent the chief inspector into a nausea spiral. Reeling, he slumped against the trunk of a wild walnut tree.

"But surely it is only natural that a chef sample his wares," Marmiche argued.

Clouseau pointed to the blue sky above. "Yes, he would! But that does not explain the six other croissants found lodged in the man's windpipe!"

"None of the six were masticated," Ponton said, still reading.

"That means they were not chewed!" Clouseau cried.

"We *know* what masticated means, you imbecile!" Dreyfus couldn't help himself.

"The point is," Clouseau continued, "someone shoved those croissants down the baker's throat—"

"*Mon dieu,*" Marmiche murmured. "What did you do?"

Clouseau shrugged. "I ordered a detailed gastronomical analysis of the croissants, of course."

"A gastronomical analysis? Of the croissants?" Marmiche asked. "For heaven's sake, why?"

Clouseau smoothed his thin mustache. "It was, for all intents and purposes, the murder weapon, was it not?"

"French pastry? The murder weapon? But that's *absurd*!" Marmiche cried.

"You would think that, wouldn't you?" Dreyfus muttered through his handkerchief. "I did. The prime minister did. *Everyone* did."

"As it turns out, the scientists made a shocking discovery," Clouseau revealed. "They determined that the croissants lodged in Jean Miguel's throat were not as buttery as the croissants the chef was baking, due to the fact that—" Clouseau paused and looked away a moment. "I'm sorry, but it is such a disturbing notion. Any Frenchman would find it hard to even consider—"

"Go on," Marmiche urged.

"These particular croissants used fat substitutes. They contained . . ." Clouseau closed his eyes and shuddered. "They contained no actual butter!"

Marmiche's jaw dropped. "You . . . you mean . . ."

"Yes!" Clouseau replied. "The killer brought his *own* pastries to the crime scene! Killer croissants! And terribly inferior croissants they were, too."

"Yes, yes, I see," Marmiche said.

Clouseau nodded. "Armed with our first clue, we set about hunting the killer."

"Wait," Marmiche said. "You hunted the killer with this clue? But how? I do not understand?"

"Yes, Clouseau, explain your strategy to the trade minister," Dreyfus said through labored breaths.

"I don't want to boast—"

"Tell him!"

"It is ingenious in its simplicity," Clouseau explained, rocking proudly on his feet. "Ponton and I have been driving around France, scouring bakeries and restaurants, sampling croissants in every town and village. When we locate a pastry of the exact same dry, inferior consistency, we shall have our killer!"

As Clouseau walked away, to observe the fresh crime scene, Dreyfus mopped his brow and turned to Ponton. "Tell me, just what have you gained thus far from this . . . this 'killer croissant' *investigation* of Clouseau's?"

Ponton touched his recently loosened belt. "About ten pounds, Chief Inspector."

"Idiot," Dreyfus muttered.

TWO

Murder on Cloven Hoof

"Excuse me, Chief Inspector?" Dr. Borg waved his hand at Charles Dreyfus. "I am ready. Assemble your people, if you please."

Dr. Flench Borg was a stout man with short-cropped gray hair, round spectacles, ears that appeared completely free of lobes, and a grimace so pronounced that the veins and tendons at the base of his neck stood out like strings on a viola. He was also the crime scene's leading forensic expert, and Dreyfus was anxious to hear what the man had to say.

Nodding respectfully at the doctor, Dreyfus asked his uniformed assistant to call together Clouseau, Ponton, Trade Minister Marmiche, and a few local gendarmes. The men tramped over the flattened grass and fallen leaves, gathering themselves around the corpse of Claude Bellafonte, where

Borg stood over it like a host at the head of a table, ready to carve up a side of beef.

"Dr. Borg comes to us from Interpol," Dreyfus explained to the group. "He is one of the finest forensic investigators in the entire European Union—"

"Excuse me?" Minister Marmiche sniffed. "Do we not have our *own* forensic investigators in France?" The trade minister's tone made it abundantly clear that he resented any interference from other members of the EU.

Borg sighed and studied the treetops as Dreyfus awkwardly explained, "Claude Bellafonte's insurance company insisted we bring the good doctor in for a consultation. Unfortunately, Dr. Borg is Norwegian so—"

"Sacré bleu!" Clouseau cried. "The pathetic wretch has my deepest sympathies. I spent a night in Oslo once, a single night that was filled with unspeakable horrors—repeated jostling by nautical-looking types, persistent invitations to sauna with naked men, the repugnant odor of pickled fish." Clouseau shuddered. "I could not wait to escape that cold, dark, herring-obsessed—"

"If you'll allow me to finish," Dreyfus interrupted, glaring at Clouseau. "I was *about* to say—because the good doctor is Norwegian, he does not speak French. And since none of us speak Norwegian, I suggest we communicate in English, a language we all understand."

"Ah," Clouseau replied, reddening slightly. "I see. Well, I for one am pleased to meet you, Dr. Borg. And, may I say, you have masked the pickled fish odor very nicely indeed!"

"The victim died on this spot," Borg began, ignoring Clouseau's proffered hand. "He was disemboweled by an unknown implement. Death occurred instantaneously."

"What a horrible tragedy, a senseless waste of something

so unique, so precious," Clouseau whispered in a reverential tone. The inspector removed his rumpled, soft-brimmed hat and bowed his head in a gesture of respect.

The others were about to join him when they noticed Clouseau was not gazing at the mangled corpse of Chef Claude Bellafonte, but the black, powdery blotch on the grass next to him—the trampled, withered remains of the enormous black diamond truffle.

"Would her shavings have graced a spectacular cream soup? Or magnificently garnished a duck confit?" Clouseau shook his head. "Sadly, we shall never know."

Borg loudly cleared his throat. "The penetration of the flesh around the victim's abdomen is indicative of the upward thrust of ripping tusks." To illustrate his point, Borg probed the gaping flesh with the tip of his pencil. The movement disturbed a horde of flies feasting on the remains.

Chief Inspector Dreyfus made a sick, whimpering noise.

Inspector Clouseau scattered the cloud of insects with his hat, then gazed at the wound. "So!" he exclaimed. "We are to assume that Monsieur Bellafonte was killed by an elephant or a walrus?"

"Certainly not," Dr. Borg replied.

"But, you said the killer possessed tusks." Clouseau snatched the pencil away from the doctor. "I can see for myself how deep these wounds are."

Clouseau attempted to probe the corpse with the pencil, but his hold slipped and the writing implement dropped through the wound, disappearing into the bowels of the corpse and out of sight. The activity stirred a single, lazy fly.

Dreyfus turned an unhealthy color.

"Oops," Clouseau murmured. He frowned at the doctor. "My apologies. I seem to have lost your—"

Murder on Cloven Hoof

Borg drew another pencil from his breast pocket. "It is highly unlikely the wounds were actually made by an animal's tusks," he continued, tapping the corpse. "What I said was that the wounds were *indicative* of the upward thrust of ripping tusks. But a number of things—several farm implements, for instance—can mimic such wounds."

Clouseau raised an eyebrow. "Then you believe our culprit is an irate farmer?"

Dr. Borg's gaze narrowed slightly as a hitch of impatience entered his voice. "Allow me to explain my logic."

"Yes, yes, by all means," Dreyfus gasped through his handkerchief.

"The other deaths of prominent French chefs appeared accidental. The first victim, Chef Dubois, drowned in a barrel of lard. The second victim, baker Jean Miguel, choked on croissants. This death, too, appears accidental. I believe we were *meant* to think a wild beast killed Monsieur Bellafonte."

"And these . . . hoof prints." Inspector Clouseau gestured to the ground around the corpse. "They belong to a hog, no?"

"Tell him," Dreyfus mumbled through his handkerchief.

Officer Lamothe stepped forward. "These tracks were made by Chef Bellafonte's truffle-hunting pig, Brigitte. The swine turned up at his master's house this morning, shivering with fear. That was the first indication we had that something terrible had happened."

"And what about these footprints over here?" Clouseau asked.

Officer Lamothe shrugged. "More of same. The man and his pig were in this clearing a while before the murderer came upon them. Certainly long enough to discover and uncover a massive truffle."

Clouseau knelt and placed his eye to the ground. For a long moment he considered the irregularly shaped prints in the soft soil.

"Several of these tracks are at least two centimeters deeper than the others," Clouseau announced. "The swine who made those tracks was much heavier than Bellafonte's famous truffle-hunting hog known as Brigitte."

Clouseau rose to his full height, faced the others. "I believe that Chef Bellafonte was murdered by a vicious trained killer peeg."

Dr. Borg blinked again. Officer Lamothe frowned, his expression skeptical. Dreyfus was so appalled he dropped his handkerchief.

"Preposterous!" the chief inspector exploded. "Idiotic! If a pig were here, why would it not attack the truffle instead of the man?"

"You must learn to listen more closely, Chief Inspector," Clouseau replied with a confident sniff. "I *said* it was a *killer* peeg. A vicious animal trained to murder. A clever one, as well. A very clever peeg. Perhaps even a smart peeg, like those smart *bums* used in modern warfare."

The group of men glanced at one another in confusion.

"Smart *bums*?" Borg asked.

"Yes, yes," Clouseau replied impatiently. "You know! The smart *bums* that drop out of jet planes and fly to the target and blow it up. Kaboom!"

Officer Lamothe raised his hand. "Smart *bombs*, you mean?"

"*Bums*. Exactly. That is what I said," Clouseau shot back.

Dreyfus was livid. "But who would commit such an idiotic crime? Train an animal—a pig, no less!—to murder a man?"

"Have you never heard of *The Ow-und of the Baskervilles*?" Clouseau asked.

"What? What did you say?" Dreyfus sputtered. "Ow-und? Ow-und?" He looked to Lamothe in frustration.

"I believe Inspector Clouseau is speaking of the *Hound* of the Baskervilles, sir. It's a Sherlock Holmes mystery written by the English author—"

"I know who Sherlock Holmes is, Lamothe! And in my estimation, even a fictional detective would be of more use to us than this . . . this bumbling fool before me!"

Monsieur Marmiche nodded in agreement. "It brings me great pain to say it, but Inspector Clouseau does not inspire the trade ministry's confidence."

Clouseau shook his head. "Chief Inspector Dreyfus, if you will *simply* allow me to explain my theory—"

"Out!" Dreyfus cried. "Get out of my sight this instant!"

With a sigh, Clouseau clicked his heels, then waved to Ponton, gesturing for him to step away as well. The two moved to another area of the crime scene.

"Ponton, my friend," Clouseau whispered, "it is clear the unbearable pressure of this case is weighing heavily upon Chief Inspector Dreyfus. Therefore, I must proceed with my investigation solo, without further taxing his overstressed mind."

Ponton nodded. "I have already checked the perimeter of the clearing and the hedgerow beyond, and I can find no evidence of anyone—or anything—entering this area beside the unlucky Monsieur Bellafonte and his more fortunate pig, Brigitte."

"Ah, Ponton," Clouseau said with a condescending pat to his partner's shoulder. "That is because you have no eyes."

Ponton's brow furrowed.

"Do not be offended, my friend," Clouseau quickly replied. "I do not say these things to diminish your considerable skills. In the streets of Paris, Gilbert Ponton is a relentless bloodhound, hot on the trail of wrongdoers, snout to the ground, tongue wagging, floppy jowls slavering. But here in the forest primeval, you are like a lost little lamb who cannot see the hungry wolf waiting to eat you up."

Ponton's brow remained wrinkled.

Clouseau cleared his throat and tightened the belt of his mackintosh. "You remain here and observe the crime scene. I shall proceed on foot."

"Proceed where, Inspector?"

"Using my considerable wilderness tracking skills, I shall follow the spoor of our viciously clever smart killer peeg. I shall track the beast back to its hidden lair."

Ponton scratched his large, egg-shaped head. "But, how? I see no trail to pursue."

Ever the patient tutor, Clouseau sighed. "Look here, my friend—" Clouseau indicated a broken branch on a spreading bush. "It is clear the killer peeg moved in this direction, breaking this branch in his flight."

The inspector led his partner around the shrubbery and the line of tall trees that separated the murder scene from a hedgerow of twisted vines and a picturesque stone farmhouse beyond.

"As you can see, Ponton, the soil here is too hard and dry to reveal animal prints." Clouseau demonstrated his theory by stomping his foot on the ground. To their astonishment, both men heard a hollow clunk.

"Hmmm. That's odd," Clouseau murmured.

Ponton nodded. "Certainly, that does not sound like solid ground."

Both men heard an animal grunt, savage and close. Ponton stared at the earth under Clouseau's feet. There was something funny about the grass around the Inspector's shoes, he noted. Ponton realized with a start that the blades were *artificial*.

"Inspector," Ponton said, "perhaps you should step aside until we can investigate this area further."

"Nonsense, my good man. The ground is perfectly safe." To illustrate his point, Clouseau stomped his foot again—much harder this time. The startling sound of splintering wood followed, and with a yelp, Clouseau plunged through a hidden trapdoor, into a dark pit beneath.

When he hit the ground, Clouseau saw stars. He shook his head and regained his bearings, blinking up at the ragged hole he'd dropped through. The blinding sunlight was suddenly eclipsed by Ponton's moon-sized head.

"Are . . . Are you hurt, Inspector?"

"No, I am fine, but—"

The Inspector's nose wrinkled. A vile stench suffused the earthen pit. The noxious mixture smelled like a combination of livestock and dung. Mostly dung, Clouseau realized, since he'd landed on a hillock of the reeking stuff.

"Sacré bleu!" He jumped to his feet.

"Inspector?" Ponton called from above. "Is everything all right? Shall I find you a rope? Get you out of there?"

Clouseau brushed himself off. "Do not be so hasty. Although the aroma down here is worse than the Paris gutter—and, believe me, my friend, this is a subject with which I have considerable experience!—I would be lax in my duty as a member of the Sûreté, if I did not first thoroughly inspect this suspicious hole, so close to the unfortunate corpse of Monsieur Bellafonte."

The Pink Panther's Just Desserts

But before Clouseau could begin his thorough inspection, he heard a wet snarl. As he turned in the direction of the sound, he spied a pair of beady eyes staring at him from the gloom.

Just then, Ponton moved his giant head away from the hole's opening, allowing the sun to fully illuminate the interior of the monster's lair.

With a sickening mixture of horror and triumph, Jacques Clouseau found himself face to face with his theory made flesh: a vicious, trained killer pig, complete with spiked leather collar, and sharpened tusks still stained with the blood of the legendary *trufficulteur*!

"Nice piggy," the weak-kneed Clouseau whispered. "Nice, piggy, piggy."

"Inspector?" called Ponton. "Did you say something?"

"Yes! For the love of God, Ponton, get me out of here!"

THREE

De Gaulling

Within an hour of Clouseau's disturbing discovery, a veritable army of professionally trained animal handlers and veterinarians arrived on the scene, further crowding the quiet forest.

The vets tranquilized the killer pig, and the handlers hauled the four-hundred-kilo monster out of its underground lair. They locked it in an iron cage, and loaded it onto a truck parked right beside the ambulance carrying the remains of its victim, Chef Claude Bellafonte.

Soon the beast was on its way to the Paris Zoological Society for further study, but the initial observations made by the vets yielded many important clues. Gathering at the edge of the earthen pit, Dreyfus, Clouseau, Ponton, Trade Minister Marmiche, and a half-dozen local authorities reviewed the evidence.

"The veterinarians believe the tusks are artificial," Ponton said, reading from his notes. "Most likely formed from a well-honed, porcelain material of incredible strength, similar to that used in dental procedures. What do you think, Inspector? You were in a position of close observation when the beast was still conscious."

"Yes, too close, if you ask me," Clouseau muttered.

"He did ask you," Dreyfus snapped.

"Asked me what?"

"About the pig's tusks!" Dreyfus shouted.

"Frankly, I could not judge whether the tusks were real or artificial. I did, however, note that they were *rah-zer* sharp. It is a fortunate thing that the creature was on a short leash."

Chief Inspector Dreyfus threw up his hands. "Oh, yes. A *fortunate* thing. A very fortunate thing. Why do the gods smile on fools, I'd like to know?"

"But if those *rah-zer*-sharp tusks were artificial," Clouseau continued, "I must say they were fitted by a skilled orthodontist." He turned to Ponton. "We shall employ an army of uniformed police, who will, of course, report to me. They will interrogate every orthodontist from Paris to Bordeaux, until we uncover the identity of the unscrupulous culprit who performed dental work on the killer swine!"

"You'll do no such thing," Dreyfus replied. "I can't think of a larger waste of resources!"

"The trap door that covered the pit was cleverly made," Ponton noted. "Nearly impossible to find—"

"Until Inspector Clouseau joined the hunt," Trade Minister Marmiche pointed out. He turned to Clouseau and gave him a respectful bow. "If it were not for you, sir, I fear all would be lost." The trade minister then shot an accusing glance at Chief Inspector Dreyfus, who silently seethed, wringing his handkerchief while imagining it was Clouseau's neck.

In the meantime, Ponton climbed down into the earthen pit. Using a flashlight, he examined the damp walls. "Inspector!" he called after a few minutes. "There are signs that a tunnel was down here once. It has recently collapsed—very recently, as the soil is still unsettled."

"And where does this tunnel lead?" Dreyfus demanded.

"Due north, sir," Ponton replied.

Everyone turned north—except Inspector Clouseau, who turned south. Officer Lamothe politely spun him, until all the men were facing the same direction. Gazing over the gnarled hedgerow, they spied a quaint stone farmhouse in the distance.

"The tunnel will lead to that farmhouse," Clouseau said. "I am certain of it!"

"My men have canvassed the area already," Officer Lamothe informed him. "That farmhouse is deserted, the doors locked."

"Then we shall have to break in!" Clouseau declared.

"Not so fast," said a local *gendarme*. "You cannot simply break in to that place. The property may appear abandoned, but it is not. Monsieur D'Arbanville owns it. He would not approve."

Clouseau lifted his nose. "And where do we find this Monsieur D'Arbanville?"

"He lives at the crossroads, seven kilometers east of here. He is the owner of a goose farm."

As the sun stretched its lengthening rays across the Périgord Vert's fields and forests, Inspector Clouseau and Ponton set off for D'Arbanville's goose farm in their tiny Metro Police smart car. In almost no time, they arrived at the rustic cottage. It sat on a low hill, surrounded by a crumbling stone wall that could have been considered old in the time of Louis XIV.

No one responded to their knock, but Clouseau and Ponton quickly located the farm's only resident behind his house, amid a flock of plump, excited geese.

The farmer was a taciturn man with a peculiarly flattened head and unkempt black hair that protruded in all directions from beneath a yellow straw hat. He wore dung-stained leather gaiters and filthy wading pants that hung loosely from worn suspenders. The man glanced at his visitors through dull milk-blue eyes in a prematurely wrinkled face that appeared to be collapsing in on itself.

"*Sacré bleu*," Clouseau whispered to Ponton. "If this man were a building he'd have been condemned long ago!"

Ponton cleared his throat. "Are you the goose farmer, Monsieur D'Arbanville?"

The man nodded once then looked away, exhibiting an almost bovine disinterest in the world around him. Clouseau could certainly understand why! Standing atop a mound of bleached guano and shed feathers, the man was completely surrounded by a sea of beating wings and squawking beaks. Casually spilling grain with one hand, D'Arbanville used the other to munch a raw onion, one tortuous bite at a time.

Over the incessant honks of several hundred agitated geese, Inspector Clouseau introduced himself and stated the reason for his official visit.

"I am told by the local authorities that you own the stone farmhouse near the town of Lalinde. Is that correct, Monsieur D'Arbanville?"

Clouseau eagerly awaited the answer with pen in hand,

his official, embossed, obscenely expensive Louis Vuitton black leather detective notebook clutched in the other.

"*Oui*, Inspector," D'Arbanville replied with a tired sigh, the smell of his onion breath nearly overwhelming the other barnyard odors.

Momentarily weakened by the toxic blast, Clouseau fumbled his designer notebook. It landed with a plop in a puddle of wet goose crap.

"Who currently resides at that farm?" Clouseau asked, staring forlornly at his prized notebook, sinking in the dung.

A sudden alertness lit up the farmer's dulled eyes. "Why, no one sir," he answered in a cunning tone. "The farm is empty."

"Yes, yes," Clouseau shot back. "We know the farm is empty *now*. But someone has recently resided there. Who was that?"

"Why, no one, sir," D'Arbanville repeated.

Clouseau stepped closer to the farmer—then stepped back again, waving away the haze of halitosis. "Do not lie to me, goose man!" he warned. "I am aware of your tricks and I know you are hiding something."

"I have told the truth," said a sweating Claude D'Arbanville. "There is no one at the farm and that . . . that is all I can say."

D'Arbanville turned his back on Clouseau. The angry inspector marched around to face the man again. "What are you hiding, you smelly, dung-stained miscreant?" Clouseau demanded, taking hold of the man's suspenders.

"No, no, please!" D'Arbanville begged. "I can say nothing. If you were really from the Sûreté, then you would know why I can say nothing. And if you are not from the Sûreté, then you are assassins! Murderers!"

The man's breath sent Clouseau reeling backward, but the Inspector never relinquished his grip on the man's suspenders.

"What are you saying?" demanded an outraged Clouseau. "Are you calling me an imposter?"

D'Arbanville tried to break from Clouseau's grip, but he only managed to throw the inspector off balance. Clouseau and the goose farmer began skating on the slick manure, their arms flailing wildly.

"Help me, Ponton!"

Clouseau's partner glanced at the mountainous pile of guano. "I'm sorry, sir." Ponton shook his large head. "I would lay down my life for you, Inspector. But this?... I really don't think so."

"Help! Help! I am being murdered!" D'Arbanville cried, still believing he was in the grip of an assassin.

"I am not a killer," Clouseau protested, "I am merely *looking* for one—the man who lived in your house!"

"I swore to the general that I would never say a word," D'Arbanville replied, regaining his footing at last.

Still clutching the man's suspenders, Clouseau steadied himself. "General? What general?"

D'Arbanville violently shook his head. "I could get into trouble if I speak."

"You are in trouble now, my good man," Clouseau promised. "Unless you would like to sink deeper in it . . ." With a choked whimper, the inspector suddenly realized that he, too, had sunk. He was knee deep in goose crap!

Relinquishing his grip on D'Arbanville, he climbed out of the muck. "I suggest you come clean immediately!" he threatened.

"But you are part of the French government, and as such, you certainly must be aware of the general's movements, his whereabouts at all time?" opined the perplexed D'Arbanville.

Finally steady, Clouseau stomped his feet to shake the loose manure off his clothing. "General? Who is this general you keep prattling about?"

"Why General Charles De Gaulle, of course," D'Arbanville replied.

"What!" Clouseau slipped and landed with a splash in the goose grime.

"I don't understand," Ponton said to the farmer. "You claim to have rented your property to General Charles de Gaulle?"

D'Arbanville nodded proudly. "The very same. The general turned up at my door one day. He told me that he saw my farm and thought it was the perfect spot to spend the summer. I rented him the property in May. The lease was good for six months."

"And you told no one?" Ponton pressed.

D'Arbanville shrugged. "It was a matter of national security. The general told me that his location was to remain secret to all but those at the highest levels of government—"

"But, sir," Ponton interrupted. "General Charles de Gaulle expired in 1970."

D'Arbanville displayed a crafty grin. "Here in the country we hear lots of rumors, but we aren't as simple as you city folk think we are. And we certainly don't believe everything we read in *Paris Match*!"

"Did you know a tunnel was constructed under your farmhouse?" Ponton asked. "One which led across your pasture and into the adjacent field?"

"Of course," the goose farmer replied. "The general needed it for security—an escape route in case he was attacked. He paid for the alterations himself . . ."

Suddenly D'Arbanville lowered his voice and whispered to Ponton in a conspiratorial tone. "General de Gaulle has many enemies, you know. Communists. Ex-Nazis. Trade Unionists. A lot of foreign governments would like to see our heroic general dead—"

"He *is* dead, you stupid, blithering fool!" sputtered Clouseau, now covered head-to-toe in filth.

"Absurd," D'Arbanville declared. "If Charles de Gaulle is dead, then who summered in my cottage?"

"Let us put aside that question for the moment," Ponton replied. "When the local police went to the farm earlier today, they found nothing but an empty house. Monsieur D'Arbanville, do you know where General Charles de Gaulle is right now?"

"In his grave," Clouseau muttered as he attempted to clean himself at a water pump.

"No," D'Arbanville replied. "The general has gone on another trip."

Ponton scratched his chin. "Another trip, you say. Then the General did some traveling?"

D'Arbanville nodded. "The general made several trips during the summer. He phoned me each time and asked me to drive him to the airport in Bordeaux."

"This imposter, this evil chef-killer, was no doubt stalking his first victim in Bourg-en-Bresse, or planning the second murder of the baker on the Left Bank of Paris!" Clouseau cried. "Bellafonte is dead just a stone's throw from here. And now, who knows into what part of France this De Gaulle imposter is traveling."

"No part," D'Arbanville said.

"What do you mean?" Ponton asked.

"When I drove the general to the airport this morning, I

noticed his tour book and map. He was flying to New York City."

Ponton used his cell phone to call the airline and check the outbound flights. He hung up a moment later, frowning.

"A flight to New York City left just two hours after the murder," Ponton said. "No one with the name Charles de Gaulle was aboard."

"There, you see?" said Clouseau. "It would be absurd for the murderer to go to New York City. Or anywhere in the United States."

Ponton blinked in confusion. "Why is that, Inspector?"

"This killer is targeting French chefs, is he not?" Clouseau replied.

Ponton nodded.

Clouseau threw up his hands. "Well, there you have it! What would any self-respecting French culinary master be doing in the home of the Whopper?!"

FOUR

Murder Most Fowl

New York City
USA—Home of the Whopper

For the past thirty minutes, twenty-six-year-old restaurant inspector Cassidy Caldwell had been moving about the Hotel Darlington's kitchen stacking up health code violations like a gambler counting poker chips.

Master Chef Etienne de Terricour had tried to ignore the petite American, fussing and squawking about his stainless-steel domain like an angry little hen. In another time and place, he might have been charmed by Cassidy's carrot-colored curls and avocado-green eyes, but the owners of this century-old establishment had flown him in from Paris to cook pheasant in pastry for eighty, not converse with a freckle-faced moppet in a shapeless business suit!

Unfortunately, the more de Terricour tried to ignore the young woman, the more determined she became to distract him. When she thrust an official-looking paper under his nose and held it there, he threw up his hands and snatched it from her.

As he studied the paper, de Terricour took a drag on his unfiltered cigarette and blew it out his flaring nostrils. His English was weak at best, and the paper's content appeared as nothing more than an indecipherable map of grid lines and check marks around the occasional recognizable word.

"Qu'est-ce que c'est? Critical violations?"

Cassidy squared the padded shoulders of her boxy brown business suit and tried to get through to the handsome Frenchman.

"A food service establishment that accumulates twenty-eight or more points from critical and/or general violations fails its DOHMH inspection—"

"D . . . O . . . ?"

"Chef, listen to me. You have seventy-two points here. You're a public health hazard. If you do not correct the critical violations right now, in front of my eyes, I am shutting you down."

"Je ne comprends pas!"

Tossing the paper down at the little woman, de Terricour turned back to his stove of simmering sauces.

Cassidy was not dissuaded. During her five-year career conducting surprise restaurant inspections for New York's Department of Health and Mental Hygiene, she'd been threatened by knife-wielding *sous*-chefs, burly nightclub bouncers, and a one-armed dart-throwing bartender with a twitchy eye and a dubious Irish brogue. She wasn't about to shrink from a big, moody Parisian in a chef's hat, even if he did win the *Saveurs de l'Europe* competition three years running.

"Stop cooking right now!" she demanded.

De Terricour turned back to the little hen, wondering what would make her go away. He had only five more hours to prepare this special birthday dinner for New York's mayor, a well-traveled business mogul who'd for years proclaimed the Croustade de Faisan at de Terricour's Montmartre brasserie one of his all-time favorite dishes.

"Zisten . . . to me," he said. "I am . . . come here . . . *only* to cook . . . *comprend*?"

Taking another drag on his cigarette, the master chef blew the smoke so close to Cassidy's face, her pale, freckled skin turned the color of moldy brie.

"All right, Frenchy, that's it!"

With a grunt of surprise from the chef, Cass plucked the ciggy from between the man's lips and stormed out the back door. Holding the burning cylinder as far from her body as possible, she marched outside, threw the filthy thing onto the concrete loading dock, and crushed it beneath her sensible, low-heeled pump.

Shuddering at the very idea of her fingers making contact with the germ-laden paper, Cassidy pulled a sanitized wipe from the canister in her shoulder bag, thoroughly cleansed her hands *and* the bottom of her shoe, then marched back into the kitchen, her curly orange ponytail bouncing.

As she tossed the filthy wipe in the uncovered, overflowing garbage can, she noticed a tall African American man striding in from the street. His black pants and white chef's jacket didn't give her pause, but his mane of long, black dreadlocks set off blaring sirens in Cassidy's brain.

"Excuse me!" Cassidy called.

The man paused, but didn't turn around.

"Make sure you put on a hair net before you start working!"

With a grunt, the man continued walking. Not caring for the kitchen worker's attitude, Cassidy began to follow him, ready to quote chapter and verse on hair restraints from the DOHMH code book. But instead of moving into the kitchen area, Dreadlocks Man turned down the short corridor that led to the walk-in refrigerator.

Throwing up her hands, Cassidy let the man go and returned to the kitchen. "Okay!" she told the chef. "I've disposed of the cigarette. That's one violation I've remedied for you."

De Terricour said nothing. He was too busy tapping a new cigarette out of his pack.

"Good gravy!" Cassidy lunged for the cancer stick.

The chef's blue eyes went wide as he lurched backward, holding the offending agent out of her reach.

"Vous êtes une folle!" he squawked.

"I am not insane," Cassidy replied. "It's the law now! No smoking in any New York City public building. You cannot smoke in here! *Non* smoking!"

The chef cursed. Finally getting the message, he tucked the slender white American violation back into its pack and returned the box to his pants pocket.

"Thank you." Cassidy straightened her clothing. "Now, let's address the rest of your infractions." She looked down at her clipboard. "You've got food temperature, prep, protection, and source issues, not to mention garbage, documentation, and facility design problems. Let's start with the food. That cheese marinating there—what is it? Cabecou?"

"Oui, Cabecou."

Cassidy remembered the cheese from her studies at New York's prestigious Culinary Academy. Cabecou was a mild goat cheese from the Périgord region. De Terricour's marinade looked like olive oil, pink peppercorns, thyme, and bay leaf. *Very nice*, she thought. De Terricour would probably serve it on a small bed of greens with a few tomato slices, little strips of duck breast, walnuts, and a drizzle of extra virgin. *Delightful!*

There was only one problem.

"You're holding your cheese above Department of Health temperature guidelines," Cass informed him. "And those hanging pheasants—take them down at once and put them in the refrigerator."

De Terricour stared at the redhead's finger, pointing at his pheasants. *"Mes faisans . . . ?"* He scratched the yellow stubble on his fleshy cheeks.

"That's right. Your pheasants. To the refrigerator! Cold box?"

Cassidy pointed down the short hallway that led to the walk-in fridge and pretended to shiver. He stared at her in complete confusion, and she exhaled in frustration. Cassidy was fairly skilled in understanding French—she just couldn't speak it to save her life. She tried twice to pronounce the word for refrigerator, but the chef simply continued to stare in perplexed silence.

"Your pheasants—" Cass began again.

"Oui, mes faisans," the chef finally said. "Zey are . . . uh, zey are to ripen. Zis is why zey must hang!"

From a culinary perspective, Cassidy understood what the chef was doing. Wild pheasant flesh tended to be reddish, but these plucked birds appeared white. In his Montmartre brassiere, de Terricour probably used wild pheasant, Cass deduced, while here in New York, he was given the farmed version. And he was probably using males, which had more flavor, but weren't as tender as the females. So, to help tenderize the meat and invoke a gamy flavor, Cass could see the chef was hanging his birds to ripen them.

The problem? He was doing it in an open kitchen—a *ginormous* no-no. But before Cassidy could further explain the food temperature violation, the chef began to curse.

"Je dois prendre plus de beurre!"

De Terricour's tall, broad-shouldered frame wheeled, and he pointed a long finger at one of the half-dozen kitchen workers fussing around the prep tables.

"You!"

"Me?" A small Latino stared at the chef with wide, alert eyes.

"You! *Apportez-moi plus de beurre!*"

"Qué?" the man asked.

Cassidy massaged her temples. The master chef was demanding to be brought more butter.

"Apportez-moi plus de beurre!" the chef repeated.

"English, *por favor*," the kitchen worker pleaded.

"Mon dieu!" The chef threw up his hands.

Cassidy considered translating the command for the worker, but thought better of it. Why should she enable this bacterial breeding ground? When the chef had stormed toward the walk-in fridge to fetch his own butter, she approached the Latino, who stood barely an inch taller than Cassidy's own five feet.

"What's your name?" she asked.

"Carlos," the man answered.

"Tell me, Carlos, is there a restaurant manager here? Someone in charge besides the chef?"

Carlos nodded. "Mr. Minucci. He's in charge. He was here earlier. He speaks French and Spanish, so he was telling us what the chef wanted. But he left."

"Left? Why?"

"Don't know." Carlos shrugged.

"He was sick," another Latino worker piped up.

"That's José," Carlos informed her.

"What's that you said, José? He went home *sick*?" Cassidy asked, confronting José.

"*Sí*," José said. "Mr. Minucci looked sick like a dog!"

"And he was working in this kitchen?" Cassidy pressed.

This time everyone nodded. "*Sí, sí . . .*"

"That's it! Stop what you're doing!" Cassidy clapped her hands at the kitchen workers, who stared with puzzled expressions. "This kitchen is closed by order of the Department of Health. You're all done here until every last violation is remedied!"

The workers glanced at each other. None of them moved.

"Don't give me any grief," she warned, pulling out her DOHMH photo ID and flipping it at them like an INS badge. "You don't want me calling Immigration, do you?"

"Immigration?" the workers murmured.

The kitchen was empty inside half a minute.

Cassidy glanced back at the stove area. The pots were simmering on their own. The chef still hadn't returned with his butter.

Well, he won't need it now!

Still clutching her clipboard, she stormed down the short dead-end corridor that led to the walk-in fridge.

"Chef de Terricour? Chef!"

Cass stared at the refrigerator's long steel handle. She imagined the metal had been shiny and silver once, but now it was dull from wear, its nicked surface encrusted with the filth of a thousand hands.

Grimacing, she reached into her bag and pulled out a sanitized wipe. She thoroughly cleaned the handle. Then, with the wipe carefully separating her skin from the repulsive metal, she pulled the heavy lever.

She knew the tall, handsome, and moody master chef would not be too happy about hearing his entire staff had been dismissed. Nevertheless, she took a deep breath for courage and marched into the vast refrigerator to confront him. After only a few steps, however, she stopped in her tracks and let out a long, loud, horrified scream.

The fridge was filled with boxes of produce, gallons of milk, vats of butter, and sides of beef. Like his dead pheasants, Etienne de Terricour was hanging right next to it all, his neck slashed, his blood pooling on the cold steel floor below him.

FIVE

Crime Seen

"**O**kay, Miss Caldwell . . ." Detective Ralph Ciccio paused and scratched the inside of his ear with the tip of his pen. "Let's go over this again . . ."

Cassidy sat in the large, empty dining room of the Hotel Darlington's elegant restaurant. The tables were covered in white linen and adorned with lush floral arrangements. The ceiling boasted antique chandeliers, one wall was lined with dramatically arched windows looking out on Fifth Avenue, and the remaining three were frescoed with an elaborate continuous work commissioned twenty years before by a popular artist.

Like the Pierre Hotel's famous trompe-l'oeil, the Darlington Hotel's colorful mural depicted dozens of famous people present and past, all dining together—from Benjamin Franklin and Mark Twain to Nancy Reagan and Madonna.

Crime Seen

Cassidy shifted in her seat, feeling as uncomfortable under the mural's painted gazes as the detective's real one. Nursing a Starbucks *venti* that he clearly wished were a single-malt scotch, the rumpled, middle-aged homicide cop sat across the table, staring at her with a blank bloodshot gaze.

"So why exactly did you clear the restaurant?" Detective Ciccio asked.

Cass sighed. Beyond the padded double doors, an NYPD forensic team was swarming the kitchen. Outside the dining room's large windows, Fox 5 and NY1 news vans were pulling up to the curb.

"As I already told you," she replied. "I was conducting a surprise inspection for the Department of Health and Mental Hygiene. The workers told me the restaurant manager left because he was sick as a dog—"

"Rubbish!"

Cassidy turned to find a stocky, swarthy man storming across the empty dining room like a well-dressed bull. Clad in an impeccably tailored Armani suit, vermilion silk tie, and matching pocket handkerchief, he wore his raven hair slicked back and a less than happy expression on his broad, flushed face.

Detective Ciccio sighed. "Mr. Minucci, I asked you to remain at the front desk while I questioned Miss Caldwell—"

"Minucci?" Cassidy met the man's intense gaze. "Are you the restaurant manager? The kitchen staff said you left. That you had been working around the food, then became sick as a dog."

"I am *Salvatore* Minucci, Miss Caldwell!"

Cass noticed the man's fists were clenched, and a vein was noticeably pulsing at his temple. "Salvatore?"

"I am the *hotel* manager! My brother, *Mario,* is the restaurant manager. He's the one who left."

"So your brother *is* sick," Cassidy charged.

"My brother isn't some kind of a . . . of a Typhoid Mario, Miss Caldwell! He doesn't have a contagious illness! He has a sensitivity to pollen! It flared up when the florist delivered all of these fresh flowers for the mayor's birthday dinner." Minucci gestured to the elaborate arrangements placed on the linen-covered tables surrounding them. "An event which you have single-handedly ruined!"

Cassidy's brow wrinkled. "What are you saying? His sickness was brought on by an *allergy*?"

"Yes! For god's sake, my brother simply had an allergic reaction to the flowers, and since he'd run out of his prescription medication, he had to return home to get more. Which is why you, madam, should be fired this instant!"

Cassidy stood up and went toe-to-toe with the looming manager. "Your brother wasn't the only reason I closed your kitchen, Mr. Minucci. How do you explain seventy-two points in Department of Health violations?!"

"Easy. You're an idiot!"

"I'm an authorized inspector, sir. And I have your paperwork right here!" She reached into her bag, pulled out the forms, and waved it in front of her. "Everything's documented!"

Still sitting in his upholstered dining room chair, Detective Ciccio gazed impassively at the arguing pair. With a sigh, he wondered how long two people could shout at each other at the top of their lungs before their voices gave out. Absently, he glanced at his watch, then he lifted his giant cup of black coffee and began to sip.

Exactly one minute later, a young Chinese American man

burst through the double doors separating the restaurant's dining room from its kitchen. "Cheech!" he cried, zigzagging around the empty tables. "What the hell's going on out here? World War Three?"

Cassidy Caldwell and Salvatore Minucci didn't bother looking up. They were still alternately yelling about pheasant for sixty and bacterial breeding grounds.

"Apparently, they're settling a beef," Ciccio informed his partner, "a contaminated beef from the sound of it. I'll put ten on the little redhead—" he shrugged. "—if you want the action."

The younger detective rolled his eyes, put two fingers in his mouth and whistled loudly. Cassidy and Minucci simultaneously quieted and stared at the new arrival.

"This is my partner." Ciccio lazily gestured to the younger man. "Detective Larry Chang."

"Chang?" Cassidy said.

"Yeah," Ciccio replied. "What about it?"

"Nothing. It's just that . . ." Cassidy shrugged. "Your names. Ciccio and Chang . . ."

"Yeah," Chang repeated. "What about it?"

"Hasn't anybody told you that your names sound like those two comedians from the seventies?"

Ciccio and Chang just stared blankly.

"You know, the guys who did those movies and records with all those jokes about cannabis?"

Ciccio glanced at Chang and sighed. "No, Miss Caldwell. No one's ever told us that." There was no irony whatsoever in his tone.

"Oh." Cassidy sank back into her dining room chair.

Detective Ciccio cleared his throat. "Now can we get back to the business at hand?"

"The restaurant violations?" Cassidy asked.

"The *homicide*," Ciccio said.

"Sorry," Cassidy replied. "But everyone has their priorities."

"What's that supposed to mean?" Minucci demanded.

"*E. coli* is a killer, too," she pointed out.

"Not in this case," Chang told her. "In this case, a perp with a razor-sharp knife is the killer. Now then . . ." Chang looked to his partner. "Where were you in your questioning?"

Ciccio flipped a page in his notebook. "Miss Caldwell here claims she found the body after she cleared the kitchen."

"Rather convenient, if you ask me," Minucci muttered.

"What is?" Cassidy demanded.

"Your, quote, 'finding the body' *after* you cleared the kitchen."

"What are you implying, Mr. Minucci?" Chang asked.

"Just that this woman, right here, had an opportunity to kill the chef herself!"

"What!" Cassidy leaped back to her feet.

"Sit down, Ms. Caldwell," said Ciccio. "No one is accusing you of murder."

"Well, I should hope not! Good gravy! I just met Chef de Terricour today. What motive would I have to harm him?"

"Jealousy, of course," Minucci sniffed.

"Jealousy!" Cass cried.

"Oh, yes." Minucci's dark eyes narrowed. "I know all about you, Miss Cassidy Caldwell. I called around. I got the scoop! You're obsessed with ruining chefs!"

"That's not true!"

"It *is* true!" Minucci turned to the detectives. "This young woman is crazy! Certifiable! She was a top student at the Culinary Academy until she called in health violations on one of the school's master instructors. She was expelled for turning in her own teacher a month before graduation! Since no restaurant would hire her, she turned in her chef's hat to become a hatchet girl for the city."

"I resent that characterization!"

"Admit it, Miss Caldwell, you're a food cop on a vengeance mission and when Chef de Terricour defied you, you became enraged, cleared the kitchen, then cut his throat in the walk-in refrigerator!"

Cassidy reddened with fury. "You're the one who's crazy, Minucci!"

Detective Ciccio stood up. "Okay! That's enough! Mr. Minucci, please *sit*."

Refusing to sit anywhere near Cassidy Caldwell, the hotel manager walked around the table. He pulled a chair out about three feet, stiffly folded himself into it, and crossed his legs.

"Ms. Caldwell, you sit, too," Detective Ciccio ordered.

Chin high, Cassidy straightened her blazer with great dignity and lowered herself back to her chair.

"Now tell us all what happened again," Chang continued. "After you told the kitchen workers to leave."

"I looked around for Chef de Terricour," said Cassidy, "but he hadn't come back from the refrigerator yet."

"And how much time would you say had passed?" Chang asked.

"Not much," Cass said. "Maybe a few minutes."

"A few minutes between the time he went back to the refrigerator and the time you found him dead?" Ciccio clarified.

"Yes, that's right."

"And did you notice anyone follow the chef into the refrigeration area?"

"Not follow him, no. But I did see a kitchen worker going

back into that area only few minutes before the chef went back there. I had come inside from disposing of de Terricour's lit cigarette—a clear violation of DOHMH regulations, by the way." Cass paused to narrow her eyes at Sal Minucci. He glared back.

"One crime at a time, Miss," Ciccio warned.

"Yes, of course. Well, as I was saying, I saw this man walking right by me without a hair net. He was an African American man. Around six feet, I guess, and pretty solidly built. And he had his hair in dreadlocks—"

"What are you talking about?" Minucci spat.

"Dreadlocks," Cass repeated. "You know those long rope-like braids—"

"I know what dreadlocks are!" Minucci cried. "I'm talking about the man you're describing. I know every employee who works at this hotel, and there's no black man with dreadlocks on staff here."

"Then he's your killer!" Cass said excitedly. "He has to be! And I saw him! I *saw* him! He was wearing a white chef's jacket—no doubt to try to blend in with the kitchen workers. And, as I said, he went directly toward the walk-in refrigerator only minutes before the chef went back there. It had to be premeditated. Certainly, the killer had a cool head."

Minucci exhaled in disgust. "Of course, the killer had a cool head. The murder took place in a refrigerator!"

"I *meant* the killer was calm and collected enough to have worn a chef's jacket to blend in, then lay low until he had a chance to attack de Terricour."

Chang glanced at Ciccio. "I think she's right about the killer being calm and collected. Forensics says the refrigerator's metal handle was wiped completely clean. There wasn't a useable fingerprint anywhere on the thing."

Cass squirmed. "The handle, you say?"

"Yeah." Chang nodded. "Forensics was hoping for a decent print. It would have been a long shot, anyway, given the amount of people who use the refrigerator on a daily basis, but the perp obviously wiped it to make sure there'd be no chance of a print being left behind."

"Well, actually . . ." Cass murmured before her voice faded away.

"What is it, Miss Caldwell?" Detective Chang prompted. "Don't be shy. Anything you can remember might help us."

"Well," Cass began again. "It was actually me who . . . uh . . . I was the one who, um . . ."

"What?" Chang coaxed. "Tell us!"

"I was the one who cleaned the handle," Cass admitted.

"I knew it!" Minucci bellowed. "She's the murderer!"

"No, no!" Cass exclaimed. "You don't understand! It's what I always carry—" She quickly leaned over and reached into her large handbag.

Minucci leaped back to his feet. "Look out! She's going for her gun!"

"Freeze!" Chang shouted. He pulled a .45 from his shoulder holster and pointed it directly at Cassidy's head.

"B-but I was just . . ." Cassidy tried again to reach into her bag.

"Don't move," Chang warned.

"I was just—"

"I mean it!"

"Get her bag!" Minucci cried.

Chang slowly moved to Cassidy's side. He threw the bag on the table. Ciccio dumped it out. "Let's see what we've got here," he muttered. "Wallet, keys, hairbrush, cell phone, aspirins, tampons—"

Cassidy reddened.

"Sorry," said Ciccio. "Disinfecting hand soap, a mother-lode of tissues, and a canister of . . . what is this?"

"Antibacterial wipes," Cassidy said. "I used a sanitary wipe to thoroughly disinfect the handle before I touched it."

"She's the killer, I tell you," Minucci continued to shout. "I demand you arrest her at once!"

"Calm down, Mr. Minucci," said Chang.

Ciccio turned to Cassidy. "Miss Caldwell, let's go back to the man with dreadlocks you claimed entered the kitchen in a chef's jacket."

"It's not a claim. It's a fact."

"Fine. Do you think you could describe him in detail? To a police artist? Let's go over the description one more time. What did he look like?"

"Exactly like him," she said, nodding at the famous mural of celebrity faces on the Hotel Darlington's dining room wall.

"Exactly like who?" asked Chang.

Cassidy pointed out Bob Marley.

Ciccio glanced at Chang. He waved him away from the table so they could talk privately. "I think this woman's got problems."

"Either that or she's watching way too much VH1 *Behind the Music*," said Chang. "First she thinks we're stand-ins for Cheech and Chong, and now she thinks the killer is a dead reggae star."

"You think Minucci's right about her?"

"What?" said Ciccio. "That she's the killer?"

"No. That she's nuts."

"I think she's marginally eccentric. But there's no way she's our killer."

"Yeah, I know," Chang said. "She's got no defensive wounds. Plus Frenchy had a good fifteen inches and a hundred and fifty pounds on her. There's just no way our little food cop here could have hoisted the victim onto a meat hook."

"Not alone, anyway."

SIX

Pie in the Sky

When Chief Inspector Charles Dreyfus arrived at his office the next morning, he found a scarlet folder marked URGENT on his polished mahogany desk.

"Mon dieu, not another one."

With a groan, he dropped into his leather chair to review the folder's contents. When he was through, he sought his usual consolation, swiveling his chair to gaze at the massive, glass-enclosed map of the City of Paris, circa 1812, mounted on the wood-paneled wall directly behind his desk.

There were many other artifacts of great historical value decorating the chief inspector's elegant office: Louis Pasteur's standing globe; first editions of the works of Hugo, Dumas, Balzac, and Jean-Paul Sartre; the shield of Sir Gilbert of Dreyfus, wielded by one of the chief inspector's ancestors during the War of the Roses. But for Charles Dreyfus, nothing held greater value than this map, which once belonged to François-Eugène Vidocq, the reformed criminal mastermind turned government informant who founded the French police two centuries ago.

Vidocq's map hung as a direct link to the great man who'd begun the finest of all police organizations in the world. During his tenure as chief inspector, Dreyfus had gazed countless times upon the yellowing canvas, while trying to solve the many vexing cases that had crossed his desk.

Like the Sûreté and the proud French people themselves, Vidocq's map had survived the July Revolution against Charles X; the Nazi occupation; the Parisian summer of burning cars; the spring rioting of royally pissed coeds; and, the most devastating trial of all, Inspector Jacques Clouseau.

Massaging his temples, Dreyfus recalled the months of restoration work required after Clouseau's last trip to his office. He could only hope the idiot was too busy with his wild-goose-farmer chase to come back to Paris anytime soon.

A knock resounded on Dreyfus's office door.

"Yes!" he called.

Officer Lamothe poked his head inside. "Clouseau is here to see you, sir."

Dreyfus shuddered. "It seems my superstitious grandmother was right," he muttered.

"Sir?"

"Thinking of the devil apparently summons the Beast."

"Excuse me, sir?"

"Nothing, nothing . . . Send him in."

"Ponton is with him, sir."

"Fine! Send them both in! Let's get this over with."

Inspector Jacques Clouseau entered with the wide grin of

a useless fool. Ponton followed, his round face as expressive as a bowl of rocks.

"We have a lead in our search for the elusive Charles de Gaulle," Clouseau announced, marching up to his superior's desk.

"Yes," the chief inspector said. "Get on with it."

"Although no one bearing that illustrious name boarded a flight out of Paris on the day of Bellafonte's murder, a passenger with the name and passport of one—" Clouseau opened his dung-stained Louis Vuitton notebook and turned a page. "Yes, here it is. One Paul Gauguin *was* aboard Flight 1069 bound for John F. Kennedy Airport."

Charles Dreyfus stared. "And?"

Clouseau handed him a piece of paper.

"What's this?" Dreyfus asked.

"Gauguin's passport photo."

"This man looks exactly like Napoleon Bonaparte."

"Indeed!" Clouseau closed his designer notebook with a snap. A cloud of dried goose guano rose up into the room.

Dreyfus gagged then coughed. "Indeed *what*? You idiot!"

Clouseau lowered his voice. "I suspect this 'Paul Gauguin,' who resembles Napoleon Bonaparte, is not, in fact the late painter Gauguin, father of modern art, but the very same man who pretended to be Charles de Gaulle! He is the serial murderer we seek!"

"You suspect that, do you?" Dreyfus replied. "Well, I should hope so. It's a fairly tiny leap of reason, even for a moron such as yourself."

"Why, thank you, sir! You flatter me, and all I can say is—"

"Be quiet! I have some news." Dreyfus picked up the red folder on his desk. "This report just arrived this morning from the Japanese National Police in Tokyo."

"Non! Another murder?" Clouseau guessed.

"And this one in Japan?" Ponton also guessed.

"Yes, *obviously*," Dreyfus replied. "Twelve hours ago, the corpse of Guillermo Gignac was found in an *unusual* state in the Ginza District of Tokyo. Like the last two victims, Gignac was a pastry chef—the head baker at Château Le Quont on the Champs-Élysées."

Ponton interrupted. "I wonder, sir. Like the others, was Chef Gignac scheduled to represent France in the World Food Expo competition next week?"

"Yes, indeed he was." Placing his palms on his polished desktop, Dreyfus rose from his chair. "Gentlemen, someone is killing the great pastry chefs of France! Even more disturbing than that, we—the Sûreté—seem entirely incapable of stopping the murders or catching the perpetrator!"

Clouseau shook his head. "But if this murder was discovered twelve hours ago in Tokyo, then the killer could *not* have been the man who flew to New York City under the name Paul Gauguin, as I had suspected. No murderer, no matter how clever, can be two places at the same time."

"You would think that, wouldn't you?" Dreyfus said, one eyebrow twitching nervously. "Yet the details of Gignac's murder actually bear your theory out, Clouseau. Don't you find that ironic? Amusing? Nauseating!"

"Well, Chief Inspector, I—"

"Excuse me," Ponton interrupted, "but how can a man, even one as clever as the villain we hunt, murder two men on opposite sides of the world within hours of each other?"

"That is not how events unfolded," Dreyfus replied, sinking back into his leather chair. "As far as the forensics experts can determine, the murder of Chef Gignac actually occurred a week ago. Only yesterday were his remains discovered."

Clouseau scratched his head. "I am afraid I do not understand."

"Three weeks ago, the Japanese conglomerate Anginsan, LLC, paid Chef Gignac a half-million francs to prepare a banquet for the board of directors' annual luncheon in Tokyo," Dreyfus explained. "Chairman Tomaga of Anginsan asked Gignac to prepare his award-winning specialties, including an array of large meat pies with flaky crusts, rich with butter, and laced with heavy sauces—"

Ponton frowned, making an uneasy assumption. "Did you say *meat* pies, sir?"

"Yes, yes, Ponton! Meat pies, meat pies," Clouseau snapped with impatience. "You know, like those little pies the English eat in their dark and musty pubs between pints of bitter ale. Small pies stuffed with spleen and bladders and entrails and every manner of questionable organ meat."

Ponton nodded. "Then Chef Gignac traveled to Tokyo to prepare this meal?"

"No," Dreyfus said. "The chef refused to fly to Tokyo. Apparently, the timing of the Japanese banquet conflicted with an international baccarat tournament in Monte Carlo. Chef Gignac has—or rather, *had*—a bit of a gambling problem. But a suitable arrangement was reached. Last week, the chef prepared several meat pies at his villa in Somme. The uncooked pies were quick-frozen, then packed in dry ice. The next day the pies were dispatched to Tokyo in a chartered airliner, with instructions for preparation of the pies. His contractual obligations met, Chef Gignac headed off to Monte Carlo . . . or so it appeared."

Sensing the end of Dreyfus's tale, Ponton felt suddenly queasy.

"In Tokyo the pies were prepared according to Chef

Gignac's instructions," Dreyfus continued, "then served to Chairman Tomaga and his board of directors, their wives, and select members of the Japanese Parliament. The meal was much appreciated, I'm told. It was only near the end of the feast, when the servers cut into the final pie, that the horrific truth was finally revealed—"

"I've got it!" Clouseau cried. "The chef used capon instead of goose! I myself was served such a meal in Vichy once. The meat was rubbery, the sauce tasteless. The crust so dry it had the texture of beach sand. It was truly a nightmare from which I—"

"Shut up, you blithering idiot!" Dreyfus pounded his desk. "The servers found Chef Gignac's severed head inside the final pie! The other pies were made with his various body parts! The Chef was the meat in his own meat pies! Do you understand now, you ridiculous popinjay?"

"*Oui.*" Clouseau blinked. "Do you suppose the diners were disturbed by the revelation?"

"Disturbed?!" Dreyfus shoved the folder of photos toward Clouseau and Ponton. "Eyewitness accounts suggest that the dining room quickly resembled the *vomitoriums* of ancient Rome—"

Although a veteran of countless crime scenes, Ponton could not stop the nausea induced by the grisly photos—not to mention the bad snails he'd eaten the night before. With a groan, he emptied the contents of his stomach onto the chief inspector's desk.

"Sorry, sir," Ponton mumbled. "Last evening's escargot . . . they did not go down well."

"*Sacré bleu,* Ponton, they did not come up any better!" Dreyfus marched to the door. "A crazed murderer is on the loose. The reputation of the Sûreté is at stake. And who comes to my office? A half-wit and a bulimic!" Throwing open the door, he bellowed, "Lamothe! Get in here with a cleaning kit!"

While the chief inspector's assistant tidied up, the men moved to the other side of the office, setting up a few chairs near the hastily opened windows.

"*Someone* stuffed Chef Gignac into those pies," Clouseau pointed out. "The victim did not bake himself."

"You think so, do you?" Dreyfus rolled his eyes.

"Who was the last person to see Gignac alive?" Ponton asked.

Dreyfus consulted the folder. Lamothe had supplemented the Japanese report with notes from the night-watch commander of the Police *Nationale*.

"The last person to see Gignac alive appears to be the new assistant chef he hired, a man who hailed from Port-au-Prince on the island nation of Haiti. Thus far, no one has been able to locate this man for questioning."

"But it is imperative we find this Haitian!" Clouseau shook a finger. "He undoubtedly possesses valuable information and must be interrogated. Who is this man?"

Dreyfus read the name. "Papa Doc Duvalier."

Ponton groaned. "So our imposter strikes again."

"It would seem so," Dreyfus said.

"*Voilà!*" Clouseau cried. "As I recall, Chef Miguel had an assistant baker who disappeared after his death by croissant! This man also used the name Duvalier."

"That must be our killer," Dreyfus said. "I also fear this imposter will strike again and again if we do not find a way to stop him."

"A serial killer?" Ponton asked.

Dreyfus shook his head. "An assassin. Or a team of them."

Pie in the Sky

"Assassins? Then you are suggesting these crimes are political?" Ponton asked.

"But, of course," Dreyfus said. "There have been five murders of prominent French chefs. Three of them here in France, the latest in New York City and Tokyo. These crimes are connected by only one thing—all the dead men were set to represent France's culinary traditions once again in the World Food Expo in Las Vegas, which they have won for twelve straight years. This has become one of the most prestigious and lucrative cooking events in the world, and it culminates with the most famous culinary contest of them all, Desserts in the Desert!"

"*Sacré bleu,* now I see," Clouseau said. "How can France win a dessert competition without pastry chefs?"

"It is worse than that, Clouseau. If France were to lose this competition, our national hegemony would be threatened. By killing these men, the assassin or assassins are not only murdering chefs, they are also threatening the gastronomic influence of French cooking worldwide!"

Ponton nodded gravely. "Now I understand why the Trade Ministry is involved."

"Yes," Dreyfus said. "Trade Minister Marmiche believes that if France should present a poor showing in this year's competition, the sales and exportation of French foods and wines would plummet."

Clouseau raised an eyebrow. "It is true. Gourmets around the world are a faddish, fickle breed. They will flock to sample the winning cuisine, ignoring all others."

"But surely French culinary traditions will endure, even if the unthinkable should occur and the French team loses," Ponton argued. "Our national cooking styles have weathered other storms—exaggerated cholesterol fears, the low-carbohydrate Atkins craze, the concession stands at Euro Disney—"

"One may draw that conclusion if one is not familiar with the facts. But history tells us otherwise," Dreyfus insisted. "In 1981, the Japanese team won the main-course portion of the World Food Expo competition by introducing sushi to the Western world. Within a decade, sushi bars had sprung up all over the planet, in every town and city!" The chief inspector's expression soured. "In a few short years and ever since, people have been choking down raw fish and swilling hot rice wine—disgusting!"

"If something isn't done to protect French culinary tradition, then Western civilization will surely be lost." Clouseau stood up and shook his fist.

Ponton glanced up at his boss. "But how can France compete when there is no team left?"

"Two members of the championship team are still alive," Dreyfus informed them. "These men are in protective custody right now, guarded around the clock."

Ponton frowned. "But two men are hardly a team—"

"Trade Minister Marmiche is scrambling to find substitutes for the murdered chefs. While these second-tier talents may not be of the same high caliber as the murdered masters, it is well known that a competent French cook is far superior to a master chef found anywhere else in the world!"

"This killer we hunt is a true villain," Clouseau said. "He hides behind false faces and false identities, and he constantly remains two steps ahead of us. I would like to introduce this miscreant to another imposter—one who would turn the tables on him!"

"A totally absurd suggestion, Clouseau!" Dreyfus threw

up his hands. "Trick the imposter with an imposter? How droll, how absolutely ridiculous and . . ."

Dreyfus fell silent a moment, suddenly struck dumb by an idea that seemed to leap full blown into his head. The ingenious scheme would trap the killer and enhance his own personal glory. And all because of Clouseau's stupid remark.

Clouseau tapped his foot impatiently. "Yes, Inspector, you were saying?"

"I was saying that your absurd, ridiculous suggestion might just be idiotic genius," Dreyfus replied. "A kind of ingenuity that is fueled by abject stupidity. Why, I believe it is your very simplemindedness that seems to attract inspiration in those around you, like air rushing into a vacuum."

Clouseau clicked his heels and solemnly bowed his head. "I am honored by your compliment, Chief Inspector."

"Yes," Dreyfus said with a weary sigh. "You would be.

SEVEN

Sûreté You Jest

As the newly appointed French minister of mental health, Virgil St. Ivey expected to deal with the occasional odd inquiry. But even he was stunned by the call he'd just received.

Chief Inspector Charles Dreyfus had made the most bizarre request he'd heard in his twenty years as a government bureaucrat, which is why the small, birdlike St. Ivey nervously drummed his fingers on the arm of his ergonomic chair.

Having arrived only recently to his post after his predecessor's abrupt retirement, St. Ivey knew he still had much to learn about the ministry he'd been appointed to head. But there was one thing he knew for certain: Charles Dreyfus had a formidable reputation.

As the head of the criminal division of the French National Police, the man wielded power and influence in the highest circles. Almost everyone knew that Dreyfus was an ambitious man.

And ambitious men were dangerous.

One rumor claimed he'd caused the downfall of Director Vallemont, the former head of the French secret service. Somehow Dreyfus had implicated the man in a sex scandal involving a transvestite prostitute and a seeing-eye dog.

No one really knew whether Vallemont had crossed Dreyfus or not. Some said he'd merely wished to eliminate a political rival. Whatever the case, Director Vallemont's secret life was exposed, his career ruined. He resigned his government position in disgrace, and committed suicide by diving off the balcony of the Paris Opera clad only in a tutu.

St. Ivey moaned. With one delicate hand, he wiped the thin film of sweat off the brow of his forehead. When someone of Charles Dreyfus's considerable influence asked for a "favor," it was hardly a request, which is why St. Ivey had acceded to the head of the Sûreté without even looking into the details of the matter.

But he realized there could be pitfalls.

"What if the Chief Inspector's scheme backfires?" St. Ivey muttered, chewing his thumbnail. "It could cause me much embarrassment . . . even ruin my career . . ."

St. Ivey sighed and straightened his bow tie. Although the Americans were noisy, tasteless cultural barbarians, they did have a pithy saying that described the best strategy to deal with Chief Inspector Charles Dreyfus of the Sûreté.

"I must cover my ass," St. Ivey murmured. Leaning forward, he touched the button on his intercom.

"Can I help you, Minister?"

"Oui, oui, Angelique. I'd like you to bring me the case files on Marquis Marcel De Salivon."

St. Ivey needed to learn more about the subject of Dreyfus's call. De Salivon was once a famous chef. Some years back, he had gone mad. Now he was permanently committed to the state's care.

Why Dreyfus wanted to impersonate the man, St. Ivey could not fathom.

"Clouseau, sit down and don't say a word," Charles Dreyfus commanded.

"Certainly, Chief Inspector," Clouseau replied with an insufferable smirk. "Your wish is my—"

"Shut up!" Dreyfus whirled and pointed to face Ponton. "Close the door and lock it. And remember, what is said in this room is to remain a state secret."

The two detectives entered, surprised to find Trade Minister Marmiche in the office with the chief inspector. Only after Ponton secured the door and the two sat down did Dreyfus speak.

"I have a plan to snare our assassin by dangling the perfect victim in front of the murderer's face, a victim too tempting not to kill. We will surround this tasty bait with an invisible wall of security, and when the criminal strikes, we shall have him."

"A good plan," Clouseau agreed. "But do you have this perfect victim?"

Dreyfus rested his elbows on his desk and confidently steepled his fingers. "Are you familiar with the career of the Marquis Marcel De Salivon?"

Clouseau's jaw dropped. "But of course! Who does not recognize the name of the greatest chef in all of France, and so, by elimination the greatest chef in the world! When De Salivon retired to Auckland five years ago, his absence left a hole in the culinary universe that has yet remained an open, sucking wound."

In a rare display of emotion, Ponton stood up, fists clenched, his perpetually hooded eyes wide. "De Salivon is a French national treasure! Are you telling us that he has been murdered by our elusive assassin?"

Dreyfus shook his head. "Never fear, De Salivon is still alive—"

"Then he is coming back from New Zealand? And out of retirement? Perhaps to lead the French team to victory at the World Food Expo!" Clouseau guessed.

Dreyfus leaned back in his chair. "In a way, Clouseau, your bovine stupidity has led you to a *version* of the truth."

Ponton took his seat again. "I do not understand."

"It is really very simple," Dreyfus explained. "As far as the world is concerned, the Marquis Marcel De Salivon *will* emerge from early retirement to lead the French team to victory."

"Huzzah! Huzzah!" Clouseau exclaimed, shaking his fist. "With De Salivon on the French team, we cannot lose—"

"However!" Dreyfus interrupted loudly. "The reality of the situation will be quite different, for the Marquis Marcel De Salivon who travels to Las Vegas next week will be an imposter. He will not be the world-class chef, but a highly trained officer of the Sûreté, ready to strike back when the assassin makes his move!"

Ponton rubbed his chin. "De Salivon will be a tempting target indeed. Five years after he announced his retirement and self-imposed exile from France, people still claim to see him. If the rumors are true, then he's been seen sipping Bordeaux on the Left Bank, dining alone in a café in Nice, and countless other sightings."

Dreyfus frowned. "Your point, Detective Second-Class?"

"What if the real De Salivon should show up? Would he not object to an imposter taking his name, even for so noble a cause as the capture of a serial killer?"

Trade Minister Marmiche cleared his throat. "There is no need to worry. The trade ministry closely monitors passports of such key citizens as De Salivon. And, I can assure you, he has not mixed with the French public since his retirement five years ago. These so called *encounters* with the marquis, they are like those Elvis sightings in America, a product of imagination and wishful thinking, not reality—"

"Enough, Trade Minister," Dreyfus interrupted. "All you need to know is that the Marquis De Salivon will remain where he is, and the National Police have obtained permission to impersonate the great chef from those in position to grant it—"

Ponton was about to ask another question, but Clouseau spoke first. "Say no more! I understand the duty that lies before me, and I accept."

"Accept what?" Dreyfus asked.

"You wish for *me* to impersonate the great chef." Standing, Clouseau placed a hand over his heart. "I realize this is a very great responsibility. No one is aware of that fact more than I. But I am sure I am up to the task and will bring nothing but honor to the institution we serve—"

"Shut up and sit down!" Dreyfus commanded. "I am the one who will be impersonating the marquis."

Clouseau blinked in surprise.

"Believe me, Clouseau, nothing would please me more than letting you play the marquis and placing you in the line of fire. But I am the one who has more than a passing resemblance to the esteemed gourmand."

Dreyfus opened the folder on his desk. "Here, see for yourself." He slid an eight-by-ten glossy photo across the desk. "This is a photo of De Salivon. It was taken just before his retirement five years ago, on the set of an American television show, during the chef's tour of American restaurants."

Clouseau studied the photograph. "I beg to differ with your assessment, Chief Inspector. In this photograph, the Marquis De Salivon does not resemble you. He looks more like a plump African woman with a large, bouffant hairstyle—"

"You fool!" Dreyfus cried. "That's Oprah Winfrey, the television hostess! De Salivon was a guest on her show. He is the man seated to her right."

"An easy mistake, sir," Clouseau replied sheepishly.

"Hardly," Dreyfus said. "But do not despair. As I recall, one other imbecilic countryman of ours failed to recognize Oprah—which means your abject stupidity qualifies you for the floor manager's position at Hermès."

"Really?" Clouseau replied. "An interesting career move. I'll keep that in mind."

"Please do." Dreyfus checked his watch. "I believe that covers everything."

"Um . . . *excusez-moi*, Chief Inspector, but before we go . . ."

"Yes, what is it, Clouseau?"

"Would you mind if I borrowed your letter opener?"

"My what?"

Clouseau pointed to the small bar of metal, shaped to look like a saber—the standard-issue letter opener for Police *Nationale* personnel.

"I have been afflicted with paper cuts of late, you see." Clouseau held up his hand. One fingertip was bandaged up with masking tape. "And my office is sorely lacking in supplies. Would you mind?"

Dreyfus sighed in disgust and waved his hand. "Take it. I have five more in my drawer."

"Ah! *Merci!*"

A sudden buzzing interrupted the meeting. Dreyfus pressed the intercom button on his phone. "Yes, Lamothe. This had better be urgent. You know I am in an important meeting and asked not to be disturbed!"

"My apologies, sir, but you'll want to hear this news."

"What is it?"

"There's been another murder, sir," said Lamothe. "The distinguished Master Chef Etienne de Terricour. It seems he was out of the country."

"Mon dieu. Where?"

"New York, USA."

"New York the city? Or New York the state?" Dreyfus asked.

"Both," answered Lamothe.

"Ah, New York, New York!" Clouseau exclaimed. "The enormous pomegranate."

Dreyfus narrowed his eyes. "The what?"

"The enormous—"

"It's the big apple, you idiot! The big apple!" Dreyfus pressed the intercom again. "Bring in the report when you have it, Lamothe."

"Yes, sir."

Dreyfus glared at Clouseau and Ponton. "Make sure you both read the file when it arrives."

"Read it? I shall devour every page of that report, Chief Inspector!" Clouseau promised.

"Good," Dreyfus muttered as they stood up to leave. "Perhaps, if I am very lucky, you will choke on it."

"Whatever France desires, sir, I shall give it to her!" Clouseau declared with a crisp, firm salute. Unfortunately, as he snapped his hand out, the inspector lost his grip on the metal letter opener. It flew across the room and smashed with great force above Dreyfus's head, right into his prized antique map of the City of Paris. The glass broke into a spider web of cracks then shattered into a million little pieces.

"Out," the chief inspector whimpered, eyes closed as bits of glass tinkled to the floor.

"*Mon dieu*, what a frightful mess," Clouseau began. "I'm terribly sorry. But do you mind if I retrieve that letter opener, I really do need one and—"

"Get Out Now!"

EIGHT

Food Cop

"**I**nspector Clouseau? The crime report from New York City has just arrived." Ponton placed the thick file on top of Clouseau's desk then waited at attention.

"*Bon!*" Clouseau gestured to a chair by the wall. "Sit down, my friend, and we shall peruse the pertinent facts together."

"I have already familiarized myself with the contents of these reports, Inspector, but I shall wait until you have studied them yourself so we can discuss the findings."

Ponton sat down across the desk from the inspector. Silently, he observed his surroundings while Clouseau familiarized himself with the American police report.

Clouseau's offices were not nearly so well appointed as the chief inspector's. In fact, the area Clouseau had been assigned was quite dismal. The faded institutional green paint on the wall was peeling, the steel filing cabinets were chipped and dented. The only view out the single narrow window was of the neighboring building's brick wall, and a thick white vertical post stood in the middle of the small office, eating up the modicum of floor space. Even Ponton, a lowly deputy inspector, had an office that was bigger and brighter.

"This material came very quickly," Clouseau marveled, fingering the pages. "Did it arrive by special courier from America? Or perhaps it was delivered in the French ambassador's diplomatic pouch?"

"Actually, the report came to Lamothe from the NYPD, as an e-mail attachment," Ponton replied. "He forwarded it to me and I printed it out in my office and brought the pages to you."

"Ah, yes, I see," Clouseau said, nodding his approval. "So the World Wide Web can be used for something beyond viewing candid photos of the beautiful Britney Spears or reading the latest Why I Hate Kevin postings on *Mon* Space, eh'?"

Ponton scratched his head. "You are speaking of Kevin Federline?"

Clouseau's eyes flashed with fury. "How many times do I have to say it?" He pounded his desk. "Don't ever, ever mention that despicable man's name to me—*ever*!"

Ponton blinked. "Of course, sir. It will not happen again."

"See that it does not," Clouseau sniffed curtly then returned his attention to the report from New York. "*Mon dieu!* Look at this! The assassin once again has used a clever disguise!"

Ponton nodded. "Yes, he impersonated the late Bob Marley. An interesting choice, given the typical profile of personnel found in urban American restaurant kitchens. Had the killer disguised himself as, say, an illegal immigrant from south of the United States border, he would not have attracted attention in the least—"

"But as the identical twin of a dead celebrity, he would naturally be remembered by a witness," Clouseau interrupted. "Which means the killer *wanted* to be noticed, Ponton. He is sending a signal."

"But why? And for whom is this message meant?"

"Crucial questions indeed, Ponton!" Clouseau rose and paced the threadbare carpet. "And here is one more: why, after pretending to be Charles de Gaulle and Paul Gauguin, did the murderer choose to impersonate a reggae legend?"

Clouseau whirled to face Ponton—and smacked into the vertical post in the middle of his office.

"Sacré bleu, stupid column!"

"Are you all right, sir?"

"Yes, yes!" Clouseau rubbed his forehead. "How reliable is the New York witness, I wonder?"

"The woman's name is Cassidy Caldwell."

"And what do we know about her?"

"She is a petty bureaucrat for the city of New York."

"Ah!" Clouseau cried, then began to pace some more. "That is very good. Petty bureaucrats are always focusing on minutiae. Zealous micromanagement is practically their given name!" He stopped and wheeled—smacking into the post once again.

"Stupid column!"

"Sir! Are you all—"

"I'm fine, Ponton! What sort of petty bureaucrat is Mademoiselle Caldwell?"

"She is an inspector for the Department of Health and Mental Hygiene."

"An inspector you say? Good." Clouseau resumed his pacing. "One can assume that an inspector has superior observation skills. One can also assume that an inspector inspects something that needs to be inspected." Clouseau suddenly stopped and scratched his head. "But I do not understand what a 'Health and Mental Hygiene' officer would investigate. A citizen's mental and physical condition perhaps? If so, how would an inspection of such a citizen be conducted? And by a woman?! Intriguing, no?"

Ponton cleared his throat. "Health and Mental Hygiene inspectors in New York City fall under their Bureau of Food Safety and Community Sanitation. They serve the same function as our food and dairy inspectors here in France."

"Ah!" Clouseau cried again. "Then this woman could be quite influential. My uncle was a food inspector in Calais. A very important job! His task was to certify that the food was pure, the restaurants sanitary for the British and American tourists who crossed the Channel."

Ponton crossed his legs. "Hard work, I imagine?"

Clouseau waved his hand dismissively. "The man hardly stirred. He lay in the sun all day and all the restaurants in the province paid a portion of their profits to him in 'consultation fees.' Last year my uncle retired to a villa in Monte Carlo with five million Euros in the bank and a mistress half his age."

Ponton's perpetually hooded eyes widened in alarm. "Do you know what you are suggesting, Inspector? That your uncle took bribes in the line of duty!"

"Yes, and look around," Clouseau gestured to his surroundings, narrowly avoiding another smack-down by the post in his office. "Do you not sometimes wonder if we are perhaps working in the wrong end of *leau* enforcement?"

"But that would mean—"

"Oh, never mind! . . . Now, listen, I intend to speak with

this Cassidy Caldwell person." Clouseau reached for the phone.

"Do you think it worth our time?" Ponton asked.

"As both a petty bureaucrat *and* a trained *leau* enforcement official, Mademoiselle Caldwell may have observed some detail our other eyewitnesses—like that revolting onion-eating goose farmer, for instance—might have missed. I intend to enlist her aid in this most disturbing case."

"Yes. Yes. Yes, sir. I understand. But if you'll just listen—"

Barbara S. Miller, M.D., Ph.D., deputy commissioner of New York City's Department of Health and Mental Hygiene, pulled the telephone receiver away from her ear. She was almost certain the nonstop tirade coming from the other end exceeded the recommended decibel limit established by the city's public health code. But the man producing it was Barbara's boss, so citing him for noise pollution was probably not a wise idea.

"Commissioner, I understand you were embarrassed," Barbara replied when her superior finally took a breath. "I understand the mayor was unhappy his birthday dinner was ruined and that you—"

With a sigh, Barbara listened for another three minutes as more masculine bellowing ensued. Finally, the phone call ended, on the other end, with a hard slam. Barbara dropped her receiver into its cradle, removed her glasses, and inhaled deeply. Like a punctured tire slowly losing air, she exhaled. Then, slowly and deliberately, she inhaled once again.

Sitting opposite Barbara's cluttered desk was an African American woman named Harriet Samuels. Both women were attractive, ambitious, and approaching fifty. There the similarities ended. Where Barbara was blonde, blue-eyed, and painfully thin, Harriet was dark-haired, dark-eyed, and pushing her seams at a size eighteen.

"Is that stress-reduction breathing you're doing?" Harriet asked her superior. "Does that work?"

"No! Where are my Advils?"

Massaging the bridge of her nose with one hand, Dr. Miller used the other to rifle her desk drawers. When she found the bottle of ibuprofen, she had an overwhelming urge to chug the whole thing.

"Come on, Barbara. What did the commissioner say?"

"You don't want to know."

With a sigh, Harriet stood up, went to the small fridge in the corner of the office and retrieved two sparkling waters. "Here, take your pain relievers with this. If you choke to death, they might just promote me, and I *really* don't want the position."

Barbara knocked back two little pills and swigged the San Pellegrino. "He wants Cassidy Caldwell fired—"

"But that young lady is the best inspector we have!" Harriet had been director of restaurant inspections for only two months, but she'd been in city management for twenty years. And she knew very well what you could and couldn't do to a union employee. "You can't fire Cassidy for doing her job!"

"I know, Harriet. I tried to tell him, but he wants her gone, out of the city. Preferably out of New York State, if we can manage it."

Harriet dropped back into the chair across from her boss's desk. "He was kidding about that, right?"

Barbara Miller just stared. "Either she goes or we do."

"Oh, hell, no! I can't lose this job! My daughter needs braces and my son is flunking out of NYU!"

"We have to think of something fast."

"Barbara, the union won't let us fire her, you know that. And so should the commissioner!"

"He knows. He doesn't care. He wants us to take the heat."

"Oh, god."

Barbara took another swig of sparkling water. "This is an unmitigated disaster."

"In more ways than one," Harriet muttered.

"What do you mean?"

"This stays between us?" Harriet whispered.

"Tell me first," Barbara warned.

"The Minucci brothers are livid about Cassidy's long list of health violations. Apparently, there's a very good reason their restaurant hasn't had an inspection in a decade."

Barbara eyed the Advils again. "I don't want to know this—"

"The Minucci's are *connected*, Barbara, and I'm not talking about Manhattan digital cable."

"I know what you're talking about."

"Well, they're royally pissed. They had some kind of financial arrangement with our former director—one he obviously failed to mention to me. Who knows how many more arrangements the man made before he retired early. And, guess what? I can't ask him."

"Why not? Sounds like we should have him investigated."

Harriet shook her head. "Juan is no longer living in Queens. He packed up his family and moved back to Caracas!"

Barbara closed her eyes. "I don't want to know this."

"You said that already and I don't care. I'm not dealing with this one alone."

"What?"

"Sal Minucci isn't just pissed about the inspection. He's convinced Cassidy Caldwell killed their guest French chef."

"That's patently ridiculous!"

"But that's what he *believes*. The police have dismissed her as a suspect, of course. She had no defensive marks on her and the man she was supposed to have overpowered, killed, and hung on a meat hook outweighs her by one-fifty at least."

"So how can Minucci think—"

"He claims she had help. The police didn't see a motive or any evidence for his accusations. So they refused to arrest her. Minucci's livid about that, too."

Barbara sighed and held her head. "Harriet, I have to tell you. None of this is making my day."

"Well, this might." Harriet reached into the pocket of her navy blue blazer and pulled out a bright pink phone message slip.

"What is that?"

"A French police inspector called the department looking for Cassidy Caldwell."

Barbara put on her glasses to look at the note. "Go on."

"I called him back since we gave the poor girl a few days off to pull herself together."

"And?"

"Apparently, Chef de Terricour is just one in what the French police believe are a series of connected chef murders."

"Chef murders!"

Harriet shrugged. "This Inspector Clouseau believes Cassidy might be able to help them recognize the perpetrator."

"I don't understand. How does that help us?"

"The inspector is traveling to Las Vegas next week to protect the French culinary team competing in the World Food Expo competition. They believe this culinary killer will show up there. So . . ." Harriet leaned forward and smiled. "If we were to assign Cassidy to their investigation as a sign of international cooperation . . ."

Barbara nodded. "We could get her the hell out of New York until this whole thing blows over and our superiors are distracted by some new disaster. This is New York City. How long could that take?"

"Is that a rhetorical question?"

"Get going, Harriet. You contact Ms. Caldwell and get her on a plane ASAP." Barbara reached for the phone and started dialing. "And I'll float this 'international food cop task force' idea with the NYPD. I have a good friend in the medical examiner's office who told me she can call in favors till the next century. That should help grease any squeaky wheels at One Police Plaza."

Harriet stood and headed for the door. "Excellent."

"And one more thing! When you talk to that girl, for god's sake tell her to stop *sanitizing* crime scenes . . . at least until forensics gets its evidence."

"Good idea."

NINE

Tough Cookies

McCarran International Airport
Las Vegas, Nevada

"**W**hat is the meaning of this unruly reception?" Clouseau asked his partner.

"I do not know, but look!" Ponton cried. "It's Elvis Presley!"

While the Pink Panther detective had spent a great deal of time in Sin City on an earlier case, Ponton had been there only briefly. Now he pointed to a tall man with a black pompadour and a glittering white jumpsuit—his very first Elvis impersonator. The experience was, admittedly, quite exciting. He had secretly wondered about the celebrated Rat Pack, the legendary mob stories, the gambling, carousing, erotic floor shows, big theatrical spectacles, and cuckoo crazy chicks.

Now was his chance to observe them—at the very least—in a professional capacity.

Behind Clouseau and Ponton, the French culinary team had just arrived in Las Vegas. As soon as the plane's doors opened, Inspector Clouseau led five jet-lagged master chefs and their personal entourages of sous-chefs down the airbridge and into the bright, spacious terminal, its tall windows framing a magnificent view of the desert landscape.

There to greet them stood a wall of reporters, cameramen, and photographers. Behind the press, an undulating crowd of fans waved cook books and placards, celebrating their favorite chefs. The rowdy mob strained against a line of harried security guards, requesting autographs, while flashbulbs popped and reporters shouted questions.

An alarmed Inspector Clouseau turned to Ponton, who was working undercover as a lowly sous-chef. The beefy French detective had taken pains to dress as scruffily as his counterparts—specifically in bèchamel-stained dungarees, an old T-shirt, and a windbreaker that would conceal the service weapon holstered on his belt.

"I simply do not understand what all of these people are doing here!"

The crowd suddenly parted. Through the rift, a middle-aged man approached, clutching a microphone.

Clouseau raised an open palm to halt the man, then looked up and down his spotless white linen suit, mauve silk shirt, and salmon-pink tie fastened by a pearl-and-diamond stickpin.

"Just *who* are you, sir?"

"You don't know? Why, I'm Chazz Eiderdown! Celebrity host of the Thirty-first Annual World Food Expo and star of the erotic thriller, *Ivory*!"

Above his excessively chiseled features, Chazz's hair had been coiffed to resemble porcupine needles. Even more disconcerting was the unnatural smile plastered across the man's salon-tanned face. His lips and features barely moved when forming words.

"Inspector," Ponton whispered, "this man has less expression than a marionette. Does that not seem suspicious to you?"

"No need to concern yourself, Ponton," Clouseau whispered with a wave. "I am surprised you have not heard of this new American style of speaking with no expression. The magazines are all abuzz with the fad. I believe it is called Botox."

"You may not know me, Inspector," Chazz Eiderdown gushed, "but I certainly recognize you!" He turned to face the camera lens. "Ladies and gentlemen, it is my pride and pleasure to introduce a modern-day Sherlock Holmes, a master of deduction and reason, a brilliant practitioner of modern criminology—the famous Pink Panther detective, Inspector Jacques Clouseau of the Sûreté!"

The subsequent flutter of camera shutters resembled a swarm of hungry locusts. The members of the French cooking team blinked, covered their ears. A few even ducked.

Clouseau was instantly won over. "Well, Mr. Jazz Eisenhower, thank you for your too, too generous praise. Let me first say that it is a pleasure to be back in America, in Las Vegas, and of course—"

Once again, Eiderdown whirled to face the camera. "For those of you who may not remember. The famed French inspector was here in Sin City only a year ago on a very public secret mission. You may recall that the incredible inspector rescued the kidnapped starlet Crystal Ray and recovered the Baby Pink Diamond—not to mention a certain pilfered Leonardo da Vinci painting called the *Laura Lisa*."

"Yes, well—" Clouseau began, but Eiderdown was already firing off his next question.

"So, Inspector. Why don't you introduce the folks of Las Vegas to the culinary masters who will represent France, starting with the most brilliant and innovative chef in all the world?"

Clouseau blinked, staring into the camera lens like a little lost deer. "*Oui* . . . er, yes—"

"Where is this master of the kitchen, this famous Marquis De Salivon?" Eiderdown said, speaking over Clouseau. "Everyone in America is anxious to meet the great man."

"Ah, well, unfortunately for us both, the marquis did not travel with the rest of the team. He arrived here a few days ago—incognito, of course, for security reasons."

Ponton heard the disappointed murmurs ripple through the crowd. The Elvis impersonator frowned, turned his back on the scene, and stalked away. Ponton watched the gleam of his rhinestone cape fade into the terminal's fluorescent hallway.

"What a shame De Salivon couldn't be here," Eiderdown said into the camera, plastic smile still in place.

"Never fear!" Clouseau replied. "The marquis will make his first appearance tonight! At the opening ceremony at the MGM Grand!"

"Well, since the Big Guy couldn't make it, why don't you introduce me to the lovely young woman at your side?"

Clouseau grinned into the camera. "*Oui, oui*, my pleasure, Mr. Eiger Sanction. May I present Mademoiselle Babette Beauford—"

"This is amazing!" the announcer cried. Stepping between

Clouseau and the camera, he pushed aside the inspector. "Ms. Beauford is Europe's most famous vegetarian chef!"

The woman who stepped forward was six feet tall and rail thin, with arms and legs like soda straws. Her long brown hair was pulled into a bun, and though her face was attractive, with high cheekbones, an upturned nose, and flawless skin, Babette Beauford eschewed the typical Parisienne's fashionista façade, wearing a plain black dress and black-framed glasses.

"It is wonderful to be here in America," Babette Beauford said in a timid voice. "And a particular joy to be here to participate in this world-class competition—"

Chef Beauford's softly spoken words were nearly drowned out by the cries of her cheering fans. Most of them were lean, pale young women with severe features, most of them also in black, holding up banners bearing slogans like VEGANS RULE and NO JUSTICE, NO MEAT!

Ponton shuddered at one sign, depicting the photo of a cow with the caption YOU'RE PRIME RIB—TO A CANNIBAL!

"And to my fans," Ms. Beauford continued, nodding to the ladies, "I'd like to say that I will demonstrate to the people of the world that fine cuisine does not involve cruelty to our fellow creatures, or the consumption of *meat*!"

"What a pleasure it is to finally meet you, Mademoiselle Beauford," Chazz Eiderdown crooned. "You have quite a following in Southern California."

Clouseau leaned toward Ponton. "Thankfully such a controversial chef as Ms. Beauford has a following *somewhere*," he whispered to Ponton. "For she is hardly a fit replacement for the *trufficulteur*, Chef Bellafonte. Trade Minister Marmiche was scraping the bottom of the root cellar when he chose this, this . . . vegetarian!"

The Pink Panther's Just Desserts

Babette Beauford was in the middle of answering another question when she suddenly yelped, swore, and scurried off. She was immediately replaced by a muscle-bound giant of a man—the one who'd just pinched her.

"Babette has a most excellent behind!" the Frenchman exclaimed. "Though the mademoiselle could use a bit of fattening, do you not think?"

Chazz Eiderdown's eyes widened, his frozen features actually showing expression. "Oh, ladies and gentlemen, it is my honor to introduce an international soccer star, a world-class surfer, a Formula One racer, and one of the most renowned restaurateurs in all of France. May I present Monsieur Arnaud Germaine, a true European Renaissance man!"

"Hmmm," Clouseau sniffed.

"What?" Ponton asked.

"In America, I believe there is a more appropriate term for Germaine."

"And that would be?"

"Eurotrash."

"Oy, oy, oy!" chanted a brace of British soccer hooligans, banging their shaved heads together.

Eyes twinkling, blond hair slicked back, the giant Germaine stepped up to Eiderdown, dwarfing the announcer. The brawny chef wore a sleeveless shirt that revealed rippling arm muscles. Twin tattoos circled his biceps—twisted thorns on his left arm, barbed wire on his right. Flashing a bright white grin, Germaine held one beefy arm high, waving to the female portion of his screaming fans.

Not everyone was cheering, however, Ms. Beauford's fans were shocked by Monsieur Germaine's chauvinistic behavior, and disgusted by his culinary specialty—wild game and rare and exotics meats. They booed.

"I remember a time when Mademoiselle Beauford was more than willing to *consume* a certain slab of meat," Germaine said, casting his icy blue gaze in the direction of the booing. "Isn't that right, darling Babette?"

Pale cheeks flushing, Babette crossed her thin arms and looked away.

"Monsieur Germaine," Eiderdown said, "you've had some fairly nasty things to say about America's greatest chefs—"

"Amateurs, the lot of them!" Germaine declared. "Worse than amateurs . . . Neophytes. Incompetents!"

Chazz Eiderdown blinked in surprise. "But what about Bobby—"

"I'd flay him alive!" spat Germaine.

"And Emer—"

"If he came to my restaurant, I'd have him tossed out on his Legasse!"

"But in America we also have Wolfgang—"

Germaine waved his hand. "Doesn't his last name rhyme with f——"

"Don't say it!" Chazz interrupted with a good-natured laugh. "This show is seen in Utah."

"Sorry, Chazz," grunted the chef.

"Any last words for our viewers—and keep it *clean*, big guy."

Arnaud Germaine thumped his barrel-shaped chest. "Eat meat. Animals taste mighty good."

"And who is this . . . interesting looking man? Please introduce yourself, sir," Eiderdown said when he spied the next chef on the queue.

Tall and gangly with bulging eyes, a prominent Adam's apple, and a perpetually startled expression, the man blinked nervously at the camera lens.

"Ha'llo," the man said in a shaky voice. "*Mon nom* . . . oh, please excuse, my English is not so good. My name is Xavier Izard. I am zee chef in a lee-tle restaurant in Baie de Mai, a ver-ree small town in zee south of France."

"You must be excited to be here."

"Oh, *oui*," Izard replied, blinking. "I am only zee substitute chef. Here to take the place of any team member who may fall ill. But I am very honored to be here. To see America is like a dream to *moi*—"

But the announcer was already moving on. He'd recognized a member of the previous year's championship winning team. "Hey, hey, hey! Let's have a big Las Vegas welcome for Yves Petit!"

"At last, true genius is represented," Clouseau whispered.

Ponton nodded. "Monsieur Petit is one of only two chefs from last year's prize-winning team who have eluded assassination thus far. He and Henri Le Rhone are fortunate men indeed—"

"Unless, of course, one of them *is* the assassin!" Clouseau whispered, his tone filled with suspicion.

Never having considered that possibility before, Ponton studied Yves Petit. Tiny and soft-spoken, with a shiny bald pate and a Salvador Dalí-style moustache, Petit did not seem the criminal type. Indeed, he seemed to lack any sort of violent potential. A genius at pairing aperitifs and appetizers, he was perhaps even better known for his tiny, origami-like edible sculptures, created with ingredients to complement any course of a meal, from soup to dessert.

But recalling the dossier he'd read on the man, Ponton also knew there was a fierce and public rivalry between him and the other surviving member of the previous year's team—seafood chef Henri Le Rhone. In fact, Le Rhone was just about to interrupt Petit's interview.

The bearded, pipe-smoking Le Rhone, wearing a thick wool sweater, leather waterproof overalls, and a threadbare fisherman's hat stepped up right behind the aperitif master.

In midsentence Petit stopped his eloquent discourse about building edible structures with pastry dough, stuck his nose in the air, and sniffed loudly.

"Excusez-moi!" Petit cried. "I detect the foul odor of rotting fish!"

"Wow!" Eiderdown exclaimed into the camera. "It's Henri Le Rhone, the world-famous seafood chef—"

Petit nodded and glanced with a sneer over his shoulder. "Yes, that is the source of the stench. I suggest the authorities remove this reeking bumpkin at once."

Squinting with his right eye at the tiny, origami-loving chef, Henri Le Rhone removed the cold pipe from between his teeth and tapped the ashes out on Petit's bald head.

"How dare you! You son of stilt fishermen, you product of the Brittany swamps, I'll—" Petit leaped for Le Rhone's throat.

Ponton quickly lunged forward and dragged Petit back.

"Enough of this senseless banter," Clouseau said, jumping between the camera and the squabbling chefs.

"It's a wrap, boys," Eiderdown said, lowering his microphone. "Let's get over to Gate 25. The Treat Restaurant chain is sponsoring a team. I think the Treat Twins are contestants."

As the camera crew—and the crowd—melted away, Ponton exhaled loudly. *"Mon dieu.* It seems this crazy place is already bringing out the worst in our compatriots."

"It is the media, my friend," Clouseau explained. "The

glare of the camera lights is anathema to the Frenchman. Americans, on the other hand, are quite used to the clownish media circus. Quite understandable, considering they are a crass culture of commercialism, glued to pernicious television broadcasts such as *Tinsel Town Exposed*, at seven P.M. weeknight on satellite; and, of course, *Hollywood Hotties*, weekends at nine P.M. Paris time. We French, by comparison, are much more reserved, eschewing the shallowness of celebrity culture and ourselves desiring privacy and dignity above all else."

"Yes, Inspector."

"Now, if you please, lead our entourage to the baggage claim, so that they may . . . you know, Ponton—" Clouseau waved his hand.

"Claim their baggage?"

"Oui, oui!"

Ponton headed toward the escalators. Inspector Clouseau, however, began walking off in the other direction.

"Excuse me, Inspector," Ponton called, "but where are you going?"

"To Gate 25, of course. The camera loves me, you know, and I need more face time."

TEN

Hit Man

After failing to attract more media attention at Gate 25, Inspector Clouseau followed the signs through the terminal to the Readi-Car Rental booth. Not surprised to find a long queue, he thrust his hands into the pockets of his trench coat and, in the manner of any self-respecting Parisian, waited for service with perfect indignation.

At long last, his turn came, and the inspector stepped up to the counter, where a platinum blonde, barely out of her teens, stood looking bored and snapping gum.

"Hello. Welcome to Readi-Car. My name is Trudi."

"My government has reserved two of your monstrous, gas-guzzling American vehicles for official Sûreté use," Clouseau declared, flashing his identification papers.

The woman stared blankly at her monitor, tapped the keyboard.

"Yeah, here it is—" Trudi eyeballed the computer screen. "You're a returning customer, I see. And will you be operating either of these vehicles, Mr. Jack Clow-see?"

"It is *Inspector* Zhawk Cloo-sew, er—Miss Trudi," Clouseau replied. "And to answer your rude and prying question, I *will* be driving one of the vehicles, my assistant will operate the other."

The woman sighed. "The Readi-Car Company will require an additional deposit for the vehicle you operate. We will need the full name of your assistant and you will be required to purchase supplementary insurance at additional cost because of your previous record with our company."

"Mon dieu! Roll over a few vehicles and the Americans brand you for life."

The woman sat back in her chair, eyed the long line of customers behind Clouseau. For a moment, Trudi's eyes were drawn to a young woman with bright orange curls at the back of the line. She impatiently tapped her foot while vigorously cleaning her hands with a sanitary wipe.

"As you can see, Mr. Clow-see, we're quite busy. Either take the reservation or cancel it. You could always try another rental car company."

"Non!" Clouseau shot back. "I am working on a vital case, mademoiselle. I have no time to comparison shop! You have forced me to agree to your company's usurious terms only because my government is paying for every expense. But be warned, I intend to take this matter up with the French embassy!"

"Are you sure you wouldn't like a smaller vehicle? A compact perhaps? According to our records, the last time you rented a Readi-Car SUV, you caused several accidents—"

"I know what your slanderous report says!" Clouseau

cried. "But I have many important passengers to ferry around your glorified desert, so I require the use of one of your obscenely large SUVs, *tout de suite*."

The woman stared at Clouseau, snapped her gum. Then she tapped the keyboard a few more times and a stack of papers began spewing out of her printer.

"Sign here, then here," Trudi commanded. "And I'll need to see your passport and that cop ID of yours again . . ."

Cassidy Caldwell stuffed the container of sanitary wipes back into her bag and glanced at her watch. Someone in front of her sneezed twice.

Good gravy, the jerk didn't even cover his face with a tissue. With total disgust, Cassidy pulled her allergy mask back out of her bag and slipped it on, covering her nose and mouth as she had on the long flight from JFK.

Bad enough that I just spent the last several hours trying to filter recycled disease-laden jet-plane air. Bad enough that I'd shared every germ, every virus in proximity with every other passenger from New York to Las Vegas. Now I have to share the car-rental line with a sneezer—and a rude and unsanitary one at that!

Cass shook her head. *And why was I exiled to Sin City, anyway?* She asked herself for the hundredth time. Her answer was the same one she'd come up with the other ninety-nine times she'd asked.

Because I did my job.

It was a concept she couldn't quite get her mind around. Landing in hot water for doing the right thing seemed so very . . . *wrong*.

She *did* appreciate the fact that Harriet Samuels and Deputy Commissioner Barbara Miller were both trying to save her career. And Cass didn't take the special assignment lightly, either—she meant business. Of couse, Ms. Samuels and Dr. Miller probably doubted her ability to actually solve a homicide. Both cited her own safety as one major reason for this trip.

"You're better off out there at the moment," Barb Miller had told her over the phone, before dispatching her to the desert. "I understand the Minucci brothers have some very dangerous connections."

Despite her superior's concerns, Cass couldn't have cared less about the Minucci brothers' *alleged* connections. Policing New York's restaurants wasn't exactly a dog walk, and she'd bumped skulls with haughty men like Sal Minucci before. Their bark was always worse than their bite.

All she wanted to do right now was secure her rental car, drive to the MGM Grand, check in, take a long, hot shower and a nap—right after she black-lighted the bedspread, sheets, pillowcases, and all the furniture in the room for any sign of organic emissions.

Fifty feet away, an older man with a broad face and slicked-back silver hair made a cell phone call. Instrument to his ear, the man checked his reflection on a polished aluminum wall. Satisfied that his white summer weight suit was spotless, his black Polo freshly pressed, he listened to three rings before the party he'd phoned picked up.

"Yeah?"

"I found her, Mr. Minucci—"

"No last names, Bruno," said the commanding voice on the other end of the call. "You never know who might be listening."

"Uh, right, Mr. Minu—I mean, *sir*."

"You're sure it's the right woman?"

"Oh, yeah, it's her. I couldn't miss that carrottop. Looks like she's wearing a traffic cone on her freakin' head."

"That's the one, all right. What is she doing now?"

"Waiting at the Readi-Car line for a rental. If she gets to the hotel, there'll be too many witnesses. So I'm gonna run her off the road, then whack her . . ."

"That could be risky. State police are pretty vigilant on the highways. And every Tom, Dick, and Jane has a cell phone to call 911 if they think they're witnessing an accident."

"Would you rather I do it quicker? I could use the silencer and get her while she's fussing with her rental car, right here in the parking lot. Then I'll use her own rental to drive her into the desert to dump her."

"What about the security cameras? They have cameras in those rental lots, don't they?"

"No problem. My brother-in-law's in private security. I know how to spot 'em and disable 'em. Just leave everything to me, boss. I'm the best."

"I know, Bruno. Don't screw it up, and let me know when it's done."

"You got it, boss."

"And one more thing."

"Yeah?"

"This Caldwell bitch cost the family a lot of money. Her demise, which is imminent—let's just say there might be a few extra dollars in it for you if her end wasn't so quick, *or* painless."

The hit man's glacial smile widened. "I hear ya. Maybe I'll just knock her unconscious here in the parkin' lot, so I can have a little fun before I dump her down some rabbit hole in the desert."

"Now you're making me happy, Bruno. Very, very happy."

Inspector Clouseau found Ponton and the French chefs waiting at the Readi-Car Rental lot. To his surprise, the culinary masters were no longer bickering. Instead they were speaking among themselves in quiet, almost reverential tones.

"My goodness, what happened to them?" Clouseau asked. "A short time ago they were at each other's throats."

Ponton shrugged. "They have simply found a subject in which they are all in agreement."

Clouseau raised an inquisitive eyebrow.

"They are sharing stories about the genius of the Marquis De Salivon."

Clouseau sighed. "Let us hope they are not disappointed when they meet the great man, eh?"

"That is why Dreyfus instructed us to keep the other chefs at arm's length," Ponton noted.

"Do you think the chief inspector's disguise will stand up to scrutiny?" Clouseau asked. "Does Dreyfus know anything about the culinary arts?"

Ponton shrugged. "I hear he has created his own recipe for a delightful crème brûlée. He intended to prepare it during the Desserts In the Desert competition at the close of the Food Expo."

"Bon dieu! I only hope the French team is far ahead in points by that time!"

As Clouseau supervised Ponton's loading of the luggage into the back of the SUV, he eavesdropped on the conversing chefs.

"I was in attendance at Balmoral when De Salivon feted the British Royal Family," said Yves Petit, eyes dancing at the memory. "Traditional Scottish haggis was served. But when the stuffed sheep's stomachs were sliced, they burst open to fill the table with the petals of the Queen Mother's favorite roses!"

Petit's rival, Chef Le Rhone, nodded in agreement. "De Salivon did amazing things at the prime minister of Canada's wedding, as well. Seafood crêpes, perfectly prepared with the most exotic marine life imaginable. Each crêpe a different fusion—pan-Asian, pan-African—even pan-Tahitian! The seasoning had astounding depth and complexity. And when the cake was cut, a flock of white doves emerged and circled the bride and groom as if rehearsed! Apparently, every amazing detail was handled by De Salivon himself—"

"I once tasted his Truffle aux Croustade," Babette Beauford sighed. "It transformed my life."

"I attended that famous Outback barbecue for world leaders, hosted by the Australian prime minister," Arnaud Germaine added, his mouth watering. "Whole roasted cows, pigs, sheep, and more exotic game, turning on two-story mechanized spits over roaring fire-pits, a design of his own and a marvelous feat of culinary engineering—"

Babette Beauford nodded enthusiastically. "I was a cook at the princess of Dubai's wedding. The three-story cake was at least thirty feet high and ten feet in diameter. It was brought in and assembled right before the guests' eyes, transported by three coaches, each pulled by three Arabian stallions transformed into unicorns by the master chefs. Their horns appeared most real!"

"Meant to symbolize the princess's irresistible sexual innocence, perhaps?" Germaine asked, eyeing his former lover.

Behind thick, black glasses, Babette rolled her eyes and looked away.

The Pink Panther's Just Desserts

*   *   *

Not far away in the same parking lot, a brutal predator waited for his prey.

Just a few minutes earlier, Bruno Ponti had slipped close to the Readi-Car counter to overhear the lot number of Cassidy Caldwell's rental. While she signed her contracts, grabbed her keys, and collected her luggage, Bruno had hurried out to the parking lot, disabled the nearest security camera, and disappeared amid the rows of cars.

What an easy job, he told himself, crouching between two midsized sedans. *Once the Caldwell bitch is distracted, I'll just come up behind her, knock her cold, and toss her inside the rental. Then it's just a short drive to the desert for a little fun . . .*

Already, Bruno could hear the clip-clopping of the woman's heels. His heart raced with excitement. His little red prey was approaching. The party was about to begin.

When Inspector Clouseau climbed behind the wheel of the SUV, he was startled to find his partner waiting for him in the passenger seat.

"Ponton? I thought you were going to ride in the other SUV, with the sous-chefs. You are certainly dressed for it." Clouseau tossed a disdainful glance at his underling's old T-shirt and stained jeans.

Ponton frowned. "I . . . I don't think they like me very much."

"What do you mean?" Clouseau demanded. "You are a reasonably charming man, and as far as the others know, you're one of them—a simple assistant chef."

"If only that were so," groaned Ponton. "But I suspect they know I am an undercover member of the Sûreté."

"Now why would they think that, my friend?"

Ponton shrugged. "On our long flight to America, the sous-chefs drank heavily and caroused for many hours. But, of course, I did not join them—"

"*Oui, oui*, you were on duty, Ponton. You behaved correctly."

"Well, they *may* have seen a passing expression of disapproval on my face."

"Nonsense!" Clouseau insisted. "I'm sure those young cooks had no idea you were observing and judging them."

Just then the vehicle carrying the assistants drove past their SUV. One of the young, hungover sous-chefs leaned out an open window and shook a tattooed arm. "Ponton, you fascist policeman! You cannot fool us!"

Clouseau stared at the passing vehicle and frowned. "Very well, Ponton," he said, starting the engine, "you may ride with me."

The inspector pulled out of the rental slot and cut the wheel sharply.

"This is a very large vehicle," Ponton observed as they rolled through the parking lot. "It must be very difficult to operate."

From behind the steering wheel, Clouseau glanced away from the view ahead, to nod at his friend. "*Oui*, I must admit, our little Smart car is much easier to handle. Driving a tanklike American monstrosity takes deft coordination and considerable focus."

Still waiting patiently between two Toyota sedans, Bruno reached for the sap in his pocket—the perfect weapon to beat Cassidy Caldwell into unconsciousness.

Clearly oblivious to her surroundings, Cassidy moved

through the Readi-Car Rental parking lot, dragging her luggage toward her assigned vehicle slot.

Bruno smiled, watching Cassidy struggle with her large Pullman and two shoulder bags. She dropped the pieces near the car's back wheels, then unlocked the trunk, and began to load in her luggage, one piece at a time. She was completely off guard now. Bruno knew it was the perfect time to strike.

Maintaining his low position, he crept toward the rear bumpers of the two parked Toyotas. He tightened his grip on the sap. *Just one good swinging lunge, and I'll knock the bitch out cold, then I'll stuff her into the trunk and off we'll go. . . .*

The hit man was so focused on his victim, however, he never noticed the sports utility vehicle speeding sharply around the corner. Bruno moved out of his hiding place, but before he could perform his hit, the vehicle struck him. The large, black, fast-moving SUV rolled right over his crouching body.

Inside the speeding SUV, Ponton glanced at the inspector.

"Did you hear that?" he asked.

"What?"

"A sort of . . . *bump*. Do you think we hit something?"

"A speed bump, perhaps, Ponton," Clouseau replied with a dismissive wave as he turned down the Readi-Car exit drive.

"A what?"

"A speed bump! They induce American drivers to keep a slow pace. To prevent deadly accidents, you see?"

"*Oui*, Inspector. Very good. Clearly, you are handling this SUV like a typical American driver."

"Ah, Ponton, you flatter me. Do not make me blush!"

ELEVEN

Love Me Tenderizer

From the moment he opened the white silk curtains in his well-appointed suite, Clouseau could not tear his eyes away from the magnificent, floor-to-ceiling view. The sun had just set over the Las Vegas Strip and the desert sky formed a backdrop of mustard yellow, radicchio red, and burnt orange Tootsie Pop. Far below, the lights of Tropicana Avenue shimmered like the translucent surfaces of multicolored aspics.

A tentative knock shook Clouseau out of his gastronomic revelry.

"Entrez, veuillez!" the inspector called.

Ponton entered.

"Ah, yes! Sit down and give me your report."

"Well, Inspector, the French chefs are safely ensconced in their individual suites. The sous-chefs are also settled, and . . . they still hate me."

"They simply don't know you as I do!" Clouseau insisted. Then he leaned forward, speaking softly. "Ponton, I never told you this, but there is a saying among the members of the Police *Nationale*. They say, 'To partner with Clouseau that Ponton must be very loyal—or a complete idiot!' You see?"

"Uh . . . no. What are you trying to say, Inspector?"

"That you, Ponton, are a good and loyal friend! What other interpretation could there be?"

"Well—"

"Back to business!" Clouseau clapped his hands. "How is security?"

"With help from Officers Lamothe and Raspail, we have secured the entire team living area. The management here is cooperating, so even the MGM Grand hotel staff must pass through a Sûreté security guard to enter this wing of the twelfth floor."

"Excellent, Ponton. And the chief inspector—I mean, 'the Marquis De Salivon.' How is he faring?"

"Chief Inspector Dreyfus is in his suite just across the hallway. He is still having his appearance altered by the specialist. Otherwise, he seems relaxed and ready for the press conference this evening."

"And what of the American woman, Mademoiselle Cassidy Caldwell? Has anyone heard from her yet?"

Ponton nodded. "She's checked in, sir. Her room is just a few doors down the hall, next to mine."

"And have you spoken with the young woman?"

Ponton glanced at his watch. "About sixty minutes ago, I went to her room and knocked, but there was no reply. I put my ear to the door and heard the shower running and a feminine voice singing—"

Love Me Tenderizer

"Ah! Our little health inspector sings in the shower, does she?"

"It would seem so. Unfortunately, when I went back just now to introduce myself, the shower was *still* running and she was still singing in it."

"Hmmm . . ." Clouseau stroked his chin. "Do you think there is a problem?"

"If I had to guess, Inspector, I would say that Mademoiselle Caldwell takes her personal hygiene even more seriously than her restaurant inspections."

Chief Inspector Dreyfus stared at the full-length mirror in his suite's spacious, marble bathroom. He greeted the image he saw with a mingling of amazement and disbelief. The makeup technician from the undercover branch of the Sûreté had finished his work thirty minutes earlier, yet Dreyfus still marveled at the result of the man's artistic labors.

"If I did not know I was looking at my own reflection, I would not have believed it possible," Dreyfus muttered, shaking a head now topped with curly, raven-black hair.

Absent were the gray highlights at his temples and around his ears—those highlights which, in the chief inspector's estimation, lent him an air of highly distinguished dignity suitable to his position. His skin was darkened by a long-lasting, waterproof dye, in an effort to match De Salivon's olive complexion. Contact lenses had turned Dreyfus's muddy brown eyes a bright green, completing the uncanny transformation into the world-renowned culinary master.

Now wrapped in the thick, white hotel robe, Dreyfus was obviously more fit than the real De Salivon. But the addition of a spotless white chef's coat—"padded" with bulletproof Kevlar body armor (as befitting his role as bait for a serial killer) would "fatten" the chief inspector's silhouette sufficiently to fool anyone. And though Dreyfus was slightly taller than the marquis, he was convinced that stooped shoulders would compensate for the additional height.

And, in any case, what person who has met the real Marquis De Salivon would remember the great man as anything less than a giant, a culinary god among men!

It was this aspect of the chief inspector's charade that Dreyfus found most daunting. De Salivon's accomplishments were epic—the stuff of legend. Artist, scientist, culinary genius, and explorer of exotic lands, the marquis was a modern Marco Polo. Some of the stories in the man's official dossier defied belief.

It was after the marquis's return from his voyages to foreign lands and cultures that both his admirers and his detractors noticed De Salivon's palate had become sharper, his preparations more complex by blending new and subtle taste experiences.

His cuisine expanded beyond the basic flavors of salty, sweet, bitter, and sour. Indeed, De Salivon began to explore that formerly unexplored territory on the culinary edge, creating dishes that were best described by the Japanese word *umami*—that taste which defies description.

A knock on the bathroom door halted Dreyfus's musings. "Yes?"

"It's Lamothe, sir," a muffled voice called. "I am about to leave your suite, Chief Inspector. It is time for me to relieve Officer Raspail at the guard station near the elevators."

"Very well, go," Dreyfus told his assistant. "I'm in no danger here . . ."

Alone at last, Dreyfus stripped off the robe and turned on the bath faucet. Soon the marble bathroom was filled with steam and the chief inspector was sinking his tired muscles into the tub of soothingly hot water.

A few moments later, Officer Lamothe—clad in casual civilian clothes to blend in with the typical Las Vegas visitors—met up with another plainclothes officer of the Sûreté. Big and balding, Assistant Officer Paul Raspail occupied a chair near the elevator doors.

"Any trouble?" Lamothe asked.

"No," Raspail replied. "Someone got off at the wrong floor. I politely sent them on their way."

"Good, fine. Go back to your room and get some rest. All of us must take care to remain extra vigilant."

"On my way, sir."

To the casual observer, the French police presence on the MGM Grand's twelfth floor was nearly invisible. A single discreetly armed plainclothes policeman occupied a chair at the end of a long hallway. The area was brightly lit by day, with sunlight streaming through a large picture window. Now that same window was dark, save for the bright lights of the Strip far below, and the pulsing lights of the McCarran Airport runways in the distance.

Thus far, it had been relatively easy to secure the area. Everyone who exited the elevator could be observed. If they headed one way, the guard knew they were guests in one of the two other wings and let them pass. If they headed another way, it was the guard's job to challenge them before they entered the hallway reserved exclusively for the French culinary team and its entourage.

If the guard encountered any trouble, he only had to use his police radio to summon MGM Grand security and the other officers of the Sûreté guarding the French team.

Seated in his straight-backed chair, Officer Lamothe heard the elevator bell chime, saw the doors slide open. A small, nervous man in his middle forties exited. He wore a suit and bow tie, and studied the room number signs as if they were hieroglyphics and he was an Egyptologist.

"May I help you?" the policeman asked in perfect English.

"I . . . I must see the Marquis De Salivon—at once!"

"That is impossible."

"Do not refuse me!"

Lamothe frowned. "You must be a fan, eh? Well, the Marquis is quite busy and cannot be disturbed—"

"But it is imperative that I see him!" the nervous man cried.

Lamothe shook his head and pointed. "The elevator is still waiting. You should go." The man didn't move, so the officer grabbed the door before it closed. "Unless you get in, I will summon hotel security and you will be arrested."

"You don't understand! This is a matter of great importance. The culinary traditions of France are at stake!"

But Lamothe refused to listen and gently pushed the little man back into the elevator car.

"You don't understand! I must see De Salivon—"

The intruder's words were cut off as the doors closed.

"Silly fan," Lamothe murmured.

When the policeman turned around again, he was surprised to see a window washer hanging on a scaffold outside the picture window. The man was busily running a squeegee across the large pane of glass. He wore dirty overalls, clutched a bucket filled with soapy water. But Lamothe was not looking at the man's clothes, or the tools of his trade. He was staring at his hair.

"My lord, but that man certainly looks familiar," Lamothe whispered to himself.

Love Me Tenderizer

Though more than one person in his life had informed Lamothe that he was hopelessly tone deaf, the window man's appearance jarred some memory in the officer's mind. Something connected to music . . .

"That's it! He must resemble a famous musician. Is it Jacques Brel? Wagner, or Dean Martin? . . ."

The window washer's identity dawned on Lamothe a mere split second before the man produced a hammer-like object and hurled it. Before Officer Lamothe could react, the heavy object slammed through the glass and into the side of his skull, knocking him unconscious!

Once Lamothe was down, the window washer jumped in through the broken window, rushed up to the officer, and rifled his pockets until he found the keycard that would open De Salivon's suite. Then he retrieved his meat-tenderizing hammer and stripped off his workman's overalls to reveal the white rhinestone-studded jumpsuit beneath. The movement dislodged a magazine from the man's pocket. The periodical landed, unnoticed, beside the still, bleeding form of Officer Lamothe.

His lower body submerged in the sweetly scented froth of vanilla bath beads, Dreyfus was lost in a steamy cocoon of comfort—until he heard the bathroom door open.

"Lamothe?" Dreyfus called, peering with difficulty through the haze of steam. "Is that you?"

A cold draft swept into the room, raising goose pimples on his flesh. As he began to rise from the tub, he caught an incongruous glimpse of a white jumpsuit, rhinestones, a black, pompadour haircut—then the spiked surface of a meat-tenderizing mallet flying toward his head!

"*Sacré bleu!*" Dreyfus suddenly slipped, splashing back

into the bath water. The loss of footing saved his life. Instead of connecting with the chief inspector's skull, the meat mallet slammed against the marble wall, knocking a good chunk out of it.

"Help! Help! I am being assassinated!" Dreyfus shouted at the top of his lungs as shards of flying marble splattered into the bath water.

Across the hall, Clouseau and Ponton heard the commotion and came running—just in time to see the killer darting out of Dreyfus's suite.

"Look!" Clouseau cried. "It's—"

So amazed to recognize the killer's disguise, Clouseau tripped over his own legs. Ponton came up behind him, tried to leap over his partner and tackle the assassin. Unfortunately, Clouseau's head lifted at that very moment, landing with a smack in poor Ponton's groin.

Howling in agony, Ponton crashed to the floor.

A few doors down, Cass Cassidy had been unable to sleep, so she'd thrown on sweats to take a brisk walk in the night air. She'd just stuffed her damp orange curls into a Yankees baseball cap when she heard the noise in the hallway and stepped out of her room to check it out.

"Stop that legendary singer!" Clouseau yelled, stumbling to his feet. "He is an assassin!"

But Cass couldn't stop anyone—the Elvis impersonator mowed her right down, rolling her end over end! Clouseau gave chase, only to trip over Officer Lamothe's unconscious form near the banks of elevators. While Clouseau struggled to stand again, the killer dived into an elevator and closed the doors.

A moment later, Raspail came running, followed by Ponton.

Love Me Tenderizer

"Inspector!" Ponton wheezed, still clutching his privates as he limped around the corner. "What happened?"

"The murderer got away," Clouseau replied, lunging for the elevator's call button. "But never fear. We should find our assassin easily, for he will stand out in any crowd!"

"What do you mean?" Ponton asked.

"The man was disguised as Elvis Presley, the King of Rock and Roll, correct?"

Ponton nodded.

"Surely such a costume is rare," Clouseau declared. "Really, how many Elvis impersonators could there possibly be in this town?"

TWELVE

Follow That Pompadour!

"**S**top! Wait!"

Angry as a wet bee, Cassidy Caldwell flew down the hotel hallway. At the end of it, she found a plainclothes French officer groaning on the carpet beside shards of broken glass and a curled up magazine. A large, bald officer, also in plainclothes, was helping him sit up.

Bing!

Cass glanced at the row of elevators. All appeared inactive, save one car, which had just arrived. Two men strode through its doors. One wore blue jeans, a loose white T-shirt, and windbreaker. He was big and broad-shouldered with olive skin, a head of dark hair, and masculine, Mediterranean features. Cass didn't know who he was, but she instantly recognized the smaller man in the trench coat with the soft-brimmed hat and cheesy mustache. Without a moment's hesitation, she leaped.

"Mademoiselle!" Clouseau cried as the doors swished closed. "What do you think you are doing!?"

"Are you kidding?" Cass replied. "That tool in an Elvis suit just mowed me down. And I am not in the mood to take any attack lightly!"

Ponton regarded the little elevator jumper. He had to admit, he felt the same way. Even now, as the paneled car descended, he fought the urge to rub his aching privates, an act he deemed less than dignified in a confined space with a female to whom he was not related.

Clouseau shook his finger. "Mademoiselle, he is not 'some tool.' He is not even an appliance. He is a deadly assassin! And I suggest, when we reach the hotel lobby, that you take a ride right back up to your hotel suite, make friends with your minibar, and forget all about it."

"No," Cassidy replied.

"No?" Clouseau repeated.

"No! You people wanted me here to assist in your investigation, so I'm assisting. As of now!"

Clouseau exchanged a surprised glance with Ponton, who took in the petite young woman's red Nike running shoes, white hooded sweatshirt, and navy stretch pants.

"Then," Ponton said, "you must be—"

"Cassidy Caldwell, United States restaurant inspector, at your service."

Ponton's eyebrow arched a fraction. "We are pleased to meet you, mademoiselle. I am Gilbert Ponton, detective second-class, of the Police *Nationale*, and this is—"

"Yes, I know, Inspector Jacques Clouseau, the famous Pink Panther detective. I just saw Chazz Eiderdown interview him on television."

"Forgive us, Mademoiselle Caldwell, for not recognizing

you," Ponton said, "but you do not look at all like the photo your superior e-mailed to us."

Cassidy pulled the baseball cap off her head. "How about now?"

"Ah, *oui*, the orange curls!" Clouseau exclaimed. "And, of course, you look much shorter in person."

Bing!

The elevator doors opened on the lobby level, and Clouseau, Ponton, and Cassidy faced a solid wall of tourists.

"Out of my way, American gamblers!" the inspector cried. "We are officers of the *leau*!"

A heavyset man in a Hawaiian shirt scratched his shaved head. "The *what*?"

"The *leau*!" Clouseau repeated, hands on hips. "Do you not understand your own English language?"

Cassidy shuddered in horror at the crush of bodies continuing to press in on them. Unable to take the barrage of potential germs, viruses, and halitosis, she grabbed Ponton's big hand.

"Excuse me!" she shouted at the top of her lungs. Then she bent low and butted her head into the human swarm, pulling Ponton along behind as she resolutely parted the crowd. The French detective's beefy form forced the wall of bodies to part even more, giving Clouseau ample room to follow in their wake.

When the three cleared the crowded bottleneck of elevators, they found themselves next to the High Limit Slots on the busy MGM Grand casino floor. Cassidy gasped in the relatively fresh air.

"Very clever, mademoiselle," Ponton's deep voice murmured. He gazed down at Cassidy, his perpetually neutral gaze flashing momentarily with a rare expression of admiration. "Where did you learn that maneuver?"

Follow That Pompadour!

"Are you kidding? Try exiting a New York City subway platform at rush hour? This was a cakewalk compared to that!"

Cassidy looked up and realized she was still holding the big, sleepy-eyed Frenchman's hand. She let it go, embarrassed, and also realized she'd grabbed him without her usual precautions for skin-on-skin contact. *Good gravy, I don't even have my face mask or antibacterial wipes!*

But there was no time to go back for them now.

"To the closest exit, at once!" Clouseau exclaimed, charging off one way on the vast casino floor while Ponton went another.

Cassidy stared for a moment at the two Frenchmen racing off in opposite directions. Frowning, she curled her upper lip and whistled sharply.

Both men froze at the loud, piercing sound—along with half the casino. When Ponton turned and realized his superior was not behind him, he waved Clouseau toward the general direction of Wolfgang Puck's Bar & Grill.

"This way, Inspector!" he called.

"You are mistaken, my friend. This way!" Clouseau insisted, pointing toward the Hollywood Theater.

"Guys," Cassidy shouted. "I *see* the jerk who mowed me down! There he goes!"

With an exchange of glances, Ponton and Clouseau once again set off behind Cassidy Caldwell's bouncing orange curls.

"Charming sound you just made there, mademoiselle," Clouseau remarked as they jogged along.

"Gee, thanks," Cassidy replied flatly.

"Where do young American ladies learn to make such whistling noises—finishing schools or at ball parks?"

Cassidy led the Frenchmen past poker and craps tables, roulette wheels, and slot machines. They continued rushing along until they reached the cavernous hotel registration area, a vast space with one massive wall devoted to floor-to-ceiling video screens, which, at the moment, were advertising an upcoming heavyweight boxing match in the MGM's Grand Arena.

Clouseau paused to consider the competitors. "Sanchez versus Jacobs," he murmured, stroking his chin. "Hmmm . . . . I wonder what the action is on that one?"

"There is the scoundrel!" Ponton shouted, catching sight of the Elvis pompadour and rhinestone jumpsuit.

Tearing himself from the digital screens, Clouseau caught sight of him too. "Stop, you!" he cried. "Stop in the name of the *leau!*"

Clouseau took the lead, racing the endless length of the registration desk, then skidding on the slick, shiny floor of the brightly lit lobby. Ponton and Cassidy followed the inspector through the bank of glass doors and out into the warm desert night.

"He's taking a taxi!" Cass cried.

Ponton spied a valet in the porte cochere, but he knew there was no time to waste. "We cannot wait for our SUV, Inspector."

"Then we shall take a taxi, too." Clouseau barreled toward the hotel's long curving driveway, but a group of blond men in tuxedoes, pouring out of a stretch limo, suddenly blocked his path.

"Out of my way, Americans!" Clouseau cried.

"Vee are not Americans," one of the blue-eyed giants protested, looking down at Clouseau with a mixture of cold detachment and ruthless disdain. "Vee are German."

Follow That Pompadour!

Of course, Clouseau thought, *the ruthless disdain should have given them away!*

"I do not care if you are—" Clouseau began, but lost his tongue for a moment when a platinum bombshell in a skin-tight gown of glittering silver spandex unfolded her six-foot frame out of the limo.

"If vee are vat?" asked the well-endowed temptress.

"Stunning . . ." Clouseau replied, his jaw slack.

"I know you!" The blonde's glossy lips curved upward. "You are de famous Pink Panther detective!" She extended her manicured hand.

"Enchanté," Clouseau cooed, kissing the woman's soft, perfumed skin. "And what brings you to the American desert, my dear?"

"Ze World Food Expo, of course! Vee come to compete and do a bit of zee business, you know?"

"A bit of zee business, of course," Clouseau gushed.

"And vat are you, such a famous detective, doing here? A little gambling, perhaps? Or are you here for a little naughtiness?"

"A little naughtiness, indeed! How charming you are, my love . . . No, I am here on police business." Clouseau leaned close and lowered his voice. "A very important and very secretive matter."

The bombshell's smoldering indigo eyes widened. "How intriguing, Inspector. Perhaps you can come to my room later and tell me more? I am Elsa, *und* I am staying wit zee German team."

"Come, Inspector!" Ponton called. "We have a taxi!"

"Oui, oui!" Clouseau called, then turned back to the platinum blonde beauty. "Until we meet again, *mademoiselle, au revoir.*"

Elsa threw the inspector a kiss. *"Auf Wiedersehen."*

Clouseau jumped into the taxi, already rolling down the drive, slammed the door, and sighed. "Ahh, Germany . . ." he murmured. "My favorite country."

"But, Inspector," Ponton countered, "you have always harbored a vehement dislike of all things German."

"Do not say such a thing, Ponton!"

"Weren't you ranting just the other day about the horrors of Oktoberfest?"

"No!"

"Yes, yes! You said if gastronomical bad taste were a crime, the first two felons would be bratwurst and beer."

"Hello *dair*! Pardon me," called the driver in a Jamaican accent. He peeked around the partition between the front and back seats. "Where would ya like ta go?"

With a start, Cass took a closer look at the cabbie—a solidly built black man with long dreadlocks—and felt her hands go clammy. The last time she'd seen a cascade of dreadlocks, they were worn by a murderer.

Clouseau pointed to the line of cars on Tropicana Avenue. "Follow that cab there."

"Really, *mahn*?" the driver asked. "You're not kiddin'?"

"No, we are not!" Clouseau insisted.

Cassidy strained to get a better look at their driver. He noticed her scrutiny in his rearview mirror, reached up to adjust it so he could scrutinize her. Before Cass could say a word, the cabbie turned the wheel, pulled out of the hotel's drive, and into the congested traffic on Tropicana.

"Ya know," said the driver in his lilting island accent, "I been doin' dis two years now, but you are de first passengers to ask me to 'follow dat cab.' Ya know, like in dose old black-and-white movies?"

Follow That Pompadour!

Cass did not recognize the man's voice—no surprise there, since the dreadlocks-wearing murderer in New York did little more than grunt at her. And she certainly knew there was more than one Rastafarian walking around. Still . . . she found it awfully coincidental that such a man should suddenly appear right after their current perp had taken off.

"Do not tarry, driver! Drive!" Clouseau cried.

"Chill now, *mahn*," said the cabbie, "you can see de traffic's all backed up."

Clouseau observed the bumper-to-bumper line.

"Perhaps I should attempt to overtake Elvis on foot," Ponton suggested. But as he opened the door, the intersection's traffic light turned green and the cab was moving again. Inside of a minute, they were turning onto Las Vegas Boulevard.

"Do not lose that cab!" Clouseau warned the driver as they picked up speed.

The Strip was just as the inspector remembered it from his last visit: a labyrinth of garish neon, flashing marquees, and structures that would drive a French architect mad.

"Look, mademoiselle." Ponton pointed. "There is your New York City."

Cassidy narrowed her eyes at the elaborate exterior design of the New York, New York Casino. "Except we don't have a roller coaster running through our skyline," she noted. "But I see your Eiffel Tower over there." She gestured to the well-lit replica of the French landmark, glowing in front of the Paris Casino.

"Ah, *oui*," said Ponton, examining it as they drove by.

"Is it really so small?" Cassidy asked. "Your Eiffel Tower?"

Clouseau sniffed. "I assure you, our French erection is much larger!"

Ponton nodded, squinting at the replica's struts and supports. "*Oui,* mademoiselle. I am no expert on erections, but I believe ours is more rigid, as well."

The spectacle of the megacasinos continued to roll by: Caesars Palace, Harrah's, Mirage, Treasure Island, the Venetian, Stardust, and Circus Circus. Finally the cabbie turned off the main drag. As simple city streetlights replaced million-dollar marquees, the neon day abruptly turned into shadowy night. The cab drove on, trailing the taxi ahead.

"Tell me, now, did I hear ya say somethin' 'bout Elvis?" the cabbie suddenly asked.

"*Oui,*" Clouseau replied. "We are on the hunt for the Elvis impersonator."

The cabbie laughed. "Why? Did de *mahn* try to kill somebody?"

"How did you know!" Cassidy blurted out.

"Chill, lady, I was jus' jokin'."

But Cassidy wasn't so sure. Still curious about the man's identity, she looked for the cabbie's license and photo. It was attached to the back of the front seat on the other side of the car. She was sitting against one window, Clouseau against the other. And Ponton sat between them, which meant Cassidy had to lean all the way across the big detective's muscular thighs to read the cabbie's license.

"Excuse me, Detective," Cassie said, her breasts pressing into his thighs as she leaned down, over Ponton's lap.

"Mademoiselle!" Ponton gasped, his perpetually hooded eyes suddenly going wide as windows.

"I'm just trying to read the driver's license," Cassidy whispered.

"Oh."

Cassie froze when she realized the man sounded disappointed. Suddenly, she was reminded of Ponton's comment about the Eiffel Tower.

"Do not get too close!" Clouseau warned.

Cassie abruptly sat up.

"He was speaking to the driver," Ponton whispered in her ear.

"Was he?" Cassidy decided it was probably good advice for her too.

The cab turned down one street, then another and another. There were blocks and blocks of apartment buildings, convenience stores, and strip malls.

"Where is the cab?" Clouseau asked the driver. "I think you have lost it."

"Chill, *mahn*, ya said not to get too close. It went down de next block." The driver shook his head. "Ya don't have no idea who dis guy is dat you're followin', do ya?"

"We already told you," Clouseau snapped. "He is the Elvis impersonator."

The next block had very few streetlamps. The cabbie pulled over about halfway down. "Okay. Here ya go, my friends. Ten dollars and fifty-five cents."

"What do you mean?" asked Ponton.

"I mean, your ride costs ten fifty-five! That cab we were followin' just dropped your *mahn* off right here. You were huntin' for Elvis, right?"

"But there is nothing here," Clouseau insisted.

"I know dis street's dark, but I saw de drop in my headlights. Your Elvis went up dat alley."

"It's pitch dark," Cassidy noted.

The cabbie shrugged.

"Pay the man, Ponton!" Clouseau commanded as he flung open the passenger door and charged into the alley.

Cassidy followed and Ponton jogged to catch up. Two dirty brick buildings flanked them as they walked along, dodging garbage cans.

"Ohhhh ...." Cassidy groaned, covering her mouth to stave off the foul, germ-filled air.

"Mademoiselle," Ponton whispered. "Are you ill?"

"No," she said, her hand muffling her voice. "I am not ill. I'm a *healthy* obsessive-compulsive."

"Excusez-moi?"

"Ask me later," Cassidy replied through her hand. "If I talk, I have to breathe, and if I breathe, I'm going to heave."

"You have made a rhyme." Ponton's eyebrow arched. "How amusing."

"There!" Clouseau softly cried.

"What is it, Inspector?" Ponton whispered.

"A door," he replied and waved the two forward.

The unmarked door stood at the very end of the fetid alley.

"Clearly we have stumbled upon a back entrance to some sort of hideout," Couseau whispered.

"Inspector, let me enter first, *s'il vous plaît*," Ponton's deep voice advised as he reached behind his back and under his windbreaker.

Clouseau nodded. *"Oui,* my friend. I keep forgetting that, as the world-renowned Pink Panther detective, I am far less expendable than you."

"He's what?" Cassidy asked Ponton from behind her hand.

"He's a lousy shot," Ponton whispered. In one smooth motion, he drew his service weapon from the holster clipped to his belt, disengaged the safety, and chambered a round. With the gun poised in one hand, he stepped up to take point and slowly turned the door handle.

Surprisingly impressed, Cassidy watched Ponton ease the

door open a crack without making a sound. Leading with his weapon, Ponton smoothly stepped inside and disappeared. A few moments later, she heard his deep voice shout—

"Do not move!"

Cassidy and Clouseau rushed in to find the French detective holding his weapon on the back of the Elvis impersonator, his white rhinestone jumpsuit and ink-black hair unmistakable.

"Turn around, *slowly*," he commanded.

The Elvis did, to show off a plunging neckline and an obscene amount of plump cleavage.

Ponton's eyes bulged and Clouseau cried out. "*Sacré bleu!* You are a woman!"

"Listen, buster, there's no need to go medieval on me. If you need a male impersonator, you've got like fifteen to choose from tonight!"

"What?" asked Clouseau.

"You heard me. They're right in here."

The woman strode out of the back hall, past the restrooms and into a brightly lit office. Over a dozen Elvises were lounging around, reading the paper, strumming guitars, or talking on cell phones.

"What is this place?" Clouseau murmured.

"1–800-GotElvis?" the female impersonator informed him. "We rent by the hour and day. Birthdays, weddings, bar mitzvahs, bachelorette parties. You name it."

"Mon dieu." Clouseau massaged his temples. "Wait till I tell the chief inspector."

"Tell him what?" Ponton asked, securing the safety on his weapon and holstering it behind his back.

"That there is more than one man impersonating Elvis, of course!"

"More than one?" Ms. Elvis laughed. "In this town? Buddy, there are thousands!"

"Do not torture me, woman. Can you not see I am distraught."

"I still think we should detain these men," Ponton asserted. "The man we chased did end up here."

"Or did he?" Cassidy asked.

"What is your meaning, mademoiselle?" Ponton asked.

"Just that the cabbie didn't match his license."

"Excusez-moi?" Clouseau asked.

"The cabbie appeared to be a black man with dreadlocks. But the license showed an Indian man with a turban. Didn't you notice?"

"Of course not! How absurd! I had my eyes fixed on the taxi we were pursuing!"

"Well," said Cassidy, "I thought it was an odd coincidence that a black man with dreadlocks appeared the moment we began pursuing your perp."

"Ah, *oui*, now I recall," Clouseau said. "This was the description of the suspect in the de Terricour murder, correct?"

"My description. Yes."

"Are you saying our cabbie was the same man?" Ponton asked.

"I couldn't be sure," Cassidy replied. "It's just a strange coincidence."

Clouseau threw up his hands. "Well, why did you not speak of this sooner, woman! We could have detained the man or written down his license plate number."

"I've already got it." Cassidy tapped her orange curls. "Up here."

Clouseau lunged for her head and began pawing through her hair.

Follow That Pompadour!

"Are you crazy!" Cassidy cried. "Get off me!"

"Hey, mister!" shouted the female Elvis. "What do you think you're doing to that little girl! Help! Help!"

"There is nothing written on your head, mademoiselle. I really think—Ahhhh!"

Unfortunately, Cassidy had no time to explain the American idiom to the French inspector. A dozen Elvis impersonators had just tackled him to the floor.

THIRTEEN

Mocktails

"What are you drinking?" Cassidy asked, sliding into the swivel chair next to Ponton.

The French detective nodded a curt greeting to the petite American restaurant inspector then frowned down at his nearly empty tumbler, sitting on the bar. "Ginger ale," he told her with a regretful sigh.

Two hours had passed since the Elvis pile-on. After extracting Clouseau from the human hillock of rhinestones and Brylcream, Ponton and Cassidy had called another cab and together carried their superior back to Charles Dreyfus, who roundly upbraided them all for allowing the perp with the pompadour to escape. Upon leaving Dreyfus's suite, Clouseau had announced that he needed a drink and headed for the casino floor. Ponton had followed.

Cassidy had veered back to her room to wash her hands—

about a dozen times with *very* hot water—and retrieve her bag before deciding to join the Frenchmen in the MGM Grand's Teatro Lounge.

"After the night we've had," she told Ponton, "I'm surprised you're not drinking something stronger."

"I would like to, mademoiselle. Believe me." He drained the tumbler. "But I am still on duty."

"When are you off?" Cassidy asked.

Ponton raised a dark eyebrow. He was sure he'd heard flirtation in the little inspector's tone. But he had little insight into women and even less into American women. Choosing not to press his luck, the French detective replied in a neutral, straightforward manner.

"Technically, mademoiselle, I'm not off duty until our plane's wheels touch Paris tarmac."

"Oh. Sorry to hear that."

The lounge was filled with couples laughing and talking. Smooth jazz flowed through the room of red banquettes and crowded tables. From behind the lighted bar, a young man approached.

"What would you like, miss?" the bartender asked.

"A Bora-Bora," Cass replied. She jerked a thumb toward Ponton. "And give him one, too."

The bartender nodded and turned away.

"What's a Bora-Bora?" Ponton asked.

"Don't worry." Cassidy waved her hand. "It's a mocktail."

"Excusez-moi?"

"A fake cocktail. No alcohol."

"Ah, *oui*. I see. Mocktail." Ponton nodded, again amused by the little American. "And what is in this Bora-Bora mocktail?"

"Three parts pineapple juice, three parts dry ginger ale, a half measure of grenadine, one teaspoon lime juice, and one maraschino cherry. Ice goes in the shaker, then the juices and grenadine. Shake well, strain into a glass, and top with your dry ginger ale and cherry."

"It does sound refreshing."

"Guaranteed to conjure images of tropical breezes and swaying palm tress." Cass smiled at Ponton, then leaned over the bar. "Hey! Bartender! Let me see those tumblers!"

The bartender looked up. "These?"

Cassidy nodded and the young man handed her the two glasses. Ponton watched her examine them, put them on the bar, and dig into her purse.

"What are you doing?"

"One can never be too careful." Cass wiped the edges with a sanitizing towelette. "Fecal fingers, you know?"

Ponton knitted his brow.

Cass waved a fresh towelette at the bartender. "Now you, please."

"Me?"

"Yes, *you*. Wipe your hands." Like an antibacterial signal flag, she waved the cloth more vigorously. With a perplexed look, the bartender took it and cleaned his hands. "Good. Now throw it away and prepare the drinks."

The bartender went back to his work, and Ponton regarded Cassidy. "This is a habit of yours?"

"What?"

"The cleaning."

"Like I told you back in the alley. I'm obsessive-compulsive."

"You are in therapy?"

"Good gravy, no! My *issue* has made me the top restaurant inspector in my department. I've received two commendations in the past six months."

"And a serious reprimand, also, I understand."

"Yes, well." Cassidy sighed. "Cleaning that crime scene was a mistake, I admit. But I didn't know it was a crime scene until I found the chef's body." She shuddered, then pounded the bar with her fist. "I really do want to help you catch the killer. For me, it's personal. You understand?"

"You knew Chef de Terricour?"

"Not really, but he certainly didn't deserve to die like that."

"No grudges, then?"

"Excuse me?"

"I studied the New York police case file," Ponton informed her.

"And?"

"And I read the statements that were taken. One Salvatore Minucci believes you take out personal grudges in your inspection work."

"Minucci's an ass."

"But, do you?"

"I call them as I see them, Mr. Ponton. Period. I don't take bribes and I don't abuse my power. And I didn't kill the chef, either. Minucci thinks that, too."

Ponton suppressed a smile. The little American was quite a package, he decided, admirable as well as adorable, even with her occasional odd quirks.

"Forgive me for prying, Mademoiselle Caldwell, but I like to know the backgrounds and attitudes of my partners."

"We're partners then?"

"*Oui.*"

She smiled. "Then please call me Cassidy."

Ponton nodded. "Mademoiselle Cassidy."

"Just Cassidy. So where are you with the investigation? And where is Inspector Clouseau?"

"The inspector and I both agreed—"

"Wait!" Cassidy cried.

"What?"

"Not you." She leaned over the bar again. "Bartender! Don't use the maraschino cherries from that condiments tray. Can't you see they're just sitting there, out in the open, where anyone can sneeze on them? Take our cherries directly from the jar, please. Thank you!" She turned back to Ponton. "You were saying?"

"The investigation. Las Vegas Metro Police are tracking down your Rasta cabbie's license plate and checking the backgrounds on any suspicious Elvises in the area."

"Not very promising leads, are they?"

Ponton grunted.

"What about the other teams here for the Expo?" Cassidy asked. "Wouldn't one of them have the strongest motive for hurting France's top chefs?"

"*Oui.* The inspector and I already came to this conclusion, which is part of the answer to your second question."

"My second?... Oh, yes, where *is* Inspector Clouseau?" Cassidy glanced around the crowded bar. Trendy couples were laughing and talking. But there wasn't a trench coat or cheesy mustache in sight.

"The inspector has gone to the guest room of a beautiful blonde named Elsa, whom he bumped into during our pursuit of the Elvis impersonator. Apparently, she is traveling with the German team."

"And the German team is important because ... ?"

"Germany has finished near the top of the World Food Expo for the past five years. And last year, they were the runners-up to France in the Desserts in the Desert part of the competition."

"I see. So if any team would benefit from France's failure in the culinary competition—"

"God forbid."

"—it would be Germany."

"Oui."

"Okay. Got it. So Inspector Clouseau is planning to interrogate this Elsa?"

Ponton nodded. "As he tells me you Americans put it, he is hoping the beautiful lady will 'present him with an opening.'"

Cassidy blinked. "Excuse me?"

"Here you go. Two Bora-Boras," said the bartender, setting down drinks the color of an island sunset. "In *clean* glasses," he added pointedly. "With cherries *from the jar.*"

"Merci," said Ponton, quickly paying the man and adding a very large tip for his troubles.

"Thank you for paying, Detective," Cassidy said, still fumbling for her wallet. "I was going to treat you, you know?"

"It is nothing, mademoiselle. You have already saved me from . . . how did you put it? Fecal fingers, have you not?"

"True."

"Then drink up."

Cassidy had barely taken two sips before they were interrupted by a large, bald man in a gray suit.

"Ponton, there you are!" he called, approaching the bar.

Cassidy recognized the newcomer. He was one of the French plainclothes officers she'd seen after the Elvis attack. She remembered seeing this one crouched on the floor, trying to help his fellow officer, the one groaning amid the broken glass, and the—

"Rolled-up magazine!" Cassidy blurted out.

"What's that?" Ponton asked.

"On the floor upstairs, near the window, where the attacking Elvis broke in. I just now remember seeing—"

"The rolled- up magazine," Officer Raspail interrupted. "I have it here."

Ponton took the item from the man's hand and read the front. "*Las Vegas Eats*. Where did you get this, Raspail?"

The officer shrugged his bulky shoulders. "It is as your lady friend just said. This was found beside Lamothe, amid the broken glass where the suspect burst in through the window. Did Dreyfus not tell you?"

Cassidy snorted. "Charles Dreyfus? Mostly what that man did was curse at us."

Ponton sighed. "The chief inspector only mentioned that Lamothe was taken to the hospital—"

"*Oui*, that is true." Raspail nodded. "I went with him. They are keeping him overnight, but they say he should be fine."

"That is very good news, my friend."

"I agree, Ponton, and this magazine was obviously dropped by the perpetrator," Raspail replied. "We have finished dusting for fingerprints."

"And?"

"Nothing. A few smudges, nothing useful. Not as far as physical clues. But I thought perhaps Inspector Clouseau would like to have a look. Unfortunately, he was not in his room."

Ponton nodded. "That is because he is pursuing a very important lead with a very beautiful woman."

Cassidy gulped her drink. "I thought you said he was pursuing 'an opening.'"

"Ah, *oui*. That, too," Ponton assured her.

"*Sacré bleu!*" A familiar voice suddenly exploded. "I need a drink!"

Mocktails

The group turned to find Inspector Jacques Clouseau marching up to the bar.

"Inspector, back so soon?" Ponton asked. "What did you discover?"

"Discover? I'll tell you what I discovered: a very large, very blond, very grim-faced watchdog in a three-piece suit, telling me the beautiful Elsa is indisposed!"

"Indisposed?"

"Apparently, the German team is allied with some Berlin-based food corporation that is planning a big presentation here at the World Food Expo. Elsa is part of the marketing team, and she will be in a planning meeting all night. All night! Can you believe this terrible news?!"

"What are your plans then?" Ponton asked.

"Plans? After my *massive* expectations were raised, then suddenly emasculated? I plan to drown my sorrows!"

"Ah, *oui*. May I respectfully recommend Bora-Bora."

"Are you daft, man? Why would I go to an island in French Polynesia to drink when there's a well-stocked bar right in front of me!"

"No, Inspector. This is a Bora-Bora." Ponton held up his coral-colored drink. "It is . . ." Ponton tossed a little, amused glance at Cassidy. "A mocktail."

"A *what*?"

Cassidy lifted her own drink. "A cocktail without alcohol."

Clouseau shuddered at the very idea. "Ghastly!" he cried, then reconsidered and patted his underling's muscular arm. "Nevertheless, Ponton, I must commend you, for staying on the straight and narrow. Yes, you are an example of honor and duty to every officer who carries a French badge!"

With great national pride, Ponton squared his broad shoulders. "Thank you, sir."

Just then, the bartender approached Clouseau. "What can I get you?"

Clouseau rubbed his hands together. "Let us begin with a martini—gin, and make the vermouth Noilly Prat of Marseilles, *s'il vous plaît*. And then I shall need a bottle of your best champagne, and, I warn you, man, do not attempt to sell me one of your inferior California sparkling whites or I shall have your head!"

The bartender hurried off and Ponton gaped at his superior with a mixture of shock and outrage. "Inspector!"

"What is it, my friend?"

"You are drinking on duty!"

Clouseau sighed with supreme disdain. "It is an elementary conclusion of logical deduction, Ponton. To require *two* French officers to simultaneously refrain from consuming alcohol is completely unwarranted and patently ridiculous when *one* has already taken it upon himself to remain sober."

"I see," said Ponton. "And I am the designated sober one?"

"But, of course, my friend! You are the one who is armed!"

FOURTEEN

In Cold Type

"What are you reading there?" Clouseau asked a few minutes later, between healthy gulps of his dry martini.

By now, Raspail had departed and the three of them—Clouseau, Ponton, and Cassidy Caldwell—had moved from the bar to one of the Teatro Lounge's tables.

"It is a magazine—" Ponton began.

"It's a clue!" Cassidy interrupted.

Clouseau raised a smirking eyebrow. "The little inspector is enjoying the game, eh, Ponton?"

Cassidy narrowed her eyes. "Watch it, Frenchy. You weren't so smug under that pile of impersonators!"

Clouseau sighed. "American women have no sense of humor."

"Both of you, stop," Ponton ordered. "Let us remain focused on our case."

Clouseau drained his martini and commenced sucking on the olive. "I am listening, my sober friend."

"Inspector, this magazine was in the possession of the man who attacked Lamothe and Chief Inspector Dreyfus. No fingerprints were usable, but I believe there is an important lead here."

"Nonsense," Clouseau replied, waving Ponton's suggestion away even as he waved over one of the lounge's cocktail waitresses. "I am sure you are reading too much into it—" Clouseau abruptly paused and blinked. "Ha!" he cried, slapping Ponton's broad back. "What do you know! I made a funny! I said you are *reading* into it! You are *reading* into a *magazine*! Is that not amusing, my friend?"

"Yes, sir?" the waitress asked.

"My bottle of champagne, *tout de suite*! The bartender has my instructions!"

"Of course, sir."

The waitress had no sooner scurried off than a new arrival tapped Clouseau's shoulder from behind. "Excuse me, but aren't you the famous Pink Panther detective?"

The feminine voice was soft yet sultry, the tone leaving no doubt about the speaker's intimate interest. Clouseau, still smarting from his monumental letdown with Elsa, turned toward the voice with an almost autonomic response.

At that point in the evening, the inspector was reasonably aware that he would have reacted positively to almost anything in a skirt. What he found when he finally saw the woman left him completely spellbound.

The newcomer was a statuesque brunette, her long, gently waving locks gleaming in the lounge's mood lighting. Her features suggested an East Indian heritage with a cocoa complexion, high cheekbones, and a hungry little smile. Her little black dress was very little, revealing long, silky legs in black leather sandals and a healthy cleavage, adorned by an antique silver chain holding a stunning onyx, its smooth black surface perfectly complementing the woman's luminous, round eyes.

The inspector gaped, utterly speechless for a solid minute.

The woman blinked her wide, dark eyes at Clouseau. "I don't mean to invade your privacy. But, you see, I saw you interviewed earlier on television. You know? By Chazz Eiderdown? And I happened to notice you here in the lounge, so I thought I'd come over and see if you . . ." The woman shrugged. "Wanted to have a drink with me?"

Clouseau continued to stare.

"What is your name?" Ponton asked, glancing with concern at his superior.

"Rita." She smiled. "Rita Saffron."

"The inspector is pleased to meet you, Mademoiselle Saffron," Ponton assured her. "Won't you sit down with us?"

"Oh, thank you!"

Finally, snapping out of his fugue state, Clouseau leaped to his feet and cleared his throat. "Pardon me! My manners!" He pulled a chair out for the woman. She gracefully sat and crossed her long, dark legs. Clouseau loosened his tie and collar.

"You must be very nervous about the competition," Rita said, her dark eyes dancing with curiosity.

"Nervous?" Clouseau replied.

"Yes. I mean, that Eiderdown interview was pretty transparent. Your new French team sure has a lot of bickering chefs among them!"

"True," Clouseau admitted. "But we French always rise above in the thick of it, you know?"

"Really? Well, I have tickets to all of the events. Even the Cast-Iron Skillet competition tomorrow in the Grand Arena. I'm so excited! I can't tell you how much I've been looking forward to a whole week of international gastronomic rivalries! It makes me want to . . . you know?" She leaned toward Clouseau's ear and whispered. "Celebrate."

"Sweet heaven," murmured Clouseau. After licking his dry lips, the inspector took a chance. "My dear, I see our waitress bringing my bottle of champagne. Would you care to share it with me?"

"Of course!"

"Perhaps somewhere more private—"

Rita grabbed Clouseau's hand and stood up. "Let's go to your room, then."

"*Oui, oui!*" Clouseau grabbed the bottle off the waitress's tray with his free hand. "*Bon soir,* Ponton, Mademoiselle Caldwell. I shall see you both in the morn—"

The inspector's final syllable was swallowed up by the crowd as Rita pulled him toward Teatro's exit.

Ponton produced a credit card for the waitress, then glanced at Cassidy and shrugged. "The inspector has many female fans."

"For the life of me, I can't see why." Cassidy pointed to the magazine in Ponton's hands. "So what is it you've found? In the magazine? Something that will help with our case, do you think?"

Ponton slid the glossy pages across the table. The colorful spread he'd been reading was a feature essay on the World Food Expo.

Cassy picked up the magazine and read the story's title aloud: "Desserts in the Desert: Why the French Team Must Die."

*   *   *

"What do you see?" Ponton asked Cassidy a short time later.

"There's a list of articles by Rex Wesson on the magazine's Web site. But no picture and no bio."

Cassidy was sitting at the desk in her hotel suite, her laptop plugged into the high-speed Internet connection. Both Ponton and Cassidy agreed that their best lead was the author of the inflammatory article in *Las Vegas Eats* magazine—Rex Wesson. And Cassidy had suggested they go to her room to do some digging into his background.

"Wesson is the magazine's restaurant critic," Cassidy informed Ponton as she studied the blurb provided by the publication. "He's a very influential food writer. Apparently, his columns are syndicated and appear all over the world, although I have never heard of him."

"Why not? You went to culinary school, did you not?"

"Let's not mince words, Ponton. I was thrown out of culinary school. Anyway, New York is crawling with its own restaurant critics. There's no need to import a syndicated column. So it's not unusual that I never heard of this Wesson character."

"All right. Let us review." Ponton began to pace the hotel room. "We know this magazine was carried by the man who attacked Dreyfus—"

"Thinking he was De Salivon, right?"

"Correct. Dreyfus is registered that way with the hotel. The announcements have made it clear to the public that De Salivon has returned from retirement to be the French team's . . . how do you say? Sure thing?"

"He's the ringer. The ace up the French team's sleeve."

"*Oui.* He is a prime target. And, *voilà!*—he *was* attacked by a man who looked like Elvis and accidentally dropped this magazine."

"But was it an accident?" Cassidy asked, scratching her head of orange curls. "Maybe it was a *Godfather*-type message?"

Ponton stopped his pacing. "A *what* message?"

"A threatening message like the ones they used in the *Godfather* movie. You know the American film?"

"Ah, *oui*. Brando, Pacino, James Caan. Making to one an offer that one cannot refuse."

"That's right."

"The bloody horse head?"

"You've got it!"

Ponton shook his head. "I must say, mademoiselle. I do not see what a bloody horse head has to do with our case. It does not even sound appetizing."

"No, listen! Rex Wesson may not have anything to do with the attempted murder of De Salivon/Dreyfus. Maybe the killer simply left Wesson's article to terrorize the rest of the French team. You know? Shake them up before the competition begins."

"Ah, *oui*. That is possible. But we still do not know enough about Wesson. Let us keep digging." Ponton gestured to the laptop. "May I?"

Cassidy rose from the chair and Ponton sat. He began working the search engines, moving into French language web pages. Finally, he called up a site put up by a French restaurant owner with businesses in Los Angeles, San Francisco, and Tokyo.

"Hmmmm . . . . It seems Rex Wesson is no friend to my countrymen. This restaurateur has put up a web page warning French chefs that Wesson is out to slam French cuisine."

"Not surprising," Cassidy noted, "considering the content of that article."

Rex Wesson had written the inflammatory article one month before the death of the first French pastry chef in France. He had slammed the hegemony of French cuisine worldwide and irresponsibly suggested that fatal heart attacks for the entire French team would be the best thing to happen to the World Food Expo in a decade.

"It is long past time we buried puff pastry and placed butter in the very grave it has dug for those whose arteries it has clogged for years," the article declared. "It is time to crown a new Desserts in the Desert champion . . ."

"And what's this?" Ponton murmured, still reading the French language Web site. "Hmmmm . . . interesting . . ."

"What is it, Ponton?"

"Apparently, this Rex Wesson always goes to restaurants incognito, using elaborate disguises."

"Disguises!" Cassidy exclaimed. "Like Bob Marley? Or Elvis?"

"One would assume he'd use more subtle personas. However, it does sound like this Rex Wesson is some sort of master of disguise—"

"Just like the killer we're looking for. You're right, Ponton. This looks like more than a message. This looks like a real lead."

"But we have found no address or way to contact Wesson—at least not through the magazine or Internet. So . . . first thing in the morning, I will visit the *Las Vegas Eats* magazine offices to inquire about the whereabouts of this Rex Wesson."

"Me, too. I'm coming with you."

"If you wish."

"Oh, I wish. My career depends on this, Ponton. The truth is . . ." Cassidy hung her head. "They're ready to can me back in New York."

"I am sorry to hear that."

She lifted her gaze, meeting Ponton's perpetually hooded eyes. "If I can help you and Inspector Clouseau solve this case, it will go a long way with getting the commissioner and the mayor to give me a second chance."

Ponton offered her a rare smile. "Then, of course, you shall continue to help us, Mademoiselle Cassidy."

"Ponton?"

"Oui?"

"You're staring at my hair. You've been doing that all night, you know."

"Have I? . . . I mean . . ." Ponton looked away, embarrassed. *"Oui*, mademoiselle, it is true. You have caught me. I am sorry."

"Don't apologize. I know it's a distracting color. Way too orange, right? If I had a fiver every time some hairdresser suggested I dye it—"

"It is an enchanting color."

Cassidy's eyes widened. "You like it?"

"Oui, it is the color of a navel orange . . . a fruit I have always found to be . . . delightfully sweet. And, how do you say? *Juicy*."

"You think my hair is juicy?"

"Forgive me. I am not very good at this sort of thing."

"At what sort of thing?"

"How do I explain?" Ponton shrugged. "You see, my sister had a doll with hair like yours."

"A doll?"

"A very lovely little porcelain thing. As a young, impressionable French boy, I found myself, on occasion . . . you know . . . *attracted* . . . to the doll . . ."

"What?"

Ponton could see he had shocked the woman's delicate sensibilities. "It is too awkward to explain," he quickly replied. "Please forget I said these things, mademoiselle. And forgive me for staring. Let us get back to work."

Cassidy checked her watch. "It's very late. Don't you think it's time we quit working—"

"*Oui.* Of course. You are right. I shall leave you then."

"Oh, no! I didn't mean you should leave!"

"Pardon?"

"I've black-lighted my sheets and everything. You don't have to worry about germs."

"*Excusez-moi?*"

Cassidy stood up and abruptly unzipped her hooded sweatshirt. "I'm no prude, Gilbert. Neat freaks get horny, too, you know."

Ponton's eyes bulged as Cassidy tossed away her hoodie, then reached around to unfasten her lacy bra. He had heard American women were sexually aggressive. He had seen *Sex and the City Girls.* He had known about *Desperate Homemakers,* but he had never believed it was true! Now that he was confronted with American horniness, he felt like a stag caught in a pair of feminist headlights. Stark performance-anxiety instantly deflated the Frenchman's romantic anticipation.

"I think I had better go now!"

"What's wrong, Gilbert?"

"You are very attractive, Mademoiselle Cassidy, but I fear we should not mix police business with . . . how do you say? Ohhhh, you know—" Ponton lunged for the door. "I shall see you in the morning. *Bon soir!*"

"But—"

The detective was down the hall and back in his room in mere seconds. Gasping for air, he slammed the door and collapsed against it. "American women," he murmured, wiping his sweaty brow. *"Sacré bleu!"*

FIFTEEN

Ms. Communication

The next afternoon, Chief Inspector Dreyfus nervously paced the length of the spacious dressing room.

"Must I go through with this ridiculous charade? Endanger myself just to participate in a silly 'cook-off' that is not even part of the official World Food Expo?"

Dreyfus's face—dyed the color of De Salivon's complexion—was flushed with warmth and shining with a thin film of sweat. Though unscathed by the previous night's attack (apart from the lump on the top of his head, the result of slipping in his bath) the chief inspector was clearly suffering from an acute case of posttraumatic stress syndrome.

"It is absurd," he continued. "A waste of time. Nothing more than a publicity stunt!"

"Exactly right," Trade Minister Marmiche replied. "And with the sorry group of second-rate talent we have representing France this year, our team needs all the good publicity it can get."

As the men spoke, they could hear the muffled roar of the capacity crowd flowing into the Grand Garden Arena. Even backstage, in the dressing room, the excitement of the audience was palpable.

On his knees in front of Dreyfus, Kevlar thigh armor in hand, Officer Raspail chided his boss like an irritable old woman. "Stand still, Chief Inspector. How can I fit you into this bulletproof body armor if you won't stand still!"

With an anguished groan, Dreyfus rigidly submitted to the fitting. Within a few moments, he was wrapped in nearly forty pounds of Kevlar plates under a virgin-white chef's coat.

"This outfit is about as comfortable as medieval armor," the chief inspector griped.

Ponton folded his arms. "Let us hope it keeps you just as safe and secure, sir." And he meant it, because he knew there would be no other way to catch the killer than to lure him out with Dreyfus as bait.

Of course, Ponton had hoped it would not come to this. Hours earlier, while Clouseau had been sleeping off his hangover, he and Cassidy Caldwell had tried to track down Rex Wesson. But they had quickly hit a dead end.

Las Vegas Eats magazine's editor in chief apologized, but assured them both that the only address she had for Wesson was a post office box in Los Angeles, which is where the magazine sent his checks. The woman also had an e-mail address, which Ponton turned over to their contact at the Las Vegas Metro Police Department.

The police captain, one Emma Titus, assured Ponton and Cassidy that she would secure a warrant to digitally trace the identity and whereabouts of the e-mail and post office box owner or owners. In the meantime, the LVMPD would run an independent search on anyone using the name Rex Wesson in the Las Vegas metro area.

All of this, Ponton knew, would take time. And they were running out of it. The most the French detective could hope for now was another attempt on their chief inspector's life—one that would serve up their killer, hopefully without actually killing Charles Dreyfus.

Inspector Clouseau stepped up to reassure his superior. "Do not fear, Chief Inspector. I have tightened security since Elvis assaulted you with a meat tenderizer. If the assassin tries to joust with you again—or if he even shows his cleverly disguised face—I will personally apprehend the scoundrel."

Dreyfus glared at his subordinate. "I am not reassured."

"It would be a terrible breach of protocol to miss this event, in any case," the trade minister declared. "To appear in the world-renowned Cast-Iron Skillet competition is an honor. Because the French team won last year's Expo, our inclusion was a given. The other teams are chosen by secret ballot."

Dreyfus sneered. "But it was not *this* French team that was victorious last year. And I am not the Master Chef De Salivon. How will I—merely the head of the most effective police bureau in the entire European Union—lead a cooking team to victory?"

"Sit on your throne and keep your mouth shut," Trade Minister Marmiche replied. "Let the rest of the team do the work. If you have to communicate at all, use disdainful glances, dismissive or rude gestures. Believe me, people are sure to believe you're the real De Salivon if you're supercilious enough."

"Why, that is a piece of proverbial cake for our chief inspector!" Clouseau exclaimed. "Charles Dreyfus may just be the most supercilious man in all of France, if not the entire EU!"

Dreyfus closed his eyes and muttered a curse. Then gingerly touched the bump hidden under his chef's hat. "If only you and your subordinates had not bungled the capture the other night, Clouseau! Alone in my shower, I was the perfect bait. No surprise the killer took it. But thanks to your incompetence, Clouseau, poor Lamothe is in the hospital, vainly hovering on the brink of death's door!"

Ponton scratched his head. "Officer Lamothe was eating a hearty breakfast and watching *The Price is Right* when I visited him earlier."

The dressing room door opened. "You Frenchies are up in five minutes!" the assistant producer called.

"How exciting," Clouseau whispered. "The Cast-Iron Skillet competition is broadcast live on cable TV's Gourmet Channel, you know . . ."

Ponton nodded. "How does the contest work?"

"The competition is truly exciting!" Clouseau gushed. "Six teams of chefs are pitted against one another in a one-hour cook-off. The goal is to create the tastiest five-course meal using a cast-iron skillet and the secret ingredient—"

"What secret ingredient?" Ponton asked.

"Fah! You are a silly goose!" Clouseau exclaimed. "The secret ingredient is not announced until the contest begins. Otherwise it would not be a *secret* ingredient. Now let us be off!"

The French team filed out of their dressing room flanked by a security team disguised as sous-chefs. Clouseau and Ponton took point, blazing a trail through the crowd for the rest of the team to follow. When the two detectives needed to communicate, they used highly advanced radio headsets specially developed for the Police *Nationale* by the best technicians in all of France.

"Listen to my every instruction, and obey my commands immediately and without question," Clouseau commanded. "Any questions?"

Ponton nodded curtly. "I understand fully, Inspector. I will follow your instructions to the letter."

"Now, go back and join the rest of the team," Clouseau commanded. "I shall call you through the radio to test out the equipment."

Ponton scurried off.

"Testing. One, two, three," Clouseau said into his microphone. He listened for a response from Ponton, but heard only silence. A few seconds later, Clouseau felt a tap on his shoulder.

"I am here, Inspector," Ponton said.

"What are you doing here?"

"I heard your command, from over the radio."

"What command?"

"I believe you said, '*Ponton, come to me*.'"

Clouseau frowned. "I did not say any such thing. What I said was, 'Testing, one, two three.' Really, Ponton, you must learn to listen more closely."

"But I did, Inspector—"

"Surely, you are not suggesting anything is amiss with this fine, and *very expensive* communications equipment! The Legion of Technical Scientists is one of France's most respected unions. And the Police *Nationale* has many outstanding contracts for sensitive equipment, this being only one."

"Well, I don't mean to imply—"

"Enough." Clouseau put up his hand. "The equipment works perfectly. Now get back to your position."

Once out of the dressing rooms, the cooking teams moved side by side through a long corridor that led to the stage—a red-carpet walk that allowed fans to cheer them, and photographers and camera crews to shoot footage from behind security ropes. Over the constant calls and applause, reporters shouted out questions to the members of each team as they passed.

At the stage door, the French chefs gathered, waiting for their curtain call. Through his soundproof headset, Clouseau heard an explosion of cheers.

At the inspector's side, Babette Beauford blinked behind thick glasses. "Am I hallucinating?" she asked.

Arnaud Germaine's handsome face curled into a sneer. Clad in a suede butcher's apron and a tool belt heavy with knives, bone saws, and cleavers, the chef folded his thick-muscled, tattooed arms over his massive chest.

"That's the Treat Restaurant team," Arnaud said in a tone of measured disdain. "The old man who started the company died last year. His granddaughters, the Treat Twins, took control of the restaurant franchise, and they have initiated . . . *changes*."

"They have turned a barely respectable American eatery into a theme park!" Yves Petit sniffed, folding his arms, too. Standing next to the enormous butcher, the diminutive chef resembled an adoring child mimicking the actions of his larger-than-life father.

Clouseau peered through the crowd and saw a most curious sight. The group that approached looked like refugees from a campy, low-budget remake of *The Wizard of Oz*. A bunch of dancing Dorothys in gingham and ruby slippers were flanked by a brace of Tin Men and Scarecrows.

As this motley crew approached, Clouseau heard an explosion of applause, mingled with a cacophony of wolf whistles. From the middle of the Emerald City set, Clouseau spied a familiar face—*two* of them in fact.

"Look, Ponton!" Clouseau cried into the headset, *"the Treat Twins are lovely tonight!"*

From somewhere behind Clouseau, a scuffle suddenly broke out. The inspector could see nothing of the altercation, but heard distinct cries of outrage, the sound of blows. A moment later the crowd parted and Ponton appeared, pushing a bruised and battered reporter in front of him. The man's face was puffed, his hands bound with handcuffs.

"I did it, sir," Ponton said proudly. "The brute put up a fight, but I followed your command."

Clouseau's eye twitched. "And what was my command?"

"I heard it clearly, sir. In my headset. You said, *'Look, Ponton, tackle the man on your right!'* So I turned, spied this suspicious-looking rascal and seized him."

"Uh . . . *oui* . . . I see," Clouseau replied. "Let us stick together now—and remove these blasted, pieces of *merde* headsets!"

Two uniformed members of MGM Grand security appeared at Ponton's shoulder. The deputy inspector turned his prisoner over to their custody, then stuffed the advanced French technology into the pocket of his Armani suit.

Clouseau turned at the sound of heels clicking on concrete, an enchanting, feminine giggle. The young women who approached were tall and slender, with large breasts, tiny waists, and sparkling blue eyes that danced with a pristine vacancy. They wore outfits meant to evoke corn-fed Midwest virtue:

matching gingham dresses, cut short at midthigh to reveal long, shapely legs, ankle socks, and ruby-red glass slippers with six-inch heels. Their long, honey-colored hair was done up in braids that fell to their delightfully curving hips in a golden waterfall, completing the double-vision Barbie Doll picture of dubious American innocence.

"Ah, the lovely and talented Treat sisters," Clouseau said, once again entranced by the fair-skinned charms of the identical twin heiresses, whose rather notorious reputation in the exclusive watering holes of the world did not match their current virtuous attire.

"Ponton, might I once again introduce the lovely Ms. Tyla Treat, and her even more lovely identical twin sister, Ms. Trina Treat."

A bedazzled Ponton kissed the hands of both twins before Clouseau stepped between them.

"Careful, Ponton," Clouseau whispered. "I was once the subject of gossip which suggested that I, Inspector Jacques Clouseau of the Sûreté, conducted a torrid affair with these two man-eating vixens. The very idea!"

Ponton blinked. "Yes, I have heard such rumors, even from that most respected of journals, *The National Midnight Star*, but I judged them to be false."

"All a result of a few innocent words, spoken before a ruthless journalist who deliberately misquoted me," Clouseau sniffed. "So heed my example and watch carefully the words you speak. We must not give the world the wrong idea, eh?"

Slender, perfectly manicured hands fingered the lapel on Inspector Clouseau's Scotland Yard-aspirational mackintosh.

"It's you again, I remember meeting you at the Louvre

in Paris! You're the famous Pink Panther detective, aren't you?" Trina Treat cooed as she melted against the inspector, then batted her sparkling baby blues.

Clouseau gulped, losing himself for a moment in the young woman's charms. "It is true, I *am* Pin-spector Pinko, the famous Inspector Detector. What . . . what are you doing here in Las Vegas, my lovely little dove?"

"We've learned to cook!" Tyla chirped. "I can boil water—"

"And I can open a can!" Trina squeaked, hopping up and down like an excited schoolgirl.

"And now we're the bosses of a whole bunch of restaurants—"

"So we made them really cool," Trina yelped.

Clouseau nodded. "*Bon! Bon!* I am duly impressed."

"Excuse the interruption, ladies . . ." A famous British scandalmonger suddenly appeared. With a Cheshire-cat grin, he pulled out his pen and reporter's notebook. "I heard that the Treat Restaurant Team was planning to prepare pork as your main dish in tonight's competition."

Tyla nodded like a Bobble-head doll. "That's right."

"Oh, delightful," the reporter purred. "Will it be something new, or the Treat's Famous Polynesian Loin, or perhaps the trademark Treat's Juicy Barbecued Loin?"

Staring blankly into an explosion of camera shutters, the Treat Twins giggled nervously. Finally, in reply to the question she didn't really comprehend, Tyla lifted her gingham and displayed a little more of her sculpted thigh. More shutters fluttered.

"Oh, but who among us can truly distinguish the difference!" Clouseau exclaimed, wrapping his arms around the twins' tiny waists in what he believed was a perfectly dignified expression of France's fellowship. "Perfection is perfection," he went on, "and both tasty treats are so tender, so succulent. Why, I myself can recommend *both* of the Treat's juicy loins, for I have found satisfaction by sating my appetite with either of them!"

"Really?" said the scribbling reporter.

"And, I must confess, I have enjoyed both of them at the same time on occasion."

"Indeed!" the reporter cried.

"A fact," Clouseau said with a smug nod. "For the perfect sensual feast, I would suggest a large serving of both of these wonderful treats! Believe me when I say that a man can find no better satisfaction than he will discover between the Treats' succulent loins! My mouth salivates at the thought!"

The interview was abruptly interrupted. "French team, you're up!" shouted the assistant producer.

Kissing both of their hands, Clouseau bid adieu to the Treat Twins. Then he turned to Ponton and placed a fatherly hand on his partner's shoulder.

"Use my highly proper behavior tonight as an example," Clouseau advised. "Notice how cleverly I deflected the conversation away from any *hint* of impropriety. Always remember, Ponton, as members of the Sûreté, we have a tradition of moral turpitude to uphold. And, as officers of the *leau*, we must take care never to offer word or deed that suggests we indulge in lewd or scandalous behavior!"

"Oui, Inspector. Whatever you say."

SIXTEEN

Into the Frying Pan

"*Live* from the famous Cast-Iron Skillet Kitchen Stadium
. . . *Inside* the luxurious MGM Grand . . . *Right* here in sunny,
high-rolling Las Vegas . . . I'm Chazz Eiderdown hosting *The
Annual Cast-Iron Skillet Competition*!"

Standing backstage, alongside Ponton and the French
team waiting to be introduced, Jacques Clouseau winced at
Eiderdown's overblown delivery—and yet it did appropri-
ately match the pulse-pounding excitement he himself felt as
the curtain went up on the live television event.

The inspector watched the show unfold on a huge HDTV
monitor, now grotesquely dominated by the announcer's sur-
gically enhanced features. Trade Minister Pierre Marmiche
was also waiting in the wings and wringing his hands with
worry.

"Tonight's Gourmet Channel Special Event comes to you

from the World Food Expo, the nation's premiere food competition. This ninety-minute cooking extravaganza is brought to you by Extra Strength Nopainatal. Remember Nopainatal . . . For fast, fast, fast headache relief in a jiffy . . ."

Eiderdown continued his nonstop patter as the camera panned back, to reveal the announcer's pseudofrontier garb—stone-washed denims, flannel shirt and shoestring tie, fringed, buckskin jacket. Eiderdown's high-gloss horseshoe belt buckle more resembled hip-hop bling than any frontier fashion Clouseau had ever seen, and the man's alligator-skin cowboy boots were so absurdly pointed, he suspected they could pierce flesh.

For Inspector Clouseau, the rustic wardrobe combined with the unnatural appearance of Eiderdown's cosmetic surgery had a decidedly unsettling effect, evoking a troubling memory from his days as a young police cadet.

He'd been assigned security duty at Euro Disney's Bastille-Day Pavilion and had engaged in an hour-long flirtation with a beautiful woman costumed as Marie-Antoinette, only to discover the object of his desire was a malfunctioning animatronic! Even now, Clouseau suppressed a shudder stirred by that unhappy memory.

Meanwhile Eiderdown directed the audience's attention to a high podium in the center of the Cast-Iron Skillet Kitchen Stadium, occupied by the dark silhouette of a man.

"Before we introduce tonight's competitors, let's give a warm round of applause to the Chuck Wagon Master of the Cast-Iron Skillet competition, Mr. Gary Kehoe!"

The spotlight struck the podium, illuminating a tall man with a narrow face and close-set eyes, that were nearly invisible behind tinted glasses. His gaunt form was draped in flowing black robes.

Into the Frying Pan

To Clouseau's surprise, more boos and catcalls than applause greeted the Chuck Wagon Master of the Cast-Iron Skillet Kitchen. Indeed, a number of audience members—mostly those who displayed the red, white, and blue of the United States flag—actually hurled food scraps, empty cups, and food wrappers at the man.

"Chuck Wagon Master Kehoe does not appear to be very popular," Ponton observed.

Trade Minister Marmiche snickered. "The Americans hate him. Gary Kehoe is—in the local parlance—a real hard-ass when it comes to rules and regulations."

Ponton frowned. "A tough referee, then. But surely fair?"

Marmiche sighed. "It depends on with whom you are speaking. This is Master Kehoe's fifth year as referee, but he is lucky to have been asked back after last year's controversial decision."

"What decision?" Clouseau asked. "Explain *s'il vous plaît.*"

"During last year's Desserts in the Desert contest, Master Kehoe disqualified a favorite American chef for using artificial food coloring to enhance the presentation of his pastry. That decision ultimately handed the French team their championship victory."

The trade minister gazed at the man on the podium. "His unpopular decision must have weighed heavily on the man—pardon the pun."

"I don't understand," Ponton said.

"Look at the man on the podium. He's a living skeleton," Marmiche explained. "Yet last year Gary Kehoe, a well-known gourmand, tipped the American measuring scales at well over three hundred pounds. More than that, I am told that Master Kehoe is now a hard, rigid, and bitter man."

"But no enemy to the French team, surely. So we can safely ignore any threat from that corner," Clouseau declared.

By now Gary Kehoe had finished his official opening remarks, and the camera switched back to Chazz Eiderdown's grotesquely perfect features.

"And now let's meet our Cast-Iron Skillet competitors," the announcer purred. "First up, a European sensation and the team to beat . . . You know who they are! The champions of last year's World Food Expo. Let's give a hearty *Oo-la-la!* to the prize-winning chefs from France!"

The Grand Garden Arena exploded with frenzied applause as the French team moved to its designated cooking space inside the massive Cast-Iron Skillet Kitchen Stadium, an array of six cooking spaces, complete with stocked refrigerators, stoves, microwaves, and ovens, set inside a giant circular stage that resembled an enormous skillet turned upside down.

Clouseau was pleased to see the audience packed with French fans. They cheered when each team member was effusively introduced by Chazz Eiderdown, finally shaking the rafters when Chef De Salivon took a bow. The inspector's heart stirred at the sight of his countrymen, waving tricolor flags, their stout hearts burning with national pride.

"Not so fast, ladies and gentlemen," Eiderdown warned. "Champions these Frenchmen were, but tonight all bets are off, which is a big deal in Vegas, lemme tell ya!"

Laughter broke through the cheers.

"The champs from France will have to face off against five culinary competitors who all want their turn to *fry* that *French* team!"

Eiderdown cackled. In the dazzling stage lights, his eyes danced maniacally. Suddenly troubled, Clouseau nudged his partner. "We shall have to keep our eyes glued to *that* one."

"First up is the Caribbean team, led by the newest sensation on the gourmet scene," Eiderdown continued. "He is world renowned for his brilliant fusion of French and Caribbean culinary traditions, along with the use of unusual ingredients and secret powders found in Haitian voodoo rituals. This unique cooking style has made Bizango, the chef's five-star restaurant in Las Ramblas, Madrid, a culinary shrine for the international set! Ladies and gentlemen, let's beat those voodoo drums nice and loud for the creator of Bokor cuisine . . . *Chef Paul-Charles Napoleon*!"

"Look, Inspector!" Ponton exclaimed as the Haitian-born chef strutted onto the stage. "This man fits the description of Mademoiselle Cassidy's New York City murderer, right down to the dangling dreadlocks."

"And his name," Clouseau pointed out. "An amalgamation of our assassin's assumed identities. *Charles* de Gaulle. *Paul* Gauguin—and the phony passport photograph of—"

"*Napoleon* Bonaparte!"

"This voodoo chef *does* appear to be our master of disguise."

"Indeed, he does."

Clouseau nodded. "But we need more evidence, Ponton. And a motive would not hurt—"

Just then, Eiderdown leered into the camera. "Chef Napoleon learned the secrets of voodoo cuisine from his father, a culinary master who was the long-time personal chef for Haitian dictator Papa Doc Duvalier—"

"*Sacré bleu.* Another connection," Ponton said. "Duvalier was the name used by the assistant baker we suspect employed butterless croissants as a murder weapon on Chef Miguel!"

"Yes, it is the same name that was used by the assistant chef who likely stuffed Chef Gignac's body parts into his own meat pies . . . . Still . . ." Clouseau tapped his chin. "It *could* be a coincidence."

At that very moment, Chef Paul-Charles Gauguin Napoleon chose to lock eyes with De Salivon. The Haitian sneered and shook an angry fist at the disguised Dreyfus.

"Did you see that, Inspector?" Ponton quickly asked. "Clearly a hostile gesture."

An unruffled Clouseau simply shrugged. "Or showmanship, my friend. A display of elan to hearten his fellow teammates. I am sure there is no personal animosity involved."

Chef Napoleon's angry fist was followed by a universally obscene gesture. A cry of outrage erupted from the spectators.

"Gosh, I hope those fellows in the control room censored that!" Chazz Eiderdown exclaimed. "It looks like the bad blood between Chefs De Salivon and Napoleon is still simmering."

Finally, Clouseau expressed alarm. "Bad blood!" he cried. "We were not briefed about a bodily fluid problem simmering among the competitors? Does the real Chef De Salivon have enemies the Sûreté does not know about?"

"Of course! What did you think?" Trade Minister Marmiche replied. "Where ego and art combine, there is always animosity. Name *one* chef on that stage who is not hated by his peers. And in the case of De Salivon and Napoleon, that enmity was earned."

"What are you saying?" Clouseau asked, eyebrow raised.

"After dining at Bizango in Madrid, De Salivon was, shall we say, less than discreet when he spoke with a reporter from *Paris Match*."

Into the Frying Pan

"De Salivon was insulting?" Ponton asked the Trade Minister.

"Apparently, Chef Napoleon's signature dish, the Chicken à l'orange, has an unpleasantly gritty texture. When the reporter reminded De Salivon that voodoo powders are used in the preparation, De Salivon was quoted as replying, 'To me, this so-called voodoo powder tastes suspiciously like tangerine Jell-O powder.'" Marmiche shook his head. "The remark caused an international incident. Needless to say, Chef Napoleon never forgave De Salivon for the insult."

"We should have been warned of this, Trade Minister," Clouseau said, massaging his forehead. "Chief Inspector Dreyfus is already in danger. This multiplies his peril."

But Marmiche simply shrugged. "If we were to brief you about all of De Salivon's enemies, we would *still* be in conference. Remember, Inspector, the French team was a target for murder long before Chief Inspector Dreyfus assumed De Salivon's identity. The real target is the French *team*."

"You are correct," Clouseau admitted. "But I shall keep one vigilant eye focused on this Chef Napoleon."

Meanwhile, on the Grand Arena stage, Chazz Eiderdown began introducing the other teams, including a group of excitable Italians from Sicily; an athletic troupe of chefs from the People's Republic of China; and the *Wizard of Oz* crowd from the Treat Restaurant chain, led by their new gingham-clad owners, Tyla and Trina Treat.

Finally, Eiderdown introduced a brace of stout men and women with powerful frames and taciturn expressions.

"*Ugh.* I smell pickled herring!" Clouseau moaned, covering his mouth.

" . . . And all the way from the fjords of Oslo," the announcer cried. "Let's give a warm hand to the team from chilly Norway!"

After the final competitors entered the Cast-Iron Skillet Kitchen Stadium, Chazz Eiderdown introduced the judges for the night's competition. The glamorously dressed men and women sat at a long table, below the stadium stage and directly in front of the audience. Ponton did not recognize one name or face, and said so.

"Minor American celebrities," Clouseau disdainfully declared. "Human flotsam washed ashore from the wreckage of failed or canceled television shows. In truth, my friend, these so-called judges are an obscure pack of worthless has-beens. The kind of no-name celebrities that only a compulsive fame-junkie would even have a prayer of recognizing."

Ponton blinked, puzzled. "But how can you be certain there are not imposters among these judges, Inspector? That none are assassins?"

"Do not worry, Ponton," Clouseau replied. "I can assure you, the young woman on the right is Kimberly Runyon, who played the title character on the failed sitcom *Myra Toval, Bar Mitzvah Singer*. And that burly bald fellow next to her is Biggin Young, star of the canceled crime melodrama *Police Brutality*."

Ponton's eyebrows lifted in surprise. "How do you know this?"

Clouseau was too busy reciting to answer. "The man next to Ms. Runyon is Jimbo Acton . . . He's the fellow who spent $100 million filming a nine-hour documentary, which the National Geographic Channel never aired. *The Search for the Real Gilligan's Island* was the title. And that lovely Japanese woman in the black leather kimono is *kaiju* actress Yuki Nakamura, who plays the title character on *Amazing Super*

Into the Frying Pan

Wonder Girl Plus. The sci-fi extravaganza was a marginal hit on Nippon Television Network, but failed to crack the European and American markets."

Ponton was still grasping for the meaning of the term *kaiju* while Clouseau pressed on.

"That fellow next to Ms. Nakamura, the wizened man with the long green hair. He is Bass Fisher, the former lead singer for the 1990s grunge band, the Dysfunctionels. You no doubt recall their only hit, 'Going Home Tumescent.' Lately, Mr. Fisher has become a minor poet in his native Great Britain . . ."

"Mon dieu," Ponton muttered.

"And next to Mr. Fisher, the man in the chef's hat . . . He's Brett Waverly. He isn't a real chef, but he played one on television in the 1970s . . . Apparently he never got over it. And finally, there's Ms. Sally Bong, star of the short-lived Watermark Channel mystery series, *Nun of That Snooping, Sister!*"

Clouseau shook his head. "Only a poor pathetic soul would even recognize this sorry lot, the kind of person addicted to useless gossip shows like *Hollywood Hot Line*, *Showbiz Chat*, *Entertainment Live Wire*, *The National Midnight Star's Celebrity Hunt,* and, that most vacuous and emptyheaded entertainment show of them all, *Bollywood Beat* with Matilda Frederique. What do you think, my friend?"

"I . . . am, uh . . . truly amazed by your extensive knowledge of the subject, Inspector, and I yield to your superior expertise in this matter."

"Bon, bon, a wise decision," Clouseau replied.

Then, to Ponton's surprise, Clouseau suddenly tossed away his hat and peeled off his trench coat. Underneath, the inspector wore a spotless white chef's jacket.

The trade minister gaped. "What do you think you're doing, Inspector Clouseau?"

"I am going to mingle with the sous-chefs and join the French team, of course," Clouseau replied. "How can I safeguard the life of Chief Inspector Dreyfus from the wings?"

Suddenly recalling the letter opener incident in Dreyfus's office and the shattered map of Paris, Marmiche frantically waved his hands. "Do not do it," he pleaded. "So much is at stake. You are a detective of the Sûreté, Clouseau, not a gourmet chef. You do not know what you are doing in the kitchen! You might cause an accident!"

Clouseau shrugged. "You fret too much, Trade Minister. What could possibly go wrong?"

SEVENTEEN

A Chemical Feast

A hush fell over the crowd. On a podium high above the Cast-Iron Skillet Kitchen Stadium, the black-robed Gary Kehoe was about to announce the year's all-important Secret Ingredient.

"For thousands of years, Asian cuisine used a pungent seaweed broth to obtain flavor-enhancing effects," Kehoe began. "In time the ancients discovered that these effects can be further enriched through the use of fermented protein products. And so the culinary masters of the ancient East gave the world the gift of soy sauce . . ."

As Kehoe went on, Inspector Clouseau adjusted his chef's coat, bid Ponton *adieu*, and slipped unnoticed onto the crowded stage. Blending with dozens of other sous-chefs, the inspector quickly located the French team.

Dreyfus/De Salivon sat in a high chair, overlooking the

161

French team. Like the chefs around him, the chief inspector was listening attentively to the Chuck Wagon Master's monologue.

"Here in the West, culinary pioneers discovered the flavor-enhancing properties of tomatoes, of mushrooms, of certain cheeses, and aged meats. Ancient Romans developed fermented fish pastes and piquant sauces to enhance their bland diet, mimicking the fermentation process used by the Asian cultures . . ."

Flashes of stage lightning and seat-quaking crashes of artificial thunder resonated through the Grand Arena to heighten the dramatic impact of the Chuck Wagon Master's delivery.

"Yet all of these advancements were merely desperate, stopgap measures in man's eternal quest for ever-more pungent, more savory foods," Kehoe declared as wind fans began to blow. "In both the East and the West, perfection in flavor-enhancement seemed to be an elusive, impossible dream!"

Dramatically, the Chuck Wagon Master ripped off his tinted glasses. His voluminous black robes billowed as the fans agitated the air. Master Kehoe's voice rose to a fever pitch. Eyes, now visible, burned with an almost crazed intensity.

"Finally, the magic substance common in all of these flavor-enhancing techniques was isolated by some great, unknown and unheralded alchemical master!" Kehoe cried. "It was discovered that this substance, found naturally in virtually all protein-containing foods, must be released through a mysterious and complex fermentation process . . . Only then can this magic ingredient fulfill its true flavor-making potential . . ."

Inspector Clouseau saw the confused expressions on the faces of the French team, heard their hushed, urgently whispered questions.

A Chemical Feast

Truly this must be some rare and exotic herb or spice!
Clouseau marveled. *Or perhaps a near-forgotten sauce, or
a cooking base known to the ancients. Whatever this secret
ingredient, I can hardly believe it is obscure enough to baffle
France's greatest chefs!*

"Today, this miraculous substance is still fermented by the
same traditional process invented exactly one hundred years
ago!" Kehoe continued.

As the Chuck Wagon Master spoke, the audience's attention was drawn to a large platform that began to drop slowly
from the ceiling.

"Mingling starch, sugar beets, sugar cane, and molasses
with specially selected strains of *Micrococcus glutamicus*,
the bacteria begins to excrete glutamic acid, a substance that
is then separated from the nutrient bath, purified, and pro-
cessed into its sodium salt . . ."

The descending platform bumped to a halt at the base of
the Chuck Wagon Master's podium. On top of the platform's
black silk tablecloth were multiple mounds of a finely grained
powder, as pristine as Tibetan snow. Crystalline specks inside the mysterious substance twinkled like tiny, mysterious
jewels.

"And, lo, it came to pass!" boomed the voice of Gary
Kehoe. "The perfect flavor-enhancement was born. Hail the
coming of this marvelous, miraculous powder . . . Tonight's
Cast-Iron Skillet Secret Ingredient . . . Ladies and gentlemen,
I give you—*Monosodium glutamate*!"

Stunned silence greeted the revelation. Audience members and participants alike were momentarily shocked. Had
Kehoe gone loopy? Had they heard the Chuck Wagon Master
correctly? Could the secret ingredient really be MSG?

Finally, after a long pause, as the reality of the situation

163

set in, an equal smattering of applause and jeers erupted throughout the arena.

On his high chair, overlooking the French team, Chief Inspector Dreyfus exploded. "Monosodium glutamate is not an ingredient!" he cried. "It is not a food, an herb, or even a spice. It is an *additive*! A chemical additive! Kehoe is insane!"

Babette Beauford shared his outrage. "I 'ave ne-vair 'erd anything so ree-diculous!"

The man she knew as Chef De Salivon shook his head. "I certainly concur!" he loudly told her. "Some no talent short-order cook could put monosodium glutamate on pulverized elephant dung and it would be perfectly palatable!"

The chief inspector's tirade was interrupted by a scream of outrage. Clouseau whirled to see Chef Napoleon glowering up at Dreyfus, shaking his fist. One of the Haitian's sous-chefs scurried away, a bucket of pulverized elephant dung clutched in his hand.

"First you compare my cuisine to tangerine Jell-O powder in *Paris Match*! Now you blurt out my cooking secrets for all the world to hear," Chef Napoleon raged in Haitian-accented French. "I vow to cast a spell of doom on you and yours, De Salivon!"

"Just so he survives this week," Clouseau replied.

Instead of focusing his wrath on the competing chef, Dreyfus fired a glance at the "sous-chef" who'd just spoken so impertinently. "What did you say, you popinjay?" Dreyfus demanded.

Clouseau blinked up in surprise at the Chief Inspector. "Are you referring to me, or the other popinjay?"

Dreyfus couldn't believe his eyes. "*You*, you bumbling nincompoop! What are you doing on stage?!"

A Chemical Feast

"Why, I am here to guard your life, 'Monsieur' De Salivon," Clouseau said with an exaggerated wink.

Dreyfus suddenly paled. "I am surrounded by open flames. By gas mains. By foreign chefs who want to do me harm. There are knives, skewers, cleavers, and spearing implements all around me . . . For the love of all things holy, Clouseau, I'm begging you, keep your distance!"

Suddenly, Chazz Eiderdown's voice piped up again. "Joining me for tonight's play-by-play action is the former championship linebacker for the Montana Bullets, as well as the founder of the Mo' Grease! Southern comfort-food restaurant franchise. Give it up for Fighting Number Fifty-five . . . *Mr. Iota Jones!*"

The spotlight barely encompassed a mountain of a man. A jovial African American wearing a super-plus-sized purple velvet tuxedo that barely stretched across his three-hundred-plus-pound frame, Iota Jones bowed and accepted the wild applause that greeted him. His smile was broad and infectious, teeth so white they outshone the drifts of MSG.

The former football star thanked his millions of fans in a low rumble. In the athlete's mammoth grip, the microphone he held appeared diminutive.

"Good to see ya', Chazz," Iota said. "It's really great to be here with all this good food goin' on. In the Jones household, we really like to eat, so I'm glad to see the Cast-Iron Skillet chefs are already firing up their ovens."

"Yes, Iota, the chefs are hard at work, but I sense some tension, too."

"You're right, Chazz. Down here in the frying pan, the controversial Secret Ingredient has really stirred up the pot simmering between the French and Caribbean teams."

"No surprise there, Iota. The French are clearly in trouble.

The Pink Panther's Just Desserts

Their culinary tradition relies on butter, truffles, vegetable or meat broth rich in herbs and spices—or even wines—to enhance flavor. The Secret Ingredient puts the Gallic team at a disadvantage, no doubt. Even the Caribbeans, familiar with jerk chicken and other dishes that use rubs or powders, have the dominance here."

"True enough, Chazz," Iota replied. "But no one has a better edge than the Chinese. These guys have used MSG for generations. It's in their blood."

"That's right, Iota. It's the Asians who devised the culinary principle of *umami*—that most indescribable of the five basic tastes. *Umami*, a loanword from Japanese, is used to describe this indescribable concept—"

"Oh, Chazz!"

"Yes, Iota?"

"You know, it was a happy laboratory accident in 1907 when Japanese chemist Kikunae Ikeda noticed the crystals left behind after the evaporation of a large vat of *kombu* broth as glutamic acid. Dang, if these crystals didn't reproduce that *mo' better* flavor the professor detected in many foods, especially seaweed! Professor Ikeda termed this flavor *umami*. Which, if you ask me, translates into some *fine* eatin'!"

"You're quite the expert when it comes to MSG, Iota."

"Well, Chazz, I'll let you in on a little secret. In the Iota Jones household, MSG stands for *Mighty Swell Grub*!"

"You know, Iota, in purely scientific terms, certain *umami* taste buds on the human tongue respond specifically to amino acids, such as the glutamic acid found in MSG. This occurs in much the same way that 'sweet' taste buds respond to sugars. And that's why our Secret Ingredient makes food taste so gosh-darn delicious."

While the banter flowed like raw sewage from a broken

storm drain, members from each Cast-Iron Skillet cooking team moved to the platform to scoop mounds of the MSG powder into bowls and saucepans.

Arnaud Germaine, the big French butcher, huddled with his fellow chefs on the French team for a strategy session. After a few minutes of spirited debate, Germaine broke from the huddle and respectfully approached Dreyfus.

"Chef De Salivon, sir, the rules are clear," he said. "We must create five dishes, from an appetizer to a dessert, each one containing MSG as an ingredient."

Babette circled the muscle-bound cook, who scowled as she declared to De Salivon, "I think we've come up with a compromised solution."

"What do you propose?" Dreyfus asked.

"I shall prepare broiled lamb," Germaine announced, thumping his chest. "It is a pungent meat and the MSG should not taint it. Lamb can be prepared quickly, before the *umami* taste sets and changes the flavor beyond redemption."

Dreyfus nodded. "And the rest?"

"Yves Petit promises an appetizer rich in glutamate," Germaine replied. "Chef Le Rhone will prepare a savory sautéed shrimp, the MSG substituting for sauvignon blanc marinade. The little one, Xavier Izard, will create a dessert of crêpes and MSG-enriched chutney. And Mademoiselle Beauford has agreed to prepare braised endives, replacing a finely spiced celery mirepoix with American canned chicken broth—which, of course, contains MSG."

"This is truly an abomination," Babette groused. "Sacrilege! Where is the freshness? The purity?" She paused to sigh in disgust and light an unfiltered cigarette.

Germaine grunted. "*Nous avons fait notre meilleur, Chef De Salivon,*" he said, shrugging his broad shoulders.

"*Oui*, I agree. You *have* done your best, Monsieur Germaine," Dreyfus replied. Then he faced the others. "An amazing performance, all of you, but what does it matter, in the end? Where is the art? You could pour MSG into a pot of steamed goat entrails and the result would be agreeable to the untrained palate!"

Another anguished cry erupted from the Caribbean kitchen.

Clouseau turned to see Chef Napoleon snatch a vat of steaming organ meat off the stove and spill it onto the floor. Sous-chefs scattered in a cloud of reeking steam and twisting guts.

"Damn you, De Salivon! Before the next cycle of the moon, you shall die a thousand deaths for your insults to my menu!" Chef Napoleon bellowed.

Clouseau scratched his chin and looked up at Dreyfus. "I do believe that man has it in for you," he observed.

In the kitchen space next to the French team, the Treat Restaurant cooks scurried around like monkeys in the land of Oz. Cameras followed Iota Jones as he observed two Scarecrows and a Tin Man.

"Oh, Chazz?" he called.

"Yes, Iota."

"It looks like the Treat team is breaking out the fourteen-inch iron skewers. You know what that means, don't you, Chazz?"

"Looks like they mean to cook up the Treat's famous Polynesian Pork Loin, Iota!"

"Oh, snap, Chazz! You're right! Like most of the foods served at the Treat Restaurants, the Polynesian loin is rich in MSG, and doggone popular, too. *For real!* The Treat Restaurants served so much Polynesian pork loin last year, the wooden skewers could make a bridge stretchin' from San Francisco to Tahiti and all the way back again!"

"That's amazing, Iota. I wonder how much MSG the Treat Restaurants use in a given day."

"That's a trade secret, Chazz. But no matter how you spell it, MSG means some mighty fine eating! You know what I'm sayin'? And at the Iota Jones household—"

A bloodcurdling scream interrupted the linebacker's good-natured banter.

"Oh, no, Iota!" Chazz exclaimed. "It appears one of the Treat twins accidentally skewered a Tin Man! My goodness, you'd think all that steel would protect a fellow, but I guess those skewers are pretty sharp."

"Sacré bleu," Clouseau cried as the paramedics wheeled the punctured Tin Man out on a stretcher. "This Cast-Iron Skillet stadium is more dangerous than the Roman Colosseum!"

"C'mon audience, give it up for the heroic paramedics of Las Vegas!" Iota Jones called.

When the applause subsided, Chazz spoke again. "While our injured player is being taken out, the scarecrows on his team are throwing papaya-soaked, MSG-rich pork loins onto the grill. I can smell that delightful scent all the way over here, Iota!"

The announcer was not exaggerating. So much grill smoke filled the Cast-Iron Skillet arena that the sprinkler system was momentarily activated, dousing the Treat team.

Their dresses soaked through, Tyla and Tina made the best of a bad situation, quickly transforming the culinary competition into an impromptu "wet gingham" contest, even as copious amounts of barbecue smoke wafted across the stage.

Dreyfus moaned. "The MSG taint is inescapable!" he

cried. "Steeped in that vile chemical salt, even raw hog's vomit would stimulate one's appetite—"

"Damn you, De Salivon!" Chef Napolean exclaimed again. "Once more, you reveal my culinary secrets! I cannot allow this to continue!" Shaking with a dangerous rage, the Haitian strode to his array of cutlery, picked up a long knife, and bent back his arm.

At that very moment, Arnaud Germaine, mistaking Clouseau for a lowly sous-chef, snapped his fingers. "You, there, with the dull expression! Wake up! Fetch me that cutting board!"

Incensed by Germaine's arrogant attitude, the inspector picked up the cutting board and waved it high. "If you want this cutting board, monsieur," he taunted, "I suggest you come and get it yourself!"

Thwap!

Clouseau froze. A long knife had suddenly struck the board and stuck there, its end quivering like a lamb's tail. The Haitian had hurled it straight as an arrow at Dreyfus's throat. Clouseau's unprofessional cutting-board taunting had inadvertently stopped the killing blade cold!

With wide disbelieving eyes, Dreyfus stared at the steel blade embedded in the thick wood.

Clouseau remained speechless a moment, then raised a wry eyebrow. "Perhaps now you can appreciate the *point* of my presence, Chief Inspector."

EIGHTEEN

Caught 'Napping

After the punctured Tin Man was whisked away, the live telecast went to a commercial. During the break, the Treat Twins changed into dry gingham and Chef Napoleon was taken into custody by MGM Grand security.

Master Gary Kehoe refused to disqualify the Haitian team, however, saying he believed Chef Napoleon was being unfairly charged, and that he was guilty of nothing more than "careless handling of a kitchen implement."

When the show resumed, a semblance of order had been restored, but not everyone in the Cast-Iron Skillet Kitchen Stadium was pleased.

"An absurd call not to disqualify the Haitians," railed Dreyfus. "Chef Napoleon tried to take my life!"

Clouseau pursed his lips in thought. "Perhaps the Chuck Wagon Master does not want to be perceived as harsh after last year's controversial decision to disqualify the American team, a decision that landed the miserable Kehoe in hot water with his fellow countrymen."

Dreyfus sneered. "The man's choice of a secret ingredient detrimental to the French team suggests he is harboring a grudge. But why is he against us? What did the French do to him?"

"Perhaps Master Kehoe had a disagreeable run-in with the real Chef De Salivon," Clouseau guessed.

"It's as good a theory as any," Dreyfus replied. "But I am not at all comfortable concurring with an idiot."

Clouseau chuckled. "You worry too much, Chief Inspector," he said, waving his hand. "It was I who came up with the theory, not an *idiot*."

The show resumed, and the sixty-minute food preparation time went by in a jiffy. Inspector Clouseau's mouth watered at the aromas conjured by his fellow Frenchmen.

Because the French were the reigning champions and the team to beat, they presented their dishes first. The judges were polite and respectful—but not overly impressed by the French team's overall effort.

All seemed to enjoy Xavier Izard's crêpes-and-chutney dish, which was the high point of the meal. But things went downhill after Japanese television star Yuki Nakamura giggled nonstop, hand over her mouth, while complimenting Chef Germaine on the subtle *umami* taste of his broiled lamb. The big butcher mistook her nervous giggling as an insult, and returned to the French cooking space with the entire team, sullen and dejected, Babette at his side.

"Where is Drey—er, I mean Chef De Salivon?" Clouseau demanded.

Babette Beauford shrugged and lit another unfiltered cigarette. She inhaled deeply and blew smoke into Clouseau's face. "The team leader must stay with the judges after their presentation, to await the verdict."

Clouseau considered this alarming news. Dreyfus was now standing behind the judges' table, all alone, his back to the audience. With the entire French team forced to return to their stage kitchen, none of the detectives disguised as sous-chefs were anywhere near the chief inspector.

I am not yet convinced that Chef Napoleon is the ruthless assassin we have been tracking from the start, Clouseau reasoned. *And, even if he is, we do not yet know whether he was working alone or with a team of culinary killers.*

Clouseau chewed his thumbnail. *One attempt has already been made on the chief inspector's life,* he thought. *Who knows what dangers now lurk in the audience? I must protect him. But to do that, I must find a way to get close to him.*

While casting about for a solution, the inspector paced to the edge of the French team's set. Two members of the Treat Restaurant team were at the edge of theirs, and he overheard them talking.

"We need to provide one loin per judge," said one sweating Scarecrow, standing over the grill.

Holding a serving platter, a second Scarecrow groaned. "Too many!" he complained as the first Scarecrow piled more loins onto his platter. "I can hardly carry what I have now."

"Like it or not, we're shorthanded. Thanks to that little mishap with the skewers," said the Scarecrow at the grill. "Management is looking for a replacement Tin Man, but don't hold your breath."

Hearing the exchange, Clouseau immediately raced off-stage.

Meanwhile, the Norwegian team was up. Their meal consisted of five courses of herring brined in MSG and pickling spice, served with various sauces and dips. The judges roundly criticized the food and the presentation, focusing most of their wrath on the blueberry torte topped with a whipped herring and cream sorbet.

The Chinese team's entry, on the other hand, was well received. Chef Ho Lung Gong bowed as his baby prawns with ginger lemongrass were showered with praise. Even the duck's-blood pudding dessert was greeted with good-natured acceptance from judges not generally accustomed to eating the chilled, coagulated bodily fluid of the dead mallard.

"*Umami!*" Yuki Nakamura exclaimed with delight at the arrival of each new dish.

Other judges, however, weren't as accustomed to ingesting the Secret Ingredient as Yuki. Documentary filmmaker Jimbo Acton was the first to succumb. "Gosh, I'm . . . I'm feeling a little woozy," he said, clutching his head after sampling the Asian team's meal.

Wizened rock star and cockney poet Bass Fisher appeared even more pallid than usual. "Crikes!" he groaned, running his veined hands through his long, stringy green hair. "Me noggin's throbbin' worse than the day I guzzled a pint o' grain and woke up havin' me bloody stomach pumped in Shropshire 'ospital . . . I'll never forget me Mum standin' over me, rainin' tears like . . . like . . . tears o' rain!"

"Goodness, Iota," Chazz remarked, "it looks like the Chinese team may have bumped some of our judges due to a bad case of Chinese Restaurant syndrome—"

"Shut yo' mouth, Chazz!" Iota Jones cried. "Don't be talkin' to me 'bout no trashy urban myths!"

"Sorry, Iota," Chazz replied, "but there *have* been reports of sensitivities to MSG, including a wide variety of physical reactions such as migraines, nausea, digestive upsets, drows-iness, and heart palpitations, among other complaints."

"Say it ain't so, Chazz," Iota countered. "In the Jones household, MSG means mo' *flava*, and *flava's* the mojo of *gooooood* eatin'!"

"Hey, looks like Bass Fisher is clutching his throat and moving his mouth, but no sound is coming out. Can you hear what the cockney poet is saying, Iota?"

The mammoth linebacker leaned over the gasping, green-haired judge. "Sounds like gurgling to me, Chazz. Now, it could be one of those beat poems he writes. Or it could be an asthma attack—"

"More likely a touch of anaphylactic shock," Chazz guessed. "Both asthma and shock are symptoms of an al-lergic reaction to monosodium glutamate. Generally, though, the symptoms of MSG sensitivity are mild. A slight head-ache, perhaps —"

Iota interrupted. "And speaking of headaches, Chazz. Remember that if the MSG *does* get you down, try Extra-Strength Nopainatal for speedy, speedy, speedy headache relief . . . When your head is killin' ya, put a pill in ya, and you'll be chillin', oh yeah!..."

As paramedics moved in and placed Bass Fisher on a stretcher, Iota Jones attempted to race the broadcast clock, speaking faster and faster before the cutaway to a hard break.

" . . . the Surgeon General warns it's real dangerous to operate vehicles or heavy machinery after takin' this medi-cation. If you experience nosebleeds-hives-or-a-sudden-speech-impediment-you-should-discontinue-use-immedi-ately-andconsultyourphysician!"

*   *   *

The Pink Panther's Just Desserts

Clanging like an aluminum bucket full of slot machine winnings, Inspector Clouseau emerged from the Treat team's dressing room wearing a Tin Man costume.

The inspector's entire body was encased in metal except for his face, which was dyed silver. The job was done so hastily that wet paint dangled from his moustache like tiny drops of mercury. Heavy metal gauntlets covered Clouseau's hands, thick pipes encircled his arms and legs. An oversized aluminum funnel with a pointed spout served as a hat.

A young floor assistant immediately spotted the Tin Man and waved him forward. "Hurry up! You're on in ninety seconds!"

Teetering uncertainly in the stiff-jointed armor, Clouseau moved to the Cast-Iron Kitchen, each footstep clanging hollowly. The costume was heavy and unwieldy. With each step Clouseau sent cameras, cameramen, and technicians scattering. On the way to the stage, Clouseau spied Ponton still waiting in the wings. The little American restaurant inspector, Cassidy Caldwell, now stood by his side.

"Hey, wait a minute pal!" bellowed a producer. "You're not the Tin Man we hired!" He raced forward to grab the inspector, just as Clouseau lifted his gauntleted hand to wave at his colleagues.

K-Klang!

Unnoticed by Clouseau, his metal glove had backhanded the producer, sending the man sprawling. Realizing his friends couldn't recognize him, the Inspector lowered his arm again.

"Three . . . Two . . . One . . . And action!" cued the director.

Chazz Eiderdown launched into his spiel and Clouseau moved toward the Treat Restaurant team, where his arrival was treated with great relief.

Caught 'Napping

"About time! The presentation's just starting," said the harried Scarecrow cook.

A Scarecrow holding a meat platter nodded. "Between losing our first Tin Man and the Cowardly Lion being banned from the stadium food preparation because of his furry costume, we're barely making do out here!"

A third Scarecrow appeared holding two Tiki torches. He thrust one into Clouseau's hand, then lifted his own. "We're going to follow the twins to the judge's table, okay?" he said, lighting both torches. "Now get behind the line, and mind your Tiki, it's an open flame."

Clouseau nodded, nearly dislodging the oversized funnel on top of his head. Clanging forward, the inspector joined the parade behind several more scarecrows bearing more platters laden with sizzling tropical glazed pork loins. Between them, Tyla and Trina Treat, hips swaying under gingham, bore trays of colorful layered drinks with tiny umbrellas, and coconut halves brimming with steaming seafood broth.

Clouseau felt a surge of relief as they neared the judges. Dreyfus/De Salivon was standing at attention behind their table, between Chef Ho Lung Gong of China and Scooner Revjii of Norway. At the moment, the chief inspector appeared safe.

I am now close enough to act, Clouseau told himself as he marched behind the Treat Twins. *If anyone tries to strike at my superior, I am more than ready to strike back, as surely and deadly as an African cobra. Yes, that is a fine comparison! I am just like that swift, dangerous, and highly elusive creature—*

Suddenly the inspector tripped over his own heavy Tin Man boots. He caught himself, but nearly dropped the burning Tiki torch. The sudden move once again dislodged the oversized funnel hat. This time it dropped over Clouseau's eyes, blinding him.

Struggling to loosen the funnel, Clouseau stumbled about, accidentally touching the scarecrow in front of him with the flaming tip of his Tiki torch. The straw sticking out of the man's shirt instantly ignited.

Still rendered blind, Clouseau heard the whoosh of the flame, felt a blast of heat. Then the inspector's ears were battered by a bloodcurdling scream.

"I'm on fire! I'm on fire!" The flaming scarecrow shouted.

The inspector dropped his torch, gripping the funnel with both hands. The heat of the fire had melted some of his silver paint, which fused it to the metal funnel, making its removal virtually impossible. His armor jangling, Clouseau heard excited cries, felt himself jostled as he continued to struggle with the hat.

Finally, the inspector yanked the aluminum funnel off his head. It came free with a sucking pop. Blinking against the bright lights, Clouseau saw the hapless scarecrow hopping about the stage, his flannel shirt smoldering.

Before Clouseau could act, six men in black flameproof gear and helmets burst into the Cast-Iron Skillet Kitchen in a cloud of fire-extinguishing fog. One of the men threw a fireproof blanket over the blazing scarecrow, smothering the flames before they could do any real harm.

"Bravo, bravo! Very good!" Clouseau exclaimed.

Unfortunately, the inspector's discarded Tiki torch ignited the black silk covering on the judges' table. As B-list celebrities scattered, and flames shot up in a ten-foot arc, the audience gasped and applauded, thinking the chaos part of the show.

Caught 'Napping

That's when a new man, swathed in fireproof gear, rushed forward and, amid the smoke and chaos, threw a heavy blanket over Tyla Treat. The girl's screams were muffled as he tightened his arms around her struggling form and began to drag her away.

A precaution to ensure the lovely heiress's safety, no doubt, Clouseau reasoned.

A second new firefighter burst onto the scene and did the same thing to the other Treat twin. Now Trina was being dragged away, her wildly kicking legs and ruby slippers the only part of her visible under a heavy blanket.

A third fireman dashed forward to help subdue Trina. A scarecrow tried to intervene, but the straw man was knocked flat for his troubles. That's when Dreyfus cried out. He lunged for the same fireman, but was quickly struck down, too.

"Mon dieu! These are not real firemen!" Clouseau finally realized. Despite his heavy armor, he managed to stumble forward, throwing himself in the path of the man who'd assaulted Dreyfus.

The two men slammed together with the force of angry Sumo wrestlers. Fortunately for Clouseau, his armor absorbed much of the punishment. The fireman was not so lucky. He flew backward and landed atop Chief Inspector Dreyfus, who was struggling to rise. Both men sprawled flat.

"That's right, stay down where it is safe, Chief Inspector!" Clouseau advised. Then he whirled to face the other fireman, who was still struggling with the feisty Trina.

"Owww!" the man howled. Trina had planted a ruby slipper in his groin. The fireman released the angry girl, only to face a determined Clouseau.

"Wait!" the phony firefighter cried—just before Clouseau pummeled him to the ground with his funnel hat.

"That is what you get for manhandling these dainty hot-house flowers of demure, virginal womanhood!" Clouseau declared.

"Let go of me you stinkin', rotten, no good son of a—" Tyla, who'd also managed to free herself, rained kicks and punches on her would-be kidnapper, even as she finished a verbal tirade that would have made a longshoreman blush.

Clouseau, now tangled in the fireproof blanket that had ensnared Tyla Treat, shook his gauntlet helplessly at the fleeing felons. "I hope you've learned your lesson!" he yelled. "If you can't stand the heat, stay out of the skillet!"

NINETEEN

Canned Ham

"**S**tay calm, sir. We'll have you out of there in a jiffy," said the rescue worker. He tapped the Tin Man costume's chest plate in what he thought was a reassuring gesture. Unfortunately, the hollow metallic clank only induced more panic in the fallen inspector.

"*Pour l'amour de dieu!* Hurry, man! Before I perish in this steel girdle!" Clouseau cried, legs and arms flailing like a flipped turtle.

After the violent struggle, Inspector Clouseau discovered he was trapped inside the metal costume. The lock had been damaged when he'd collided with the man who'd assaulted Dreyfus.

Unable to strip off the heavy metal that imprisoned him, Clouseau was forced to watch helplessly while the would-be kidnappers fled the arena. No one made a move to stop them.

Both hotel security and the audience took them for part of the show.

Immobilized, the inspector now lay in the center of the darkened Cast-Iron Skillet set, surrounded by a half-dozen real firemen and rescue workers.

"Don't worry, Tin Man," a fireman called from across the room. "They're bringing in the jaws of life to cut you out of there."

"*Oui! Oui!* Let me be devoured by the Jaws of Life," Clouseau moaned. "Better that, than suffocation in this hellish iron coffin!"

The crowd parted. Two big men raced to the inspector's side. Between them they carried the heavy cutting tool. Carefully, they began slicing away the dented armor.

Despite Clouseau's howls of panic, things went fairly well, and Clouseau was soon free. Ponton reached down and helped his fellow Frenchman to his feet.

"*Mon dieu*, Ponton! What an ordeal! Never again will I don steel britches!" Clouseau vowed. The inspector glanced fearfully at the gigantic scissors that had cut him free, then checked to see if all of his bodily parts were intact.

"You have stopped the attempted stabbing of the chief inspector *and* saved the Treat twins from kidnappers," Ponton proudly declared, handing Clouseau his trench coat and hat. "A marvelous example of French courage—and both on live television."

The inspector waved away the compliment. "How is our intrepid superior faring after this ordeal?"

Ponton sighed. "A physician is treating him now. I'm sure he will recover."

A relieved smile crossed Clouseau's features. Clad once again in what he regarded as his uniform, he felt his dignity return, oblivious to the fact that his face was smeared with silver makeup, his legs still encased in Tin Man pants.

"I should question him," he said. "Perhaps Chief Inspector Dreyfus noticed something I might have missed."

Ponton shook his head. "I wouldn't do that now. He is naturally upset. He actually blames you for starting the fire—"

"Tut-tut, *mon ami*, you do not have to make excuses for the chief inspector. I am sure he is embarrassed and ashamed that he was not able to stop the kidnappers single-handedly, as I have done. Blaming me is a natural reaction to his feelings of inadequacy. He has done this before, as you well know. But I always forgive his shortcomings. We must learn to rise above, Ponton!"

Ponton shrugged, deciding to let the fire-starter subject drop. "Unfortunately, for our case, Dreyfus was not the target this time. He was merely collateral damage."

But Clouseau shook his head. "I would not be so certain of that, my friend. Would not a failed kidnapping be the perfect *cover* for *murder*?"

Ponton looked doubtful. But before he could reply, Cassidy Caldwell joined them.

"I just spoke with a local detective," she said. "The kidnappers got away clean. They ran off-stage, dumped their helmets and firemen's gear in the dressing room, then mingled with the casino patrons to make their escape."

"But how could this be!" Clouseau exclaimed. "The MGM Grand is one of the most secure facilities in the world!"

Cass shrugged. "The kidnappers convinced everyone they were part of the act, even the show's producers. The Treat Twins are drama queens. They've pulled stunts like this before—though their pranks usually involve one or both of them taking off their clothes."

Clouseau's eyes glazed over at the very suggestion. "Ah . . . how mischievous they can be, those wonderful, free-spirited little innocent cherubs . . ."

"Innocent cherubs?" Cassidy snorted. "Clearly, you haven't Googled them."

"Perhaps the kidnappers' disguises will yield a clue," Ponton suggested.

"Maybe, but we'll never get near them," Cass said. "Everything's been confiscated by the Las Vegas Metro police."

Ponton exhaled in frustration. "Then we are back where we started. Stymied. At an impasse."

Clouseau stepped forward to console his partner—and felt something hard crunch under his metal boot. He lifted his foot, looked down, and noticed a flat pile of yellow powder on the floor.

Ponton dropped to one knee, sniffed the substance. "Sugar," he declared.

Cass joined him on the ground. The ex-culinary student examined the powder more closely and shook her head. "This isn't sugar. This is marzipan. There's another piece over there."

Ponton scooped up the object—a small, pale blue chunk of candy. "It looks like a tiny toy tank. See the little turret and the cannon."

Cass Caldwell dug into her handbag. After snapping on a latex glove, she took the object from Ponton and studied it. "Good gravy! I recognize this. It's a *marzi-panzer*."

"Ah, yes, of course," Clouseau murmured, nodding sagely. "A marzi-panzer." Then he turned to Cassidy and spoke in a soft, calm voice. "Please, mademoiselle, tell us?"

Cass blinked. "Tell you what, Inspector?"

"What the devil *is* a *marzi-panzer*!" he shouted, suddenly hysterical.

Canned Ham

"Easy, Inspector," Cass said. "It's a candy, made of sugar. And it's manufactured by only one company, a German restaurant franchise called Beitermann Foods, LLC."

Ponton folded his arms and arched an intrigued eyebrow. "And how do you know this, *ma petite*?"

Cass sighed. "Last year I had a run-in with these guys at the annual Food and Franchise Fair at New York's Javits Convention Center. The executives from Bietermann were handing these out to attendees. I made them stop."

"And why is that?" Ponton asked.

"Because this candy is an accident waiting to happen!" Cass reached into her bag and pulled out a clear plastic pipe three inches long and about an inch around. "This plastic tube is used to check for choking hazards. It's the same size as a child's esophagus."

Cass dropped the *marzi-panzer* into the top of the plastic tube. The candy lodged inside the pipe instead of falling through it. "You could kill a kid with this candy," she said. "Not that those creeps at Beitermann Foods give a damn. They even complained to my boss, tried to get me fired."

"What happened?" Ponton asked.

Cass shrugged. "Rules are rules. The candy was a choking hazard, and they were forced to withdraw the product."

Ponton nodded, betraying a little smile of admiration for the petite American.

"These Germans seem rather ruthless," Clouseau mused. "Which is not unusual, given the events of the twentieth century—not to mention the effect of sauerkraut on my digestive tract. However, do you suppose they could have something to do with the murders of our chefs?"

"I don't know about that," Cass said. She shook the tube

until the *marzi-panzer* fell into her palm. Then she held the confection up to the light. "This clue right here tells me they sure had something to do with the attempted kidnapping of the Treat Twins."

"Mon dieu," Ponton said. "Do you think the Beitermann Food group is aligned with the German team?"

"I don't know," Cass replied. "But we can find out. They have a franchise seminar tonight. It's listed in the Expo guide. I believe Beitermann is pitching their new theme restaurants to the American market."

Clouseau nodded. "I believe I shall attend this seminar—in disguise, of course."

Ponton sighed. "Then perhaps you should advise me now, Inspector. Will we once again be needing the Jaws of Life?"

A gentle, almost timid knock cut through the silence of the dimly lit suite.

"What is that horrifying noise!" Dreyfus bellowed.

Officer Raspail sat up, blinking. Realizing he'd dozed off, the policeman jumped out of his chair. "Someone is at the door!"

Dreyfus moaned. "With every tap my head feels as though it is about to explode," he cried. Sprawled across the bedspread, the chief inspector adjusted the ice pack he held against his throbbing temple, moved it to his bruised forehead. "I gave strict orders that I was not to be disturbed. Tell them to go away!"

With the security chain in place, Officer Raspail, opened the door an inch and peered into the hallway. He saw a stranger. The short, middle-aged man wore a suit and bow tie and twitched nervously when he saw Raspail.

"I must see Chef De Salivon," the man hissed. He glanced

down one hallway, then another, as if he expected to be menaced at any moment.

"You should not be here," Raspail shot back. "This floor is secure. Where is your badge, your security pass?"

"Please," the other cried, his voice louder now. "I must see De Salivon. It is a matter of life or death!"

The little man pushed against the door. The chain stretched with a metallic click.

"Raspail! Where are you?" Dreyfus called. "I need more ice!"

"Sir! I must speak with you at once!" the little man insisted.

"That's it!" Raspail muttered. He released the chain and stepped into the hallway, locking the door behind him. The little man backed up a step.

"Please, I must see De Salivon!"

"Why is that?"

The man lowered his eyes, to stare at the pattered carpet. "I . . . I cannot say. I will only tell the Marquis De Salivon."

Another deluded fan who believes Dreyfus is the real *De Salivon*, Raspail thought. Then he cried out. "Dumas! Where are you?"

A short, towheaded man with close-set eyes and a barrel chest, appeared at the end of the hallway. He spied the intruder and frowned.

"I'm sorry, sir. He must have gotten past me," Dumas said sheepishly.

Raspail's eyes narrowed. "I should report you for this."

"I stepped away for only a moment, sir. For the doing of the business, you know?"

Officer Raspail frowned. "I'll look the other way this time. But don't let it happen again."

"Please," the diminutive stranger gasped, hands wringing. "I must speak to De Salivon . . . It's a matter of life or death!"

The two Sûreté officers exchanged glances. "Do you think he's telling the truth? About this *matter of life and death* thing?" Dumas asked.

Raspail studied the intruder. The little man was frail, quaking. His clothes appeared classy but disheveled, eyes wild and full of fear. The officer shook his head. "He's harmless, just a deluded fan, and not our murderer."

"You are sure?"

"Officer Lamothe reported a confrontation with this very man—right before he was attacked by Elvis. It's in his statement taken at the hospital."

Raspail gazed at the stranger once again. This time his eyes held no suspicion, only pity.

"He's harmless. Or crazy. Either way, he doesn't belong here. Escort this man to the elevators while I fetch the Big Boss some ice."

TWENTY

Party Line

"*Sacré bleu*! There's quite a draft in here, eh Ponton?"

"I am perfectly comfortable, Inspector," Ponton replied. "A little warm, in fact."

"*Absurde!*" Clouseau insisted. "It feels like a blast of frigid Antarctic air has swept through this place!"

The pair had just passed through the MGM's Grand Pool area. The expansive complex of five swimming pools, waterfalls, soothing whirlpools baths, lush vegetation, and a meandering, manmade river shimmered like an enchanted tropical paradise under the clear night sky and bright desert moon.

It was only after they entered the air-conditioned comfort of the elegant Conference Center that Clouseau felt a chill.

"Of course *you're* comfortable," the inspector complained to his junior partner. "You are wearing pants, shirt, a suit of clothes."

The Pink Panther's Just Desserts

Clouseau paused at a full-length mirror to check his disguise. The phony beard, black as a moonless Sahara night, mingled perfectly with his own dark moustache. The Inspector's prematurely gray hair was hidden under the *keffiyeh* crowning his head. The square of white cotton cloth was held in place by an *egal*—a rope circlet that wrapped around Clouseau's forehead. Below the traditional Arab headdress, Clouseau wore a spotless white *dishdasha*, a modified form of bedouin garb worn in more progressive Arab nations. The billowing cotton robes reached to the floor.

"But, Inspector, surely you are wearing a suit as well? Under the *dishdasha*, I mean?"

"Certainly not!" Clouseau exclaimed. "My disguise must be as convincing as possible, and that involves scrupulous attention to detail and absolute accuracy."

"But, Inspector, Arab businessmen wear European clothing under their robes. Suits and trousers. Did you not know that?"

"Really? Is that so?" Clouseau tapped his chin. "I think I must have confused the Arab sheiks with those other men who run around in women's clothing, the ones across the Channel—"

"Monty Python?"

"Scottish highlanders." Clouseau sighed. "Well, there's nothing to be done about it now. We have arrived."

At the door of the spacious, well-appointed Convention Center meeting room stood a friendly young woman in Bavarian peasant garb. She was all smiles in her greeting, under copious ringlets of bouncy blond hair.

"*Willkommen* to the Beitermann Food Franchise Investment Prospectus," the cheerful woman said in heavily accented English. She slipped Clouseau and Ponton brochures, then led them to a table, where she opened a laptop computer.

"Mein name *ist* Heidi. May I please haff your names?"

Clouseau bowed deeply. "I am Prince Abdullah Mullah Dullah al Lullah, of the Royal Family of Toofar."

"Danke," Heidi replied, typing the name into the computer. "And your comrade?"

Clouseau glanced disdainfully at Ponton. "This infidel? This nonentity? He is no one of importance. My servant, my bodyguard. Nothing more. His name is Gilbert."

Heidi nodded. "Very good. I am sorry to say you've arrived late. We are very punctual here at Beitermann, so the presentation has already begun. But never fear . . . The best is yet to come."

She handed each of them a plastic nametag. "Elsa will lead you both to a seat."

Clouseau turned, shocked to see the beautiful platinum-blonde bombshell he'd met the night before. Quickly masking any recognition, the inspector greeted the statuesque blonde as a stranger, reasonably certain she could not penetrate his clever disguise.

For the night's business event, Elsa had shed her shimmering silver spandex gown in favor of an ebony business suit tailored to show off her luscious figure. Her platinum-blonde hair, which had draped down her form as freely as a glorious bolt of silk the night before, was now rolled into a twist so tight it slightly altered the shape of her eyes. The woman's pale features seemed spectral against the inky blackness of her attire. Only Elsa's cherry glossed lips and ice-blue eyes showed any hint of color.

"Prince Lullah, please follow me," Elsa said in a firm voice that belied the flirtatious sidelong glance Clouseau was sure she'd displayed. He followed her swaying hips through the doors and into the conference room.

The dimly lit chamber was filled with row upon row of padded black chairs, most of them occupied by men and women in business attire. All eyes were drawn to the glare of a single spotlight illuminating a podium on a raised stage. Behind that, half-hidden by shadows, an austere group of men sat at a long table. All had square heads, flat faces, and flesh of a bonelike pallor. They stared unblinking at the audience with chilly eyes.

Clouseau shuddered. "What is this, Ponton?" he whispered as they continued to follow Elsa to the middle of the room. "A seminar or a funeral?"

"You are right, Inspector," Ponton softly replied. "There is something rather ghoulish afoot."

On the raised stage, a wizened old man in a beautiful Helmut Lang suit slowly moved to the podium. His arrival was greeted by enthusiastic applause, but the speaker quickly silenced the audience with a stiff-armed salute.

Elsa turned to Clouseau. "Vee are just in time. Our leader is about to speak," she whispered, her blue eyes flashing with anticipation.

Clouseau noticed a parade of men in tight, black jumpsuits entering from a side door. The group, all athletic and young had shaved heads and stern expressions. They circled the conference room, dropping a single guard at each exit as they moved.

The inspector's attention was suddenly drawn from the guards by Elsa, who placed a soft, manicured hand on his arm. "Prince Lullah, please sit here . . . *und* I vill sit next to you," she instructed, leaning close enough for Clouseau to feel her sweet breath tickle his cheek.

The inspector took the seat between Ponton and the lovely German woman. Acutely aware of Elsa's close proximity, the inspector attempted, with only marginal success, to direct his attention back to the man at the podium.

"Willkommen! Willkommen jeder!" the skeletal old man said in a surprisingly strong voice. *"Mein* name *ist* Horst Spikel. Though I have been to America before, it vas many years ago, however. So my English is not so good, maybe."

The man's broken English and self-deprecating manner was greeted with a smattering of chuckles and applause.

"I vant to thank you all for coming at this late hour," Horst Spikel continued. "The Food Expo is very busy for us all. But I think you will find zis meeting of value, and perhaps quite profitable . . ."

Clouseau was surprised when Elsa subtly moved her chair closer—close enough to touch her silky thigh against his own. The inspector shivered again, but this time it had nothing to do with the air conditioning or his lack of pants.

"Ask me why I am here, in America, speaking to all of you?" Spikel said. "I *vill* tell you why. It *ist* because I *love* America! Yes, yes! I vas taught to love America many years ago, by a great man. My mentor vas an American, and he used to say, 'Colonel Spikel, once vee were enemies. Now vee are friends.'"

Horst Spikel grinned at the audience. "Zat is zee vay I feel. I love America, and believe zat vee are all friends, comrades in arms, so to speak!"

Applause filled the room. Elsa leaned close to Clouseau. "Are you really a prince?" she cooed.

"Yes," Clouseau replied.

He felt Elsa's hand touch his knee, stroke his thigh. "*Und* are you very rich, Prince Abdullah Mullah Dullah al Lullah?"

Clouseau's chill fled in a hurry. Now he was getting warm under his cotton robes. Beads of sweat appeared on his forehead. "Yes, I am immensely rich," he told Elsa. "I own an oasis next door to the king's palace."

Elsa squeezed Clouseau's thigh. "*Und* do *you* have a palace?"

Clouseau nodded. "Several. But I mostly live with my fellow bedouins in a luxury tent at the oasis. It is convenient, you see. Being near the goats and all . . ."

"Do you have many tents at zis oasis of yours?" Elsa asked as her hand continued to explore.

Clouseau glanced down at the lap of his robe and swallowed hard. "Oh, yes," he rasped. "I have many tents . . . and a great big pole, as well."

"There ist somezing very special about friends," Spikel said at the podium. "We share secrets vit our friends—and business opportunities, too. I, myself, have a secret to share. *Und* a lucrative financial opportunity, *und* I invite all of you, my American friends, to take advantage!"

Spikel signaled the audio-visual technician with a stiff-armed gesture, and a power point's projected beam filled a screen above the old man's head.

Clouseau shifted uncomfortably as Elsa's gentle touch continued to distract him.

"All of us know zat theme restaurants are zee newest, hottest trend in zee food service industry," Herr Spikel declared cheerfully. "Every year, millions flock to zese restaurants *und* bars built around a central concept, a catchy or appealing theme . . ."

While the man spoke, pictures of famous franchise restaurants appeared on the screen.

"Vee have all been to Zee Heavy Metal Café, to Hollywood Flavor. Vee satisfy more zan one appetite at Boobies. We devour fish at zee Perfect Storm's Trawler. *Und* what *junge oder mädchen* does not love der fun zee *kinder* have at zee Incredible Sea Monkey's Seafood House?"

Elsa cooed in Clouseau's ear. "I vould like to introduce you to *my* monkey, Prince. It is so soft and furry *und* inviting. Friendly, too."

"By the sands of the Sahara, control yourself, woman!" Clouseau hissed. "Do you not already have a male friend to satisfy you?"

Elsa's lovely face curled into a sneer. "I vas *supposed* to meet a member of the Sûreté for a passionate tryst last evening. But like all Frenchmen, der limp, pathetic fool must have lost his nerve and failed to appear."

"Indeed," Spikel proclaimed. "Truly successful themes have spawned whole tourist towns. Two such places we have closely studied in America: Hershey, Pennsylvania, and Colonial Williamsburg."

The screen went black for a moment. "But zere is a problem with such places. It ist very difficult to keep zee theme fresh," Spikel said. "Fads come and go. Empires rise *und* fall, franchise icons fade. Zoo, how is a franchise owner to stay ahead of der pack? To anticipate new trends? New visions for a brave new world?"

Spikel paused, glared at his audience. "I say, look to history, my American friends. Look to the past, comrades! Nostalgia *always* sells. Let us harken back to a time and a place when zings seemed better, simpler . . . When life vas uncluttered by all zee modern complications *und* inconveniences."

The inspector felt Elsa lean toward him. Her lips moved so close to his ear they tickled his lobe as she whispered, "Are you not moved by vat you hear?"

Clouseau realized, under the thin *dishdasha,* he was very moved, indeed!

"Here at Beitermann Food Group, LLC, vee believe vee haff found that theme. Zee first of our new franchise restaurants opened in Argentina to wild acclaim *und* instant success. Since then, vee haff opened profitable franchises in Paraguay *und* Venezuela . . ."

Spikel fixed his audience with an imperious stare. His eyes seemed to smolder with a savage fire.

"But like all great and noble endeavors, this new franchise requires living space in which to thrive!" Spikel declared. "*Und* vee are bringing zis new restaurant concept north, to the United States of America. *Damen und Herren*, I present you with zee boldest theme concept of zee twenty-first century . . . I give you . . . *Happy Fritzie's Reichshaus!*"

On the screen, above Herr Spikel's outthrust arms, appeared the image of a massive, flat-roofed, squat building with walls of gray, unpainted concrete. Completely encircled by a narrow strip of windows, the entire structure resembled a World War Two gun emplacement, down to the horizontal "cannons" spouting theatrical smoke from three turrets.

On the roof, poles waving flags of a dozen different nations flapped in the wind. In the center, raised higher than the rest, a red banner emblazoned with the words *REICHSHAUS* in Gothic script, slowly unfurled.

Herr Spikel continued his spiel. "Happy Fritzie's Reichshaus is a family restaurant with an historical feel, represented by a cheerfully harmless iconic character zat perfectly embodies fun and frolic."

The image on the screen morphed into "Happy Fritzie," a fat, red-cheeked Bavarian man in lederhosen and black boots, a German-style tankard of frothy beer in one hand, a knockwurst in the other.

"Everything at Happy Fritzie's invokes the nostalgic feel vee all haff for zee good days of zee 1930s, from zee marvelously authentic décor to zee dedicated, trained, and uniformed staff . . . Yet despite the old-time milieu, Happy Fritzie's features a surprisingly contemporary menu . . ."

Again the image morphed.

"Each chain restaurant vill feature unique dining areas, with their own distinct style of décor," Spikel said proudly. "For family-style eating, try zee 'Barracks.' For a more formal setting, zee 'Reich Chancellery,' and for good-time parties *und* pub fare, hit zee 'Beer Hall Putsch.'"

"*C'est absurde*," Clouseau muttered as each image went by.

"*Und* zere is fun *und* games for zee *kinders* to be had downstairs, in zee 'Bunker,'" Herr Spikel said with what he assumed was a paternal smile. "Zee *kinders* can romp *und* play on an exact replica of zee 'Tiger Tank,' or frolic on an ice slide. Vee do not yet haff a name for zis chilly attraction. But vee are leaning toward calling it zee 'Russian Front.'"

Clouseau glanced at Ponton. His sleepy eyes were bulging in horror. "*Sacré bleu*," he whispered.

"It *is* amazing, is it not?" Elsa gushed to Clouseau. "Our leader's vision surpasses all others of the food service industry! Soon zee inferior franchises vill crumble under Happy Fritzie's boot!"

"But décor is not why people come to a restaurant, correct?" Spikel continued. "*Und* zat is why vee have created Happy Fritzie's menu of unique, signature dishes. For breakfast, try our 'Luft-Waffles,' so light and airy zey might fly! For lunch, try our 'Fatherland Franks' or 'Kriegsmarine Knockwurst'—both come vit Happy Fritzie's famous 'Helmet o' Sauerkraut' . . . *Und* believe me! All of Happy Fritzie's wieners are thick and delicious."

"Naughty prince!" Elsa exclaimed in delight. "You're not wearing underwear."

Clouseau tried to focus, but the woman was like an octopus. He winced when he felt Elsa's strong hand grip his own "Happy Fritzie."

"I am sure your wiener is thick and delicious, too, my Prince," she whispered throatily.

"Madame, please," Clouseau whimpered. "Control yourself!"

Herr Spikel droned on. "Desserts are not forgotten at Happy Fritzie's. Vee serve many confections, including 'Reichshaus's Marzi-panzers,' in dozens of delicious fruit flavors, *und* chocolate, too."

Clouseau heard a crunching sound. He turned to see one of the guards eating something.

"At Happy Fritzie's, vee know how you Americans prize convenience, so each location will feature a drive-through window with easy to read menus, just 'Take zee Third Reich, and follow zee signs, to Happy Fritzie's!'" Spikel paused to cackle at his own joke.

"Now! Down to zee real business. Zee best part of our Happy Fritzie franchise, is zee blitzkrieg vee plan to launch to take America by storm! By year's end, vee vill haff over three hundred locations operating in North America. How is zis possible, you ask?"

Spikel paused. Above his head, a map of the continental United States appeared. Red dots showed where each restaurant would be located. Soon the red dots filled the map, revealing a very familiar pattern to Inspector Clouseau.

"Ponton!" he hissed. "That map! I've seen it before."

Spikel grinned proudly as his battle plan was unveiled. "Vee will soon begin negotiations with a vell-known American chain of restaurants to take over their locations and transform them into Happy Fritzie's restaurants—"

"Where have you seen the map, Inspector?" Ponton asked.

"On the 'Little Boy's Activity' placemat at my favorite Treat Restaurant! It is a map of the Treat locations. It is always printed right next to the 'Connect the Dots to Draw Trina Treat's Backside' puzzle."

Ponton blinked in surprise. "You mean—"

"Oui," Clouseau said. "Cassidy Caldwell was correct. These Beitermann thugs did attempt to kidnap Tyla and Trina. Clearly, they were going to hold the girls hostage until the Treat family relinquished their ownership of the properties."

Clouseau heard a crunching sound again. He looked up in time to see one of the burly guards pop a marzi-panzer into his mouth. The inspector leaped to his feet, suddenly recognizing the man. He pointed an accusing finger.

"You, sir, are a villain! A kidnapper. You tried to grab those lovely, innocent flowers, the Treat Twins!"

Stunned, and obviously guilty, the man dropped his marzi-panzers and groped at his belt for a weapon. Suddenly the exits burst open and the room was filled with dozens of American tactical officers in body armor, toting machine guns.

"FBI!" a man in a dark suit cried as he charged into the conference room, his ID badge held high. "I have a warrant for the arrest of Herr Horst Spikel, his daughter Elsa Spikel—"

The Pink Panther's Just Desserts

The woman at Clouseau's side screamed and jumped to her feet. She tried to flee, but Clouseau tackled her. His *keffiyeh* headdress fell away and Elsa took a second, shocked look at the Inspector's face.

"You! You are not an Arab prince!"

"No, my dear," the inspector informed her. "I am that limp, pathetic Frenchman whom your fellow countryman obviously turned away last night before we could consummate our attraction."

"Unhand me, you duplicitous frog!"

"Gladly!" Clouseau replied as two female agents rushed forward to cuff and lead away their prisoner.

"I also have warrants for each member of Beitermann Foods, LLC," the head agent declared.

One of the ghoulishly pale, dark-suited men at the table jumped to his feet. "This is an outrage," he cried. "What is zee charge?"

"Attempted kidnapping and extortion, buddy!" the agent replied. "And that's just for starters." Then the agent turned to his tactical assault team.

"Line 'em up and cuff 'em, boys," he commanded. Then he turned to the audience. "Ladies and gentlemen, I'm terribly sorry, but this presentation is over. Happy Fritzie's crew is about to explore that uniquely American-themed experience we like to call 'the Federal Pen.'"

TWENTY-ONE

Meat Grinder

Late the next morning, Chief Inspector Dreyfus called the French police detail to his hotel suite. Inspector Clouseau, Detective Second-Class Ponton, Raspail, Lamothe, and the rest of the officers took seats in the living room area, on couches, chairs, and at the dining room table. Trade Minister Marmiche was also present.

Pots of hot coffee and overflowing baskets of fresh baked muffins, buttery croissants, and cream cheese stuffed bagels kept the Frenchmen contented as Dreyfus paced back and forth, updating them on the state of their case.

"Chef Napoleon spent the night cooling his Haitian heels in the Las Vegas jail," Dreyfus informed the team. "But a local judge is letting him out on bail before the first World Food Expo event this afternoon."

"Outrageous!" Clouseau declared, jumping to his feet.

"His attempt on your life has been recorded by the television cameras! I caught the knife myself!"

"Sit down, Clouseau, I reviewed the tape with the Las Vegas police. And, although the side-effect of your taunting Chef Germaine with his own cutting board *appeared* to have saved my life from a crazed killer, Chef Napoleon and a local judge both disagree."

"How can this be?" Ponton asked.

"At the bond hearing earlier this morning, the chef said the charges against him were false. He claimed that he often juggles knives in his restaurant as entertainment, and he was about to do so again for the Grand Arena audience, but in the heat of the competition, his aim was off."

"That is absurd!" Ponton declared.

"I agree, Detective," Dreyfus replied. "But, unfortunately, we are in another country's jurisdiction."

"And what of Napoleon's suspected connections to two murders in France?" Ponton pressed.

"Yes, yes, I know," Dreyfus sighed. "The local police captain, one Emma Titus, interrogated him herself. Apparently, he has produced an airtight alibi. He has been working from morning till night every day in his restaurant for the past three months without even one day off. He has produced witnesses."

"Members of his culinary team, no doubt," Clouseau guessed.

"Correct. And, yes—" Dreyfus held up a hand. "Do not even pose the notion. I have already considered that they could be lying for him."

"Can we not pressure the local authorities to hold Chef Napoleon until the end of the World Food Expo?" Ponton asked.

Meat Grinder

This time it was Trade Minister Marmiche who answered. "I have already tried. But there is equal pressure to release him—from the World Food Expo organizers themselves. Do not forget, Chef Napoleon is well known and has many fans. They expect to see the Haitians compete with Napoleon rather than without."

Ponton folded his arms. "Then we are back in the position of guarding the lives of the French team?"

"Yes," Dreyfus replied. "And I am back to acting as the decoy De Salivon. So listen carefully—I want everyone to be on their toes! Look alive! This competition will be heated and danger may be lurking around the next pot or pan!"

Clouseau leaped up and saluted. "You will have my utmost attention, sir!"

Dreyfus reached for his Kevlar vest. "That is what frightens me the most."

Each day of the World Food Expo would bring a new "course" of competiton. That day's was "Appetizers and Hors d'oeuvres." The final day would bring the most prestigious event of the entire week—"Desserts in the Desert."

As the returning champions from the year before, the French team would not have to compete until each evening's "final battle." The key question was: who would win the right to be their competitor each day?

By three o'clock the first day, the French team was already worried. Since noon, they had watched in stunned disbelief as teams from China, Italy, Spain, and the Treat Restaurant succumbed to a new, upstart pack of culinary mavericks from Australia.

Dubbed "the Bandicoots," this eclectic mix of world travelers and big-game hunters specialized in the preparation of rare and exotic meats, seafood, and vegetables. Round after round, the Bandicoots had been smashing the competition, moving from underdog to front runners in a very short time.

By early afternoon, the French team could see that their man Yves Petit had his work cut out for him. Petit was the chef who would be representing the French in the day's Appetizers and Hors d'oeuvres final battle, scheduled to begin at six o'clock that evening.

Petit could see that he'd be squaring off against a formidable opponent—one he had never before competed against. When that realization dawned, he tossed aside his carefully planned menu and demanded his sous-chefs bring him foie gras, the freshest batch of pig intestines they could possibly find, and a final, mysterious ingredient whispered to a sous-chef from Ecuador.

Vegetarian chef Babette Beauford was horrified. "This is how you fight back? By transforming our kitchen into an abattoir?"

"The kitchen *is* an abattoir, mademoiselle," Petit sniffed. "Only a fool would mistake it for anything else."

Insulted, Babette turned on her heels and stormed off to her suite. Yves Petit forgot about the exchange the moment it was over.

Locked up in the privacy of the team's fully stocked rehearsal kitchen backstage, he and his personal sous-chefs set to work planning a new menu, using the most exotic cuts of meat they could find.

Meanwhile, the highly placed Japanese team was the next to go up against the Australians. Chef Miyama Ido of Osaka prepared a bold assortment of three types of hibachi barbecued Takifugu—a highly toxic blowfish considered a delicacy in Japan.

Meat Grinder

The World Food Expo's master of ceremonies, Chazz Eiderdown, was mightily impressed.

"Chef Ido centered his appetizer tray around the most prized of the edible species, *T. rubripes*, the Tiger Blowfish. This species also happens to be the most poisonous! But the chef also included lesser known toxic species such as *T. pardalis*, *T. vermicularis*, and *T. porphyreus* for a balanced, well-presented tray. Let's listen to the great man describe his meal . . ."

Unfortunately, Chef Miyama Ido was an aged man who spoke only halting Japanese. The audience at home and in the arena heard the voice of a translator, a young Japanese woman, instead.

"To achieve a high degree of *umami*, I grilled the fish with the skin intact, and I blended the fish's deadly liver and testicles into a glaze that contains just enough poison to offer a pleasing sting on the tip of the tongue . . . without the fatal side-effects of a tetrodotoxin overdose, of course."

But not even the thrill of risking slow death by asphyxiation impressed the judges. Gary Kehoe greeted the entry with visible disdain, and the other judges seemed critical of both taste and texture. A Japanese judge went so far as to state that blowfish should not be prepared in any way but in soup—the culinary equivalent of charging Chef Ido with heresy.

By contrast, the judges were much more impressed with the Aussies' take on the Korean delicacy *t'talk ttong jip*.

"There's no precise translation for the name of this Korean comfort food—at least not one we can use in prime time," Chazz Eiderdown explained to the audience with a wink and a nod. "The FCC has its standards, you know!"

Inspector Clouseau examined the dish on a high-definition television monitor. When the camera offered a close-up, he studied the plate. The dish looked like fried skin of fowl, cut into bite-sized pieces and sprinkled with sesame seeds, garlic, shallots, and lemongrass, and served as finger food on a Wasabi and rice flour cracker.

"To me, you know, it simply looks like chicken parts," Clouseau remarked with a shrug.

"It *is* chicken asshole," Arnaud Germaine replied.

The inspector whirled to face the other man. "Monsieur Germaine, I am a highly decorated police inspector. I may not have your culinary credentials, but that does not give you the right to insult me, you, you . . . *meatpacker*!"

The burly man chuckled. "You misunderstand, Inspector. *T'talk ttong jip* is a traditional Korean dish *made* from chicken *anus*."

"Chicken . . . ?"

"Asshole."

Clouseau reddened. "Ah, I see, monsieur . . . you confused me there for a moment . . . and, uh, I thank you so much for clarifying that up."

The judges scores soon made it official. The Japanese were defeated, and the Bandicoots moved up to the highest level. At last, they earned the right to compete against the previous year's champion team—the French—in a television face-off that would be going out live to an East Coast prime-time audience. In this final round, the two battling chefs were expected to create three distinctly different appetizers each for presentation to the judges.

When the time came, Clouseau, Ponton, and Cassidy reported to the wings for the big event, staged inside the MGM Grand Garden Arena.

From the outset, it was clear that Yves Petit had tried to beat the Australians at their own game. His first appetizer was traditionally French, a fois gras served on what appeared to be thin, circular crackers. Curiously, Yves Petit described his dish as a "French-Asian fusion." The reason became apparent when he divulged the ingredients.

"The braised fois gras is placed on a bed of Szechuan-style Siberian ox penis," Chef Petit explained. "The ox penis is sliced paper thin, marinated in cilantro and black peppers and flash-fried to make the flesh both stiff and chewy. Each translucent slice has a naturally-occurring hole in the center, perfect to hold a fresh, green scallion sprig!"

Next came a rare delicacy from Ecuador, glazed *cuy*— guinea pig—roasted over an apple wood fire. Served whole, the *cuy*'s tiny ears and toes were charred stumps, the eyes burned, hollow pits. The lips were curled back to reveal a tiny pink tongue, scorched at the edges.

Chef Petit sliced the abdomen so that bite-sized pieces could be stabbed with a toothpick. The skin seemed crispy and fatty. When he reached the rump, something dark brown and clotted slid out of the *cuy*'s behind.

"*Chungo!*" a Central American judge exclaimed, obviously excited.

Clouseau paled. "*Mon dieu*, is that—"

"Organ meat," Arnaud Germaine explained. "Very savory, exceedingly gamey. Though I'm not generally an admirer of *cuy*, I must salute Yves's choice of a mango glaze. Truly inspired."

For his final entry, Chef Petit surprised everyone when his sous-chefs wheeled a cart bearing a covered tray tall enough to hold a wedding cake. Petit had to climb a ladder to lift the silver cover.

It was difficult to determine what struck the judges most profoundly—the spectacle of a six-foot food sculpture that resembled the trunk and twisting branches of a bare tree with gray-brown bark; or the rank, overpowering stench of fetid organ meat that immediately filled the judges' area.

"This is traditional African American chitlins . . . with a twist," Petit announced, a cloth over his nose to block the smell. "Served with a simmering Roquefort and Gruyère cheese fondue, the hog intestines are stuffed with red peppers and onions and roasted until they are hard and chewy. *S'il vous plaît*, treat this sculpture as a fruit-bearing tree—"

"Strange fruit, indeed," Clouseau murmured.

"—simply break off a piece, like so, and dip it into the bubbling cheese . . ."

While the judges seemed duly impressed by the architectural skill involved, the chitlins were not a gustatory hit. Master Gary Kehoe ordered the pork-gut sculpture removed and fans brought in as soon as the judges sampled the fare. Yves Petit was grim-faced as he stood stiffly behind the judges while the Australian team made their "challenge" presentation.

Fortunately for the French team, the Australians seemed to take up where Petit left off by further horrifying the judges. Their first offering was a Filipino treat called *balut*, topped with a bright yellow whipped butter concoction.

Although the dish looked like a tray of deviled eggs, it was quickly evident that this "delicacy" from the Philippines bore no resemblance to the popular American finger food.

Chef Rolfe Pennsbury of the Australian team explained the delicacy. "These fertilized duck eggs are allowed to develop for ten to fourteen days before boiling. When cracked, the *balut* has a slimy texture and a mild egglike taste that is perfectly complimented by the lightly whipped saffron butter . . . . Now don't be afraid of those feathers or the tiny bones, the feet, or the wings—they are tasty delights to be savored, mates!"

But not many of the judges "savored" the taste. Even Gary Kehoe put aside his portion after only a nibble.

Next came what looked like a paté on a thick, fried cracker. But both the audience and the judges had, by now, come to the conclusion that looks can be deceiving.

"A sauté of mealworms—the larvae of *Tenebrio molitor*—topping a patty of ground, fried cricket," Chef Pennsbury proudly announced.

Because this rather disgusting dish resembled escargot, the judges were a little more accepting. Yves Petit's spirits, which had been heartened by the first round, fell once again.

For their final entry, the Australians brought out trays containing what looked like large prawns. "Parched locust was discovered by explorer William Dampier while visiting the Bashee Islands in 1687," Chef Pennsbury explained.

From his observation spot offstage, Ponton groaned.

"What is it?" Cassidy whispered beside him.

"I cannot imagine eating locust."

Cassidy laughed. "It's not that bad."

Ponton stared in amazmnt. "You—Mademoiselle 'Fecal Fingers'—can say this?"

"The enemy is E. coli, Ponton, not rare gourmet delicacies. As long as you don't mind the legs getting stuck between your teeth, locusts can be quite tasty."

"*Oui*," Clouseau interjected behind them. "You know, while considering a stint in the French Foreign Legion, I imagined a delightful recipe for locusts—a little butter, a little white wine, fresh tarragon." He kissed the tips of his fingers. "The perfect, impromptu desert meal. I wonder how the Aussies have prepared them?"

The Pink Panther's Just Desserts

Onstage, Chef Pennsbury was explaining just that: "In our modern take on this ancient recipe, we use Taiwanese swamp locust because of their size and creamy taste, and because their arthropod shells are relatively thin. Care must be taken to cook only live locusts. Postmortem is very rapid in insects and the fetid flesh tastes very unpleasant . . ."

The judges found the spices interesting, the shells nicely crunchy. Unfortunately for the Bandicoots, the failure to use enough butter, left the locust meat somewhat dry and unpalatable, and it was clear that the judges were not impressed.

After a short deliberation to calculate their scores, the judges returned their verdict. It was a frowning Gary Kehoe who made the announcement. "The First Course gold medal for this year's World Food Expo goes to France's Yves Petit, the champion of Appetizers and Hors d'oeuvres."

TWENTY-TWO

Midnight Snack

After the official medal presentation, the French team honored Yves Petit with a victory dinner at Michael White's Fiamma.

The restaurant's menu, which featured modern Italian cuisine culled from every region on the Peninsula, ranged far enough and wide enough to satisfy the varying tastes and demands of the discerning team members—with the exception of the Marquis Marcel De Salivon.

Fatigued from a long day of carting around Kevlar and fretting about Chef Napoleon's release, Dreyfus bowed out of the dinner, choosing to remain in his suite under Ponton's watchful eye. Cassidy Caldwell also returned to her hotel room.

All of the other chefs, however, as well as Clouseau and the other French plainclothes officers, were now seated in a large booth in a quiet corner of the ultramodern restaurant. They began the evening by toasting Yves Petit's success. Even Babette Beauford joined in, the ugly exchange between herself and Petit earlier in the day seemingly forgotten.

Arnaud Germaine was elegant in tailored Armani, and quite boisterous, continually engaging the shy Xavier Izard in conversation, drawing the man out of his shell. Seated next to Izard, Babette wore a strapless black evening gown, her hair down instead of in its usual severe bun. Though the woman refused to abandon her black, heavy framed glasses, Clouseau found her softer look most enchanting.

The taciturn Henri Le Rhone, wearing his rustic fishing cloths, drank heartily as he sampled a number of dishes on Fiamma's seafood menu. Though he joined in the toasts to Petit, it was clear no love was lost between the two.

Over several bottles of select wines, and a delicious array of dishes, the genial good fellowship continued. Everyone was inebriated by the time the aperitifs were served—with the exception of Babette, whose turn it was to compete the next day.

Petit noticed Babette's teetotalism and poured a glass for her. "Drink with us, my little vegetable diva," he urged, his words slurring as he pushed the wine toward her.

"No, no," Babette insisted, checking her delicate silver wristwatch. "It is already close to ten o'clock and I still have work tonight. I must compete tomorrow."

Petit snorted. "You! Compete? They'll eat you alive . . . like that little guinea pig."

Babette gaped in shock, unable to believe the man had so rudely and publicly insulted her.

Through bleary eyes, Yves Petit addressed the chefs around him. "Time was a real chef could select his ingredients when the markets opened, cook all day and into the evening, and then close the wine shops with his friends. But this wilted flower," Petit shot a derisive look at Babette. "She is afraid of life. She does not smile, she never laughs, and she does not drink. She probably does not even—"

"Enough!" Arnaud Germaine warned.

But Petit did not stop. He stood up on shaky legs and stared down at Babette Beauford, who was now flushed with humiliation.

"Look at her!" Petit cried, loud enough to draw the attention of half the restaurant. "Babette the vegetable diva. She wants to be a world-class chef, but she won't even eat meat!"

Clouseau was appalled by Yves Petit's ugly, ungentlemanly display. At booths around them, heads turned. Among them, the inspector noticed several of the judges, including Gary Kehoe.

This is quite disasterous! Clouseau realized. "Sir, you are causing a scene," he whispered to Petit, hauling the man back down to his seat.

"Don't touch me, pig!" Petit cried. "You policemen all stink like chitlins."

"Shut up! Just shut up!" Babette insisted, rising to her feet. Her eyes were glistening behind her glasses. She was very obviously near tears. "I do not have to sit here and listen to this rubbish! I have hours of work to do, so I am going back to the kitchen to prepare my menu . . ."

Then the woman shot a glare of naked hatred at the drunken Petit. "And if you come anywhere near me tonight or tomorrow during the competition, this vegetable diva will shove her paring knife right into your ear!"

All eyes followed Babette as she gathered her dignity,

spun on her sensible heels, and stalked out of the restaurant.

"Ah, my Babette," Arnaud Germaine murmured. "There goes one helluva woman."

Upstairs, in the Grand Tower, all was quiet. Ponton exhaled with great relief when Officer Lamothe arrived, just after midnight, to take over sentry duty in the De Salivon suite. The long day finally catching up with him, Ponton locked the door behind him with a weary sigh, happily leaving the demanding Chief Inspector Dreyfus in the care of Officer Lamothe.

On the way back to his hotel room, Ponton passed Cassidy Caldwell's suite. To his surprise, he noticed her door opening.

"Oh, hi!" she said, stepping into the hallway.

The sight of Cassidy's carrot curls made Ponton's fatigue almost magically vanish. "Can you not sleep?" he asked.

She sighed. "Strange bed. And I was getting a bit . . . peckish."

"Excusez-moi?"

"I was getting a little hungry, Gilbert—and before you run away again—what I'm hungry for is food, not . . . you know . . ."

"Oui, mademoiselle. You must pardon my reaction last evening. You, uh . . . *surprised* me."

"Yeah, I noticed . . . So, I guess it's true about you Frenchmen then? You're into the whole romance thing."

"Romance *thing*?"

"You like to move at a slower pace, notwithstanding your immediate superior."

"Ah, *oui.* Inspector Clouseau has always been . . . how do you Americans say it? Hot to trot?"

Midnight Snack

"Good gravy, Gilbert, we 'Americans' haven't said 'hot to trot' for at least fifty years." Cass shook her head. "French TV must still be airing old reruns of *Happy Days*."

"Ah, *Happy Days*! Fonzie and Potsie, *oui*? And Joanie and Chachie. Very amusing, although not as humorous as *Green Acres*."

"Small world, isn't it?"

Ponton smiled. "If you are hungry, mademoiselle, then why did you not call the room service? I am told it is superb. The sous-chefs are ordering up all the time—not that they talk to me about it, but—"

Cass shook her head. "I can't order room service. Who knows how long that stuff sits out on a tray? And then they have to bring it up through all these dirty, public hallways, where people can sneeze on it, or even touch it." She shuddered.

Ponton nodded. "I have a suggestion. I am hungry, too. Why do we not both go down to the French team's kitchen? I have the key in my pocket. The pantry is fully stocked. We can make something for ourselves."

"I don't know. Babette Beauford might be there, working. She's competing tomorrow."

"If she is there, we will simply leave," Ponton replied. "Or, who knows? Perhaps she will welcome two willing tasters."

Cass smiled, liking that idea. She took his muscular arm. "Okay, Gilbert, you win. Let's go."

The team kitchens were backstage, in the wings of the Grand Garden Arena. Though it was late, the halls around the kitchens were still busy, and the cooking smells ranged from intriguing to mouthwatering. When Ponton and Cass reached the French team's kitchen, the door was locked.

"See," Ponton said with a grin. "Mademoiselle Beauford has retired for the night."

He unlocked the door and they stepped inside. The kitchen was dark, the only sound the hum of the massive Sub Zero refrigerators. Ponton fumbled for the light switch on the wall, and banks of fluorescent lights sprang to life.

"Good gravy!" Cass shouted and abruptly turned away.

Ponton caught her in his arms and stared at the bloody mess sprawled across the countertop.

"Is it . . . Is he?" Cass stammered.

"Oui. It is Yves Petit. And he is quite dead."

Pushing Cass behind him, Ponton leaned closer and examined the victim in the harsh light. The diminutive chef seemed even smaller in death. His eyes were open and unfocused, his mouth gaping in surprise.

"Mon dieu, the knife!" Ponton exclaimed. "The knife that killed the man is still in his ear!"

TWENTY-THREE

A Diva Takes a Fall

After Ponton reported the murder, it took nearly twenty minutes for Officer Lamothe to locate Inspector Jacques Clouseau. He finally found him at Fiamma, swilling aperitifs with Henri Le Rhone and a very pretty waitress who had gone off duty.

Lamothe whispered the dire news in Clouseau's ear, which seemed to sober the inspector faster than a dash of ice water to the face or a gallon of strong, black coffee poured down his gullet!

Clouseau rose on unsteady legs, muttered his excuses, and left the restaurant. Chef Le Rhone was too far gone to notice his departure. When the still-befogged inspector reached the French kitchen, he discovered the Las Vegas Metropolitan Police Department had arrived ahead of him.

Though ribbons of yellow police tape crisscrossed the

doorway, Inspector Clouseau barged through. A horde of crime-scene technicians and forensics experts surrounded the counter in the center of the kitchen. The inspector stepped forward, to get a glimpse of what they were doing—only to be confronted by an imposing Amazon of a woman with shoulder-length straw-blond hair and a face as pointed as the Wicked Witch of the West's.

"Ah," Clouseau exclaimed with a crooked, drunken smile. "The lovely Detective Van Dyke—Kirsten, if I may be so bold."

Clouseau took the woman's hand and kissed it. His lips touched latex gloves. Detective Van Dyke sniffed the pervasive scent of alcohol that permeated the air around Clouseau.

"You may *not*," she said coolly, withdrawing her hand.

Clouseau was unperturbed. "And your boss, Captain Tight-ass. Is she here? If so, please send her my regards."

"It's *Titus*. Emma Titus. And she's a *captain* now, so watch how you pronounce it, Inspector." Detective Van Dyke glanced nervously over her shoulder. "I'll break the news to her that you're back here again. But right now, I have someone to track down so I've got to go . . ."

"Always busy, eh? You elusive little minx."

Detective Van Dyke wasn't sure what she'd heard. The inspector was slurring his words. "Excuse me?" she asked.

"Never mind," Clouseau replied. "Here comes the graceful and curvaceous Mademoiselle Tight-ass now."

Captain Emma Titus approached Clouseau with determined strides. She stood a head taller than the Frenchman, her business suit's charcoal color nicely accented her creamy complexion and its cut stylishly displayed her shapely figure. The woman's long red hair was swept back into a perky ponytail that bounced around her long, slim neck. There was nothing perky about the woman's demeanor, however, or the scowl with which she greeted Inspector Clouseau's arrival.

"What are you doing back here?" Captain Titus demanded. "Nobody told me you were a part of the French protection detail."

Clouseau pouted. "Is that any way to greet the man who helped your department solve the Baby Pink Diamond theft and the kidnapping of Crystal Ray?"

"Beginner's luck," Titus replied. Then she jerked her head in the direction of the activity inside the busy kitchen. "The stiff. Is he one of yours?"

Clouseau frowned, nodded. "May I see him?"

Titus led Clouseau to the counter. "Excuse us," she told the technicians working over the dead man. They parted and the inspector swallowed hard when he saw the lifeless face of Yves Petit.

"Another victim of our serial killer," the inspector sighed.

"Yeah, I heard something to that effect from the couple who stumbled upon the body."

Emma Titus stepped aside, and Clouseau finally noticed Ponton and Cassidy slumped together on a bench in the corner. Ponton's arm was draped protectively around Cassidy's small shoulders. The pair were being questioned by three detectives. One of them was Captain Titus's aide, Detective Erika Mann.

"I need to speak with them," Clouseau said, taking a step forward. Emma Titus stopped him with a restraining palm to his chest.

"You can have your little chat when our interrogation is over. Meanwhile, they belong to me."

"But surely you know that members of the French team have been stalked. Assassinated—" Clouseau declared.

"I think the whole story sounds fishy. I have a much more likely suspect—"

Clouseau's jaw dropped. "*Non!* You've solved the mystery already. Good job! We have been hunting this assassin for months! Do you have the culprit in custody?"

"We expect to make an arrest shortly." Emma Titus's expression was smug, and her self-congratulatory mood infectious, spreading to the rest of the forensics staff.

"I'm not surprised the Sûreté was stalled," Captain Titus continued. "Here in the United States, our law enforcement agencies use logic, reason, and cutting-edge investigative technology to hunt down perps. That's why two out of three homicides in America are solved within twenty-four hours. And by the way—those statistics are a little bit better here in Las Vegas."

Captain Titus fixed her gaze on the French detective. "While we wait for an arrest, would you like to examine the crime scene?"

"*Oui,*" Clouseau replied. "And perhaps you will reveal the identity of your suspect . . . *and* explain your deductive reasoning to me, Captain."

"It would be my pleasure, Inspector," Titus replied imperiously.

They approached the corpse. Clouseau leaned over the dead man, noted the knife in his ear, the clotted blood.

"The blade entered the ear and was driven into the brain," Emma Titus explained. "Death was nearly, but not quite instantaneous, which explains the look of surprise on the deceased's face . . ."

"The blood runs down his shirt, stains his pants," Clouseau

observed. "Petit was on his feet when he was assaulted."

Captain Titus raised a manicured eyebrow, nodded. "Mr. Petit *was* standing up—"

"*Chef* Petit," Clouseau corrected pointedly as he stared at the body. "*World Food Expo Gold Medal Award-winning Chef Petit . . .*" He slipped off his hat, clutched it to his heart. "Let us give the dead their due, madamoiselle."

Titus realized the alcohol he'd consumed had made Clouseau maudlin. She rolled her eyes. "You can see by the angle of the knife that *the victim* was killed by someone shorter than himself. The penetration was made with an upward thrust . . ."

"Curious," Inspector Clouseau said, rubbing his chin. "Yves Petit is a very short man."

"Indeed," Emma Titus replied. "According to copies of the passports I've obtained, Mr. Petit was the shortest *man* on the French team."

"What are you getting at, Captain?" Clouseau demanded.

At that moment, Kirsten Van Dyke returned to the kitchen, leading Babette Beauford. The petite French woman seemed very confused. She was bleary-eyed, sans glasses, hair touseled, wrapped in a thick robe, as if she'd been rousted from sleep. The vegetarian chef gasped in horror when she saw the corpse on the countertop.

"Ms. Beauford, come closer, please," Emma Titus commanded.

Detective Van Dyke gave her a push and Babette stumbled forward. Her stare fixed on the corpse, the woman's eyes widened more with each step.

"Do you recognize the engraving on this knife?" Emma Titus asked.

Babette drew her glasses out of her robe and put them on.

She studied the blade for a moment then looked away and nodded.

"It belongs to me," she said.

"And did you not threaten to stick a knife into the ear of this very man in the dining room of Fiamma earlier this evening?"

Babette's jaw went slack. "Surely, you don't think—"

Clouseau stepped forward in outrage. "How can you suggest such an absurd theory?"

"I was there, Inspector." It was Kirsten Van Dyke who spoke. "I was eating with my fiancé in the same dining room. I witnessed the entire confrontation with my own eyes."

Emma Titus faced Clouseau. "You were there, too, Inspector. You heard the suspect threaten the victim, did you not?"

"Oui, oui . . . But I am sure Babette was only speaking out of the anger of the moment," Clouseau insisted. "The murderer must have overheard the exchange and mimicked the crime in order to implicate her, or perhaps—"

"Excuse me, Captain," Erika Mann interrupted. "We lifted one good fingerprint off the knife. It's a positive match with the fingerprints Interpol provided."

"Prints of whom?" Clouseau demanded.

But Emma Titus ignored him. Instead, she addressed the stunned vegetarian chef. "Babette Beauford, you are under arrest for the murder of Yves Petit, a French citizen—"

"No." Babette gasped for air. "I'm innocent!"

Detective Van Dyke grabbed the woman's arm, fighting the chef as she began to struggle.

"You have the right to remain silent," Emma Titus continued. "Anything you say can be held against you in a court of law . . ."

*   *   *

Shortly after Babette's arrest, an emergency meeting of the French team was convened. Chief Inspector Dreyfus was furious to learn of the murder, even angrier to discover Inspector Clouseau was drinking on duty.

"The murderer was devilishly clever," Clouseau said.

"Babette? Clever?" Arnaud Germaine shook his head doubtfully.

"Not her, you baboon!" Clouseau cried. "I am speaking of the *real* killer."

"I do not understand," Ponton said. "If the killer wished to sink the French team, then why not go after Chef Germaine here? Or Henri Le Rhone? Yves Petit already won the gold medal. His job was done."

Clouseau leaped to his feet, paced the De Salivon suite. "Ponton, you miss the assassin's true plan!"

"Which was?"

"To frame poor Mademoiselle Beauford, removing her from the competition!" The room suddenly began to spin. Clouseau sat down, clutched his head in his hand. "I should have foreseen this development. I blame myself!"

"I blame you, too," Dreyfus cried. "And when we get back to France, I'll see that you pay for your stupidity."

"Chef De Salivon, calm yourself," Trade Minister Marmiche pleaded. "Recriminations will not win the competition tomorrow morning."

"Nothing will," Arnaud Germaine said. "Without Babette, we are sunk."

Clouseau observed the muscle-bound chef, felt a stab of envy. Despite the copious amounts of alcohol the big man had consumed, Germaine still seemed clear eyed and composed. The same could not be said for Henri Le Rhone.

"The butcher is correct," slurred the seafood chef, clutching his aching head. "It's one o'clock in the morning. Babette is locked up in the local version of the Bastille, and I *do not* do salads or vegetables. None of us do."

"I do," said a soft, timid voice.

Trade Minister Marmiche, who'd been slumped in his chair, suddenly sat up. "Izard? Was that you who spoke?"

The little chef nodded. "Back home, in Baie de Mai, in zee south of France . . . My brother-in-law . . . My sister's husband. He's a vintner who distills an excellent champagne vinegar. I told him zat he should bottle it, but Marcel tells me he only makes a ver-ry small amount—"

"What are you saying, man?" Marmiche demanded.

Izard shrugged. "Mademoiselle Beauford has already selected many excellent vegetables. With the champagne vinegar, and perhaps some of my grandfather's truffle oil—"

"You have these ingredients with you?" the trade minister asked hopefully.

Xavier Izard's head bobbed like a plastic bath toy. "*Oui, oui . . .*"

Marmiche looked at the others. "You are the team," he said. "So you make the decision. Should we allow Xavier Izard to take Babette's place?"

Dreyfus nodded. Henri Le Rhone frowned as he weighed their options. "What choice do we have?" he asked, then nodded too.

Finally, Arnaud Germaine patted Izard on the back—so hard it nearly bowled the little man over. "Xavier Izard is our substitute chef. I say let the man cook!" Germaine declared.

TWENTY-FOUR

Femme—Fatal

It was two o'clock in the morning when Inspector Clouseau finally returned to his suite. His mood was foul—a result of the dressing down he received at the hands of Chief Inspector Dreyfus—and his mind was still fogged by alcohol. Drunkenly, he fumbled in his pocket for the card key, slipped it through the slot.

Stumbling through the door, Clouseau was stopped in his tracks when he found himself staring into a pair of familiar, dark, almond-shaped eyes.

"Hello, Jacques," Rita Saffron purred seductively from Clouseau's bed. "I've been waiting for you. What took you so long?"

"Work, my little Shiva. But how did you get in?"

The statuesque brunette sat up in bed, shook out her silky, raven locks. Clouseau recognized the black onyx dangling enticingly near her ample cleavage. Rita Saffron was wearing little else, and her naked, cocoa-hued flesh gleamed in the dim light of the bedside lamp.

She lifted one dainty hand. Pinched between two fingers was a key card. Rita nibbled the plastic edge with sharp white teeth. "You gave me the key, remember?"

Clouseau blinked dazedly. "I recall *losing* one . . . and, at the moment, little else about that night."

The woman pouted her ruby lips. "Are you angry with me?"

Clouseau shook his head, as much to clear it as to deny the woman's assertion. "No, no, my saucy dove. Not at all."

She grinned, and the light caught her high cheekbones and predatory smile. Rita Saffron crossed her long, silky legs and patted the sheets beside her. "Come to bed, silly boy."

"Into the breach, dear friend," Clouseau muttered. The inspector ripped off his hat, tossed his rumpled mackintosh over a chair, took off his suit coat and slumped onto the bed. Rita began to knead his shoulders, unbutton his shirt. Clouseau groaned in animal satisfaction.

"Did you have a very hard day, darling?" Rita asked.

"You cannot imagine . . . What I went through . . . Not even including . . . Yves Petit's horrible murder," Clouseau muttered between sighs.

Rita Saffron's eyes went wide with surprise, though she continued the massage without breaking stride.

"A little more . . . to the left, my dear," Clouseau mumbled.

Rita Saffron reached out with one hand, to open the tiny handbag she'd left on the nightstand. She toggled the switch on the miniature tape recorder hidden inside, then resumed Clouseau's massage.

"Right here?" Rita asked.

"Oui, oui," Clouseau said, exhaling the stress.

"It must have been terrible for you . . . the murder . . . . Tell Rita all about it."

"It *was* terrible," Clouseau said, nodding languidly. "Now the police think Babette Beauford is the murderer . . ."

"But she can't be the killer," Rita cooed, her hot breath tickling Clouseau's ear. "She has to prepare the vegetable dish in the competition tomorrow."

Clouseau giggled, close to hysterically. "She won't be doing that . . . Not from the local lockup, or wherever the police have taken her!"

The inspector was interrupted by a knock.

"Coming," Clouseau called, rolling out of bed. Rita Saffron ducked under the sheets as Clouseau stumbled to the door. A waiter stood there, with a bottle of champagne on ice, two glasses.

"Thank you, my good man," Clouseau said. He fished in his pocket, came up clutching a fistful of Euros. But to his surprise, the waiter had fled—without waiting for his tip.

"Champagne!" Rita Saffron cried. "How delightful!"

"Yes, I must agree," Clouseau replied, assuming Rita must have ordered it. "Champagne is always a delight."

Clouseau lifted the bottle to find that the waiter had already popped the cork. He poured—rather sloppily, handing one glass to Rita. He filled the other to the brim.

"Oui, that *is* what I need. More alcohol," Clouseau decided, placing his glass on the night table beside him. Rita set her glass on the other table, near her leather shoulder bag.

"Where were we," she said softly, her deft hands caressing the small of his back.

"Oh, you know," Clouseau said dreamily. "You were doing

that wonderful massage thing, and I was moaning a lot . . ."

Rita put her hands on his shoulders and Clouseau was soon moaning again. Kneeling behind him on the bed, she pressed her naked breasts against his back while stroking his neck.

"That feels soooo good . . ."

"I want you to forget your troubles," Rita purred. "Forget that there is no one to compete tomorrow . . ."

"That little fellow . . . Xavier Izard . . . He will substitute . . ." Clouseau grunted.

"But he is an unknown, a nobody," Rita replied.

Clouseau snorted. "You think he's a nobody . . . Wait until you see De Salivon . . ."

Again Rita's reaction was shock. "The Marquis De Salivon is the greatest chef in the world. I can't wait to see him prepare the dessert."

Clouseau giggled again. "The real De Salivon is great, perhaps . . . But we have . . . only my boss . . . the phony gourmet!"

Rita's nimble fingers continued to probe Clouseau's soft spots. "Are you saying De Salivon is not the real De Salivon?"

Clouseau's grin was crooked, his tone bitter. "That's exactly what I am saying . . . my little minx . . . The real De Salivon continues his exile from public life . . . To be replaced by Chief Inspector Charles Dreyfus . . . The Captain Bligh of the *Police Nationale*! The Simon Legree of the Sûreté!"

Clouseau blinked, spied the champagne bubbling in the glass. "Enough of this," he cried. "Let us toast—"

Drunkenly, Clouseau swept his glass off the nightstand, spilling it all over himself. "*Mon dieu*, what a mess!"

"Go to the bathroom and dry yourself off," Rita said. "I'll be here waiting for you when you get back."

Clouseau, dripping, stumbled to the bathroom and closed the door. As soon as he was gone, Rita dived across the bed and grabbed the tape recorder. She rewound the tape a little and checked the sound. The recording was perfect.

Rita grinned and tucked the recorder back into her purse.

"This calls for a toast," she said, lifting her glass. "To me, the journalist who came here for a simple culinary scoop, and who's leaving with the Pulitzer Prize-winning story of the year!"

Rita Saffron drained the glass, set the empty crystal aside. She took a deep breath, which oddly failed to fill her lungs. Suddenly she felt dizzy, flushed. Panicking a little, she struggled for breath, even as her heart began to race—even as the poison took effect.

As her respiratory system became paralyzed, she felt her limbs move convulsively. She tried to speak, to call for help, but her vocal cords seemed to be frozen, too.

"Here I come!" Clouseau called as he flung open the door. The inspector emerged from the bathroom wrapped only in a towel. His desire for the young East Indian woman quite evident, despite the copious amounts of alcohol he'd consumed.

Rita Saffron, eyes wide, moved her lips, but no sound emerged.

"Struck speechless with desire, eh?" Clouseau crowed. "There's no shame in it. You would not be the first!"

Eyes bulging, Rita staggered to her knees, reached out her arms imploringly.

"Here I come, my dear," Clouseau cried, galloping across the suite. He caught the woman just as she toppled over the side of the bed. Clouseau rained kisses on her slack lips, her flushed cheeks for several long moments before he noticed that something seemed strangely amiss.

"Who ordered the champagne, Inspector?"

Hands free, Captain Emma Titus squinted to read the label on the bottle. Behind her, Detectives Kirsten Van Dyke and Erika Mann worked over the corpse.

"Ms. Saffron must have ordered it. I certainly did not. Just look at the label, it's a California sparkling white, for heaven's sake . . . Oh, but what does it matter now?!"

"It matters a great deal," Captain Titus replied.

Clouseau placed his wrists together and offered them to the captain. "Why don't you just arrest me? It is my fault. It is I who killed that poor woman . . ."

Camera flashes burst suddenly, filling the suite with muted lightning as Titus's lieutenant snapped multiple crime scene photos.

"What happened, Clouseau? Tell me again."

The inspector shook his head. "It's all a blur . . . I remember we were laughing. We've done this before, you see? And then . . . then I spilled my champagne and went to the bathroom to clean myself. When I came out again, she reached for me . . . we embraced . . . and she expired from the force of her desire for me!"

Emma Titus froze for a moment. "What?"

Clouseau looked up at her with tortured eyes. "What other explanation can there be, Mademoiselle Titus? My masculine charisma was too much for a simple American woman—even one with roots in the exotic East." Clouseau's head dropped into his hands. "Lust for me killed the beauty!"

Emma Titus suppressed her amusement behind a veil of professionalism. "You didn't taste the champagne?"

Clouseau raised his head. "No, as I told you, I spilled it on myself."

Emma turned her back on Clouseau, exchanged a look with Erika Mann, who was testing a few drops of the liquor, drawn out of the bottle with a long glass tube.

"It's laced with potassium cyanide, Captain." She raised one eyebrow. "Almost enough to kill Inspector Clouseau's ego."

Clouseau lifted his head. "Potassium cyanide? Are you saying poison was involved?"

"Undoubtedly," Emma Titus replied. "And you were the most likely target."

Clouseau leaped to his feet—dropping his towel. Emma Titus, Kristen Van Dyke, and Erika Mann all yelped in horror and looked away. "Then Rita Saffron tried to kill me?"

"Not likely," Emma replied, shading her eyes. "She's the one who drank the champagne, remember. And please see to your missing towel, sir."

"Oh, *oui*," Clouseau said sheepishly. Towel in place again, he blinked. "The assassin. The man who murdered Yves Petit! He tried to kill me. I told you Mademoiselle Beauford is innocent!"

"We've got enough evidence to hold Ms. Beauford and she's still our prime suspect in the murder of Chef Petit. This . . . crime is a separate issue."

Clouseau folded his arms and pouted. "You will find you are wrong in this."

"Did you know Ms. Saffron was taping your conversation?" Emma asked.

Clouseau frowned, shook his head.

"Your friends . . . Gilbert Ponton, and that woman with the curly orange hair—"

"Ms. Caldwell?"

"Yes. Give them a message, from me."

"Of course."

"The other day, they were in my office, trying to track down the whereabouts of a restaurant critic named Rex Wesson."

"*Oui*, they told me of their theory, that Mr. Wesson is a master of disguise and he is also quite adamant that the French team should lose this year's World Food Expo."

"Well, it seems Mr. Wesson won't live to see the outcome."

"What are you saying?"

"The e-mail from the FBI came through about an hour ago on my Blackberry. Their traces identified the owner of Rex Wesson's post office box and e-mail address. It seems 'Rex Wesson' is a pen name. The real name of the person your partners were looking for is—or was—Ms. Rita Saffron."

"Rita Saffron is Rex Wesson?"

"That is correct."

Clouseau's eyes widened in shock. "Mademoiselle, I assure you, as a master of disguise myself." He pointed to Rita Saffron's voluptuous naked form. "*That* is the most extraordinary impersonation of a woman I have ever seen!"

TWENTY-FIVE

Too Many Cooks

"**M**ove that disgusting hog this instant!" Chef Henri Le Rhone's voice boomed at precisely eight o'clock the next evening. "Bad enough that meat smoker of yours takes up half the space in the kitchen. Now you have your sour, smelly dead pig guts all over the countertop."

Arnaud Germaine continued gutting the hog carcass. "Leave me alone, Henri. I have work to do. Izard did his job today, he won another gold for France, but he hogged our kitchen for far too long—now it is my turn to use it."

"Tomorrow's Main Course event requires a meat *and* a fish dish, Germaine. Your pig is only half an entry," Le Rhone insisted, "so move it or I shall have my sous-chefs impale you with this razor-sharp spike!"

Behind the raging seafood chef, four assistants struggled under the weight of a three hundred pound swordfish, its silver scales dripping with the ice in which it had been packed.

"The animal stays where it lays, Le Rhone," Chef Germaine replied. "I'm not finished stuffing it yet, and I won't be finished until midnight at least. Come back then!"

"Do not presume to give orders to me, Germaine," Le Rhone roared, "or I swear I shall split that meathead of yours!"

The butcher ripped his cleaver free from the cutting board and waved it under the fisherman's nose. "You know, my fish-smelling friend, you have been in my face all day. No wonder Yves Petit hated your guts—they smell like day-old fish and so does your personality."

Le Rhone stepped aside, waved his sous-chefs forward like a Napoleonic-era officer ordering a cavalry charge. "Attack! Attack! Run Germaine through!"

Hearing the din from the other side of the door, Clouseau and Ponton rushed into the team's kitchen and separated the feuding men.

"This is the third confrontation today," Clouseau complained. "You could not even watch Chef Izard win the Salad and Vegetable course medal without bickering!"

"That is because La Rhone would not stop shouting out asinine suggestions from the wings," Germaine declared.

"You are the asinine one, Germaine!" La Rhone spat.

"Stop it!" Clouseau demanded. "We are spending more time guarding you two from each another than from the still-at-large assassin!"

"Well, he was the one who started it this time. Germaine threatened me with his meat cleaver!" Le Rhone accused with a stabbing finger.

"That was a simple misunderstanding," Germaine replied with a grin that suggested he was lying through his teeth.

"It does not matter," Clouseau informed them. "You are close to leaving me no choice. If you do not shape up, I shall report your bickering to the judges. Then one of you will be disqualified!"

"Ha!" Germaine snorted. "It better not be me who is disqualified. France cannot win the Main Course event tomorrow with dead fish alone!"

"You know, Germaine, we do not need you," Le Rhone threatened. "Xavier Izard has proved himself today. He won the gold meant for Babette Beauford. I'm sure he can stuff a swine as well as a common butcher such as yourself, and join me in winning a gold medal tomorrow!"

Germaine replied with a mirthless grin. "Oh, I am well versed on how to butcher a swine! Let me show you how it is done—"

Arnaud Germaine lunged toward Le Rhone, cleaver raised. The seafood chef squealed and backed out the door—right into the arms of a startled Gary Kehoe.

"Oh, Judge Kehoe! Please ... Please forgive me," Le Rhone stammered.

"I've come in response to your complaint, Chef Le Rhone," Judge Kehoe said evenly.

Because this was his first opportunity to see the controversial and much-feared Judge Kehoe up close, Clouseau observed the man with interest. Despite the judge's obvious surprise when Le Rhone slammed into him, Kehoe's face remained as stern and impassive as a wax dummy's. Only his eyes seemed to contain any vitality. They burned with a near-fanatical intensity.

Clouseau was suddenly reminded of a particularly harsh schoolmaster he had when he was twelve years old. The man spanked him with a cane for the slightest infraction.

The Pink Panther's Just Desserts

His beatings were so humiliating, Clouseau recalled. *Not at all like young Sister Marie's sweet punishments. Ah, such exquisite agony!*

Clouseau quickly quelled his too-happy childhood memory.

"Please explain the problem," Judge Kehoe demanded.

Le Rhone cleared his throat. "I have insufficient space in which to prepare my swordfish. I request to be assigned space in another kitchen. Preferably a kitchen of my own, if one is available!"

"Where is Chef De Salivon?" Kehoe asked. "It's his duty, as team leader, to arbitrate disagreements between you."

Clouseau stepped forward. "Unfortunately the marquis is, uh, indisposed . . . . He was injured during the Cast-Iron Skillet competition, as you may recall. So he fatigues quite easily now. And he is trying to conserve his strength for the 'Desserts in the Desert' finale."

Gary Kehoe nodded, apparently accepting Clouseau's explanation without argument. Silently, he paced through the kitchen. First the judge examined the stuffed pig on the countertop, and the enormous steel meat smoker dominating one wall. Finally, Judge Kehoe glanced at the massive fish still cradled in the aching arms of the overworked sous-chefs.

"I see your point," the judge conceded. "Fortunately for you, the Haitian team has been disqualified."

"Disqualified!" Clouseau cried.

"Apparently the Drug Enforcement Agency had a problem with one of Chef Napoleon's secret powders. The entire team has been deported."

Judge Kehoe focused his gaze on Le Rhone. "You may move into their empty kitchen and prepare your dish there."

"Thank you . . . Thank you, sir!" Le Rhone gushed.

Without another word, Kehoe turned and strode out of the room.

"The wisdom of a Solomon," Clouseau said, awestruck.

Ponton blinked in surprise. "But only this morning you called Judge Kehoe a dirty rotten scoundrel who was biased against the French team. You said he should be *shot*."

"So I did," Clouseau replied. "But a man may change his opinion, no? Even a man such as I, whose opinion is always the correct one."

Arnaud Germaine cursed, a long, loud stream of colorful invectives. He turned away from the stubborn meat smoker and glanced at the clock on the wall.

"Nearly midnight," he muttered.

For the past four hours, he had been working to prepare his pig. After carefully marinating the flesh, he stuffed the cavity with an amazing array of succulent ingredients, from game fowl to black diamond truffles, whole onions, garlic cloves, and herbs. Then he carefully sewed the beast up again and hung the pig on a long iron skewer with stout chains.

The finished product now weighed over two hundred pounds, and it took all of Arnaud Germaine's considerable strength to mount the hog in the mammoth closet-sized meat smoker. He'd had the device flown in from his home in France at great expense, but it was worth it to the chef, who did not trust any other smoker in the world to treat *his* meats.

Working entirely alone, so as not to give away any of his culinary secrets, Germaine filled the hopper with soaked wood chips, specially imported from the Forest of Ardennes, then closed the smoker's iron doors.

Before igniting the fire under the saturated oak wood, the chef paused to swill Beaujolais from the bottle. He silently toasted Xavier Izard for winning the gold that day. The late Yves Petit for winning it the day before. Then, when he was drunk enough, he had another swig in honor of Babette Beauford, wondering how his feisty little ex-lover was faring, locked up in an American jail.

When the bottle was drained, Germaine put a match to the gas jet until he heard the whoosh of burning propane. For a moment, he allowed himself a smile of satisfaction.

"Ah, yes," he murmured in drunken French. "By morning, my pork and the stuffing inside will be permeated with the same smoky, woody taste that has been part of mankind's culinary vocabulary since Cro-Magnon man roasted bloody chunks of woolly mammoth flesh on a spit outside his French cave!"

Germaine washed up, splashing cold water on his face before cleaning his knives. He was about to go to bed when he heard the propane cut out. He hurried over to the smoker and touched it. *Cold already!* When he tried to re-ignite the smoker, it burned for another five minutes, then failed again.

The butcher groaned in frustration. He had built this smoker himself and Germaine knew the problem was with the valve, which was clogged. The fire would only burn for a few minutes before the gas would shut off. To fix the problem, Germaine would have to dismantle the machine and clean the valve, a task that would take at least an hour.

He was about to start work when the kitchen door opened behind him. Germaine turned his back on the open smoker, the pig still inside, and faced the intruder. He saw a silhouette standing in the gloom.

"Who's there?" he called.

The person stepped forward, into the light. Germaine's eyes narrowed. He placed his hands on his hips.

"What do you want?" he asked.

Instead of replying, the intruder dropped into a crouch and hurled something. Germaine saw a flash of silver, coming at him too quickly to dodge. Then the meat mallet smashed into the side of his head, and Chef Arnaud Germaine's world faded to black.

"Inspector! Inspector! Open the door," Ponton's deep voice bellowed. "We have a crisis."

Clouseau's eyes opened. Sun streamed through the window, bathing his suite in a golden glow. It was morning in Las Vegas, and Clouseau smiled at that thought.

Then the pounding on the door resumed.

"Yes, what is it?" Clouseau cried, leaping out of bed and donning his slippers. When he opened the door, Ponton pushed past him and slammed it again.

"Ponton! What the devil has gotten into you?"

The detective's usually hooded eyes were wide, almost frantic. "They are missing . . . both of them," he said in an incredulous tone, as if he could not believe his own words.

"Who is missing?" Clouseau asked, his own tone paternal, even slightly condescending, as if Ponton was overreacting to a situation the inspector could easily solve.

"Arnaud Germaine and Henri Le Rhone," Ponton replied. "They are not in their rooms, nor in the kitchen. Nor did they leave any messages as to their whereabouts. Lamothe just brought me the news."

Clouseau slipped his mackintosh over his flannel Euro-Disney pajamas, placed the soft-brimmed hat on his tousled hair.

"We must investigate this for ourselves," he declared, rushing out the door.

The Pink Panther's Just Desserts

When they arrived at the French team's kitchen, Clouseau and Ponton found a dozen sous-chefs milling around outside the entrance. None would go in the kitchen, however.

"What are you doing here?" Clouseau demanded.

"Officer Lamothe . . . he told us Germaine and Le Rhone are missing. He said foul play is suspected, so the kitchen is a possible crime scene and off limits."

"Bah!" snorted Clouseau. "How do we even know if it's a crime scene if we do not enter?"

"I'm not going in there," one of the sous-chefs whimpered. "Someone is killing us one by one. I don't want to be next."

Ponton addressed them. "Do not despair. We are doing our best to keep you safe. If you fear to enter the kitchen, stay back. The inspector and I shall investigate ourselves." Reaching behind his back, Ponton pulled free his service weapon.

A frightened young sous-chef stepped out of the pack. He gazed up at Ponton with grateful brown eyes. *"Merci,"* he whispered.

"Vive le Ponton! . . . He is armed and dangerous!" the other sous-chefs began to cheer. *"Oui, oui, Merci! . . .* Keep us safe, Ponton!"

"Never fear," the detective replied. "I shall do my best."

But to both men's surprise, the kitchen was not only empty, there was absolutely no sign of foul play. The area was neat and tidy. Germaine's carving knives were spotless, lined up on the counter. The floor had been swept, and the place smelled clean and fresh.

Not even Mademoiselle Cassidy would find fault here, Ponton mused as he continued the search. Inside the walk-in refrigerator, he found the stuffed pig skewered and ready to be placed inside the smoker.

"Everything seems normal," Ponton said, holstering his weapon.

But Clouseau shook his head. "If everything is normal, then why is the stuffed hog *not* smoking inside the meat smoker?"

The two detectives exchanged horrified glances. Slowly they turned and faced the iron smoker. Clouseau grabbed the handles, took a deep breath, steeled himself, and ripped open the door.

"Mon dieu!" Ponton exclaimed when he saw the trussed-up figure hanging inside.

"About damn time someone showed up to get me out of here!" Arnaud Germaine groaned. Blood trickled down the side of the man's head, but otherwise he seemed fit. Ponton cut the ropes and helped the chef out of the iron contraption.

"The smoker is turned on," Clouseau declared, examining the control panel. "You were supposed to be asphyxiated!"

"I know. Thank god the valve is clogged," Germaine replied, rubbing his aching, rope-chafed limbs.

"Fortunately for you, monsieur, your attacker was ignorant of that fact."

Germaine scowled. "That is because Henri Le Rhone is an idiot."

"What are you saying?" Ponton cried.

"I'm saying that Henri Le Rhone attacked me. Last night, while I was working, he came in here at precisely midnight and threw a meat mallet at my head. I passed out. When I woke up again, I was tied up inside that damn smoker. I only managed to spit the apple out of my mouth an hour ago. I yelled myself hoarse but no one heard!"

Ponton blinked. "But where is Le Rhone? His suite is empty. His bed was not slept in. And he is not here—"

"You forget, Ponton," Clouseau replied. "Chef Le Rhone moved to the Haitians' kitchen."

"We must go there now," Ponton insisted.

"Send in my sous-chefs while you're at it," Germaine said. "I need to get my stuffed pig into the smoker *tout de suite*, and I still have to fix the valve!"

They found Trade Minister Marmiche at the door to the Haitian team's kitchen. An MGM Grand security guard was with him, but the French official seemed relieved to see Clouseau and Ponton arrive.

"Something is wrong. Henri Le Rhone is locked inside, and he will not come out," the trade minister explained.

"Apparently, the feud that's been simmering between Chef Germaine and Chef Le Rhone has boiled over," Clouseau said. "Le Rhone tried to kill Arnaud Germaine—"

"Sacré bleu!"

"Don't worry, Trade Minister. Germaine is in good health."

The trade minister's relief was evident. "But what about Le Rhone? I know he's in there. I can smell the food he's cooking."

Clouseau sniffed. *"Oui,"* he said. "And it smells delightful."

The inspector pounded on the door. "Chef Le Rhone? It is I, Inspector Jacques Clouseau. Open up in the name of the *leau*!"

Silence greeted his command.

"Very well, then. Stand back! I shall break down the door," Clouseau declared.

"But, Inspector, it's a steel door," Marmiche said.

"No matter." Closeau waved his hand dismissively. "I am

a trained martial artist." He backed up, lowered his shoulder. "Make way!" he warned.

"Wait—" the security guard called.

But Clouseau was already charging. He hit the door full-on then bounced backward, into the wall on the opposite side of the corridor. Spinning helplessly, the inspector rebounded off the wall and stumbled against the door again.

The wind knocked out of him, Clouseau slumped to the floor. Holding his aching arm, he looked up to see *two* MGM security guards standing over him.

"Am I seeing double?" he asked them.

Trade Minister Marmiche stepped up and jerked his thumb toward the newly arrived security guard. "He says he has the key to the door."

"Then why didn't he say so!" Clouseau cried.

As Ponton helped the inspector to his feet, the newly arrived guard unlocked the door. Clouseau pushed past the man and entered the kitchen. The appetizing scent of simmering broth, herbs and spices and vegetables parboiling immediately assailed his nostrils. Clouseau spied the source of it: a massive stainless-steel pot cooking on a gigantic burner. The cauldron was so large, a stepladder was needed to reach the lid.

"What is that?" Clouseau asked, pointing to the mammoth pot.

"I believe it is called a *lobster pot* because it is used to boil *lobsters*," Trade Minister Marmiche replied flatly.

Clouseau snorted. "It's large enough to be a walrus pot. And do you not think it is a hazard left unattended?" The inspector turned to his junior partner. "Search the premises, Ponton, while I see what's cooking."

While Ponton searched the room, the inspector climbed

the stepladder. At the top he touched the lid. "Hot," he complained, licking his fingers.

Trade Minister Marmiche tossed him a pot holder, and Clouseau lifted the lid.

A cloud of steam roiled up to the ceiling, tantalizing Clouseau's taste buds. Salivating, he peered into the stew—only to find the "stew" staring back at him.

"Gack!" Clouseau choked, tumbling backward off the ladder. He hit the floor hard. The gong from the clattering lid boomed inside the kitchen. As the echo faded, Trade Minister Marmiche and Ponton hurried to the inspector's side.

"What is it, Inspector?" Marmiche demanded. "What's wrong?"

"It is . . . It is Le Rhone," Clouseau rasped. "He is the main course . . . Le Rhone is cooking in his own pot!"

TWENTY-SIX

Parboiled

"We really have to stop meeting like this, Inspector," Captain Emma Titus said. "For one thing, there are no vacancies at the morgue, and my homicide investigators are working overtime cleaning up after the Sûreté's messes."

Seated in a metal folding chair, shoulders slumped, Clouseau appeared deaf. His sullen gaze wandered over Emma Titus's shoulder, toward the gleaming pot in the corner of the kitchen, where a temporary platform had been erected around the massive cauldron. That platform was crowded with pathologists and forensics experts. A crime scene photographer moved among them, videotaping the action.

When he spoke, Clouseau's tone was glum. "Please spare me your gloating, Captain Tight-ass. Just tell me if your crime scene experts can offer us any details that would help solve this crime?"

The Pink Panther's Just Desserts

Emma Titus sat down across from Clouseau, who was flanked by Ponton and Cassidy Caldwell. Under their impatient stares, the captain flipped back her red ponytail and opened the manila folder in her lap. After scanning the notes she'd scrawled, she cleared her throat.

"These results are preliminary, and subject to confirmation through laboratory tests."

Clouseau waved her concerns aside. "Just give us your theories."

"Okay," she replied, taking a breath. "For starters, the murder of Henri Le Rhone was an animal-rights activist's revenge fantasy come true. You all know how a lobster is boiled, right? It's cooked alive."

"But before it hits the water, the lobster's spine is severed by a cut to the base of its head," Cass said. "That way it can't feel the scalding pain of the boiling water—presumably."

Captain Titus nodded. "In *this* case, the victim's spinal column was severed before he was placed—alive—inside the pot—"

Cassidy gasped. Ponton froze. And Clouseau felt his stomach lurch.

"The water was not boiling, however. It appears that the heat was increased slowly. Eventually Chef Le Rhone boiled to death, but his final expiration took many hours."

Emma Titus looked up from her notes. Three sets of shocked and horrified eyes were staring back.

"Well," she said with a shrug, "anatomy being what it is, those seafood chefs would tell you the same thing. The poor bastard didn't feel any pain."

Clouseau put his head between his legs. Ponton covered his mouth. And Cassidy appeared to be turning a whiter shade of pale.

Parboiled

Emma Titus decided it was time to change the subject. "Inspector, did you say that Le Rhone attacked one of his French colleagues right before he was murdered?"

"That's right." His head still down, Clouseau answered with a muffled voice. "It was at precisely midnight. Arnaud Germaine remembered exactly."

"No." The captain pursed her lips then shook her head. "That's impossible, Inspector. According to the victim's internal temperature at the time his body was discovered, Henri Le Rhone had been cooking for twelve hours, give or take an hour—at most."

Clouseau's head rose, his expression one of astonishment.

Ponton glanced at his watch. "But it is not even nine A.M. yet. That means—"

"That means Henri Le Rhone was already in the pot by nine or ten P.M. last night, at the latest. Either your assault victim is mistaken about the time he was attacked or about the identity of his attacker, or he is lying."

"There's a third possibility," Cass Caldwell said. "The killer was disguised as Le Rhone."

Clouseau nodded. "That is correct. Captain Titus should know that the serial killer we seek is a master of disguise."

"It makes sense, doesn't it?" Cassidy said. "Why not assume the identity of the man you've already murdered? He can't do anything about it."

Emma Titus looked away in thought. "That does make sense," she finally conceded, "considering that the victim's clothing and personal effects have not been located."

Inspector Clouseau lifted his chin. "Then the killer is still out there," he said.

To Clouseau's surprise, Emma Titus sighed and said,

"Yes, and it appears you were right, Inspector, about Babette Beauford. I hate to say it . . . but . . . I *am* big enough to admit a mistake. There's obviously another killer loose, and it was that person who murdered Yves Petit. I will do my best to have the charges dropped and Ms. Babette Beauford released from custody before the end of business today."

Ponton grunted in disgust.

"Something on your mind, Detective?" Emma Titus asked pointedly.

"Nothing, Captain," he said. "Just that poor Babette will get out of your jail just in time to congratulate another chef on winning her gold."

Clouseau nodded mutely in agreement, his attention distracted by the stretcher being wheeled in. Three men in plastic body suits and face masks reached into the man-sized stainless-steel pot.

"Well, I've got to go," Emma Titus said, rising. "I'll let you know if we learn anything new with the autopsy. All right, Inspector?"

Clouseau did not reply. His attention was now completely focused on the grim tableau in front of him. Once again, he felt his stomach churning.

"You know, Inspector, you're welcome to join me," Captain Titus offered, touching his shoulder.

"Join you?" Clouseau murmured, his bile rising.

"For the autopsy."

Just then, the pink, parboiled remains of Henri Le Rhone were hauled, dripping, out of the pot of broth. The sight finally too much for him, Clouseau shuddered, retched, and abruptly emptied the contents of his stomach on Emma Titus's shoes.

*   *   *

Parboiled

"Good news! It is now official," Trade Minister Marmiche announced when he hung up the phone. "Captain Titus has secured Mademoiselle Beauford's release. She will be free within the hour. I've dispatched Officer Lamothe to fetch her."

The French culinary team, the French police detail, and Cassidy Caldwell were gathered in De Salivon's suite. The Trade Minister was on the phone, "Chef De Salivon" by his side. When Dreyfus saw Clouseau, his eyebrow began to twitch.

After informing them of Babette's imminent release, Marmiche placed his hands on the desk. "Now that Mademoiselle Beauford is returning to us, Chef De Salivon and I need to know how we stand," the trade minister began. "What is happening with today's competitors in the Grand Garden Arena?"

"The Chinese and Australians have been knocked out of the Main Course competition," Chef Germaine replied. "The Norwegians and Americans have also fallen. Tonight, it appears we will be facing one of our usual foes. The Germans or the Japanese."

"And are we ready?"

Stroking his bandaged head, the big man frowned. "My stuffed pig is in the smoker now, but it will never be seasoned properly in time to meet the deadline. And, unfortunately, it was refrigerated all night, so it will probably not cook evenly." Then a smile curled the corners of Arnaud Germaine's mouth. "That said, I will easily beat the Germans or the Japanese!"

"Except that we have no seafood chef," De Salivon/Dreyfus said glumly. "And the Main Course event requires a fish entrée as well as a meat dish or we will be disqualified.

I would volunteer, but as team leader, I am only permitted to compete in the final round. However, Trade Minister Marmiche and I have been discussing this problem, and we agree that another solution is now available to us . . ."

"That's right," Marmiche nodded. "Mademoiselle Beauford will be free to volunteer *her* services. Prepare the seafood course. Le Rhone has already purchased a beautiful three hundred pound swordfish. She can work with that."

Germaine blinked. "Work with what? She is a strict *vegetarian*, Trade Minister. She will never filet and cook an animal, even a swimming one."

"But surely she can compromise, for France—"

Arnaud Germaine cursed. "I would *never* ask her to do such a thing, and neither will you, Marmiche! Babette has sacrificed enough for this team!"

"All right, forget the swordfish then," Marmiche argued. "The dish need only contain *one* seafood ingredient. Anchovy paste, perhaps? Or a fermented fish sauce from Asia—"

Germaine crossed his muscular arms and glowered at the trade minister. *"Non!"*

"I . . . I can cook fish," offered a quiet voice.

Everyone turned to face the speaker. Only Cassidy Caldwell was not surprised at his identity.

"Izard? What do you know about cooking fish?" the trade minister asked. "Anyway, you are merely a substitute chef—"

Germaine cut him off. "A substitute chef who won the gold for us yesterday!"

Cass Caldwell ignored the bickering men and focused her attention on Xavier Izard. This was the second time the shy little chef stepped in to save the day. It brought back memories of student rivalries from her old days in cooking school, and she began to wonder about the man.

Curiously, for someone who outwardly seemed to lack all ambition or charisma, Chef Xavier Izard was fast becoming the Little Chef Who Could—and that got Cass thinking.

"You see, my cousin," Izard said. "He is in zee navy. He traveled to Vietnam many times. He bring back with him a wonderful recipe for poached fish, and some delightful sauces that are not found anywhere in Europe. To poach the fish I would use jasmine blossoms and ginger and—"

"How convenient," Cass muttered.

"What are you saying, Chef Izard?" De Salivon/Dreyfus asked. "That you have these sauces?"

"Oui, oui! Of course. I brought zem with me."

Germaine liked the idea. He could see that Chef De Salivon was nearly convinced, but the trade minister was still wavering.

"Look, Marmiche," Germaine said. "All Izard has to do is take the silver. Even if I only take a silver medal, too, *god forbid*, we can still win the entire competition with the gold tomorrow—and surely Chef De Salivon will bring us the gold!"

"It's . . . so risky," muttered Marmiche, breaking into a sweat as he glanced at Dreyfus.

"We might as well give Izard another chance," Germaine insisted. "We have nothing to lose."

The trade minister chewed his lip, paralyzed by a bureaucratic funk.

Dreyfus could see that a decision was required, so he made it. "You have my blessings, Chef Izard," he said, waving his hand as imperiously as the real Chef De Salivon might have done. "Good luck!"

The Pink Panther's Just Desserts

*   *   *

That night, after the conclusion of the Main Course event, Dreyfus returned to his suite with Officer Lamothe as his escort. They paused at the front door.

"Anything else, Chief Inspector?" Lamothe asked.

Dreyfus nodded. "See that all the chefs return to their rooms, then post guards at their doors."

Lamothe blinked. "That may not be possible, sir. They are in a celebratory mood. Who can blame them? Another gold medal and a silver!"

"Explain to them that this is for their own safety. By now, even this confederacy of egomaniacs should realize they are in danger!"

"Perhaps, as head of the team, De Salivon should issue a statement," Lamothe suggested.

Dreyfus rubbed his chin. "Good idea . . . Tell them that De Salivon sends his congratulations. Tell them that the marquis is overjoyed that Chef Germaine won the gold and Izard the silver for France, but he regrets there will be no celebration tonight. For their own safety, they must *remain in their suites*."

Lamothe saluted. "Very good, sir. I shall convey your congratulations and follow your instructions to the letter."

As Dreyfus unlocked the door to his own suite, he pondered what the morning would bring. *Both glory and danger, in equal measure*, he mused. *Glory when the one dessert I know how to prepare—my grandmother's famous crème brûlée. Danger because it is the final opportunity for the elusive assassin to strike.*

Dreyfus struck what he thought was a noble pose.

Well, I will face both eventualities. And perhaps some day, many years from now, this affair will make an excellent chap-

Parboïled

ter in my own memoirs, which may ultimately stand beside the writings of François Eugène Vidocq's himself!

On the floor of his suite, Dreyfus discovered that a square white envelope had been slipped under his door. It was addressed to "De Salivon," and written in a spidery, unsteady hand.

Hmmmm . . . an obsessed fan, no doubt.

Dreyfus tore open the envelope. Inside was a note scribbled by the same shaky hand, on MGM Grand stationery.

> WE MUST MEET.
> I FEAR I AM BEING WATCHED.
> WILL TRY TO CONTACT YOU WHEN IT IS SAFE.
> URGENT THAT WE SPEAK.

The note was signed "Virgil St. Ivey, French Minister of Mental Health."

Dreyfus cursed. "St. Ivey, here?" he muttered. "Why would the fool bother me? Why would he jeopardize my secret undercover identity!?"

Dreyfus folded the letter and thrust it into his pocket.

"That bureaucratic buffoon will have to find me. I have no time to seek him out. It is my moment tomorrow, and I must rehearse. Both my crème brûlée *and* my masquerade must be perfect, as befitting a future hero of the Sûreté!"

TWENTY-SEVEN

Culinary Conspiracy

Sal Minucci stepped out of the McCarran International terminal and into the harsh desert day. Squinting against the glare, he donned a stylish pair of tinted glasses and waved down a cab.

"MGM Grand. ASAP," Minucci told the driver. "I'm not here to sightsee."

Adjusting his silk tie, Sal cursed the necessity of this trip. But, as his Neapolitan grandfather used to say—

"If you want a job done right . . ."

Sal sighed, watching his cab swerve onto the highway. He didn't know how the hell Cassidy Caldwell had managed to whack a professional hit man, but there was no doubt in Sal's mind that she'd done it.

Bruno Ponti had spoken to Sal from a rental car parking lot just a few days earlier. He'd been mere minutes away from abducting Caldwell. After some desert fun and games, Ponti was supposed to bury the girl and send Sal her driver's license—the usual hit man's confirmation that he'd gotten the job done.

Instead, Sal got the news that Bruno Ponti had been the one hit, *literally*. His broken body had been struck by a vehicle and found hours after he'd expired. *Supposedly* he'd crawled between rows of parked cars after the vehicle's impact.

Sal didn't think so.

He figured the Caldwell bitch must have done the job on Bruno herself. Then she'd dragged his dead body off the road to make a clean getaway.

Which means that bitch is due for some payback, Sal thought. *Major-league payback . . .*

Unfortunately, Sal's superiors didn't feel the same way. Not even his brother, Mario. They all told Sal to drop his vendetta against the young woman. Nobody would back his hiring a second hit. It wouldn't bring them anything but trouble, they claimed. Just get on with business as usual, they warned him. Forget about it!

But *forgetting* had never been a part of Sal Minucci's vocabulary. Once he'd checked into the MGM Grand, he intended to reassemble the pistol in his suitcase, screw on the silencer, and use it to drill a hole into Miss Cassidy Caldwell's murdering guts at first opportunity. Then he was going to watch her bleed to death, right before his eyes. And, if he was very lucky, she'd beg for her life while he was watching.

Sal smiled for the first time in a week.

Though he was righteously pissed that he had to do his own dirty work, the thought of watching Carrot Top beg for mercy held an additional, nostalgic charm. A chance to relive the bad old days of his less than sophisticated youth more than made up for any inconvenience.

Then I'll have a nice meal at Wolfgang Puck's, do a little gambling, a little shopping, and be on the first plane out tomorrow. Piece of cake.

Sure, Minucci knew there could be a snag or two. He knew the girl was here working with the French police. But even her pals in the Sûreté wouldn't be able to keep her safe 24/7. And, thanks to Sal's longstanding Vegas connections, he already had a backstage pass to the World Food Expo's sold-out finale event, Desserts in the Desert.

Yeah, I'll get to her, Sal thought, feeling that old sweet rush of anticipation. *Easy as pie.*

Two hours before the big live telecast of the Desserts in the Desert finale cook-off, the French and German teams were summoned to the Grand Arena.

Such meetings were routine. The chefs expected to hear platitudes about putting on an entertaining show and the importance of good sportsmanship.

Even so, the Germans glared at the French with undisguised hostility. Clouseau took note of its members—two burly male chefs in their middle years, a young slender male chef with tattoos and piercings, one very well fed female chef, said to be the best baker of their crew, and their team leader, a big man named Chef Horst Kunckle.

Kunckle wasn't as well known as Arnaud Germaine throughout the EU, but Clouseau had heard that his mastery of butchery was nearly as good.

"We are making a last-minute change in the game rules," Judge Gary Kehoe explained to both assembled teams. "The entire world knows about Chef Marquis Marcel De Salivon's famous three-story wedding cake, created for the daughter of the financier, Sheik Ramar Rhaimeedi of Dubai . . ."

All eyes turned to Dreyfus. Still in character, he nodded humbly in response to the praise. In truth, however, he suddenly felt queasy.

"This feat of culinary engineering is unrivaled," Kehoe continued. "And so to honor that achievement, both teams will be required to create a sculpted dessert. Shape, character, and ingredients are yours to select. The only stipulation is that the dessert must stand two feet high at a *minimum*. The higher the dessert, the higher the points, but keep this in mind—members of your team must carry your dessert through a gauntlet of steps and ramps and deliver it to the foot of the judges' podium intact. In this way, we will test how sturdy your construction truly is. The gauntlet is a difficult challenge. I designed it myself. Good luck."

After the announcement, Ponton and Clouseau departed for a meeting with MGM Grand security. Cassidy remained behind, listening in as Dreyfus huddled with the French team and Trade Minister Marmiche.

"What do I do?" Dreyfus whispered to Marmiche. "My plan was to create a silky crème brûlèe. But I cannot sculpt a towering dessert with crème brûlée!"

Trade Minister Marmiche's face went pale against his finely tailored black suit. "I fear we have lost the competition before it has even begun."

Suddenly Xavier Izard appeared at their side. "I can sculpt desserts," he said.

"Surprise, surprise." Cassidy Caldwell's voice was laced with sarcasm. No one seemed to notice.

"My uncle, he was a scaffold builder," Izard explained.

"I learned zee trade before I became a chef. And I 'ave often molded little candies out of choc-olat'. Once I even made zee Eiffel Tower. It was only a few centimeters tall, but zee concept is zee same no matter zee size."

"A chocolate Eiffel Tower . . . That's brilliant!" Marmiche exclaimed. "A culinary delight, and a show of national pride! I must go back to my suite, phone Paris at once. The prime minister's public relations office will be thrilled. Excuse me."

"I must 'ave some ingredients from zee team kitchen," Izard said a few minutes after consulting with Arnaud Germaine and Babette Beauford.

"Go," Dreyfus commanded. "If we do not have it, we will get it. Whatever you need."

Cass considered the little chef. She couldn't believe that no one yet suspected the way-too-handy Xavier Izard of the murders. *Could I be wrong?* she wondered. *I have no real evidence to bring up to Gilbert and the inspector, only my general observations . . .*

But those observations were damning indeed.

Right from the beginning, Izard had profited from the deaths of the French chefs. Before coming to America, he'd been an obscure cook in a small town, recruited for the French team only because so many of the more famous veterans had fallen victim to a mysterious assassin.

He benefited again when Yves Petit was assassinated and Babette was arrested, and again when Le Rhone turned up dead. In Cass's view, this was all too much to be mere coincidence. So, when the little chef hurried back to the French kitchen, Cass decided to follow the man and ask him a few questions.

As her old Irish grandmother used to say—

Culinary Conspiracy

"You have to squeeze an orange to get the juice!"

In this case, Cass believed squeezing Izard might just yield some juicy responses. Maybe nothing directly incriminating, she thought. But if she brought his replies to Gilbert for cross-checking, she might catch Izard in a lie. Perhaps that would be enough to convince the inspector to squeeze him further.

Unfortunately, Cass lost sight of Izard in the Grand Garden Arena's network of backstage hallways. She was further delayed by a crush of people suddenly emerging from the broadcasters' lounge.

After fighting her way through the human swarm, she finally made it to the French team's kitchen. Izard had left the steel door unlocked. She pushed it open and stopped dead.

A small man in a suit and bow tie was sprawled on the kitchen floor. A large butcher knife protruded from his still-heaving chest. Xavier Izard was kneeling over the man, his hands stained crimson, his white chef's jacket saturated with blood.

Cass gasped. Izard looked up at the sound, eyes as frantic as a cornered animal about to be slaughtered.

"It's you!" Cassidy cried. "You're the killer!"

"Non! Non! I did not do anything," the little chef insisted, stumbling to his feet. He saw Cassidy gazing in horror at his chef's coat, stained crimson.

"Ignore the blood, *please*, mademoiselle . . . It is not mine. That man, there. He . . . he bled all over me!"

"Well, what the heck did you expect him to do after you stabbed him!"

"Non! I stabbed no one!" Izard exclaimed. "When I came into zee kitchen, a man wearing a mask and all in black was waiting for me. He had a knife—" Izard pointed to the blade

still quivering in the victim's chest, "—that knife, right there! This stranger in black . . . he lunged at me. But zis little fellow with zee bow tie . . . he jumped out from behind the meat smoker and threw himself between us. Zis brave man took the knife meant for *me*! He saved my life!"

Cass blinked. She didn't know what to believe. Then the door opened behind her. She dropped into a fighting crouch, half-expecting to be attacked by Izard's accomplice.

Cass hadn't used her judo in months—not since she'd begun a surprise inspection on a rat hole of a pub in midtown and the owner had sent his biggest bar bouncer to eject her. *Mistake.* The bouncer ended up in traction, and the pub in bankruptcy. In any event, she was certainly prepared to apply her martial-arts skills should she need to use them.

As it turned out, she didn't. It was Clouseau who'd entered the kitchen. He pointed to the body on the floor. "*Sacré bleu!* Who is he?"

"I have no idea," Cass replied. "Chef Izard here *claims* he was attacked—"

"By the man with the mask, the one in black?" Clouseau asked.

Cass blinked in surprise. "The man in black? You're telling me he's real?"

"Ponton and I saw him flee this room with blood on his hand. MGM security guards were with me. They gave chase and are hunting him now."

"Then it wasn't Izard?" Cass said. "But, you see, I thought he was the one all along who—"

Ponton burst into the kitchen. "The guards are notifying the LVMPD. They lost him in the crowds and fear the intruder will escape the building."

"Call for an ambulance, Ponton, then escort Chef Izard

back to the arena. See that he remains safe. I shall take care of things here," Clouseau commanded.

Ponton dialed 911 on the kitchen phone and summoned help. Then he and Xavier Izard headed off to the arena, both carrying the ingredients the chef needed to make the French team's final and most important entry of the week.

"Win one for Le Gipper!" Clouseau called as the pair bolted out the door. He tossed a glance at Cassidy. "Is that not what you Americans say?"

"Not in this century. But it doesn't matter."

The inspector knelt down to examine the victim. His expression was filled with pity. "A single stab wound to the heart. No doubt death was instantaneous."

The man on the floor let out a loud gasp.

Cassidy yelped.

"Merely a muscle spasm," Clouseau assured Cassidy, waving his hand. "Quite common postmortem."

The man's eyes opened wide. He stared in horror at the knife sticking out of his chest, and began to flail his arms and legs wildly, trying to rise.

"Oh, *mon dieu*," Clouseau muttered. "Uh, stay where you are, sir! Try to remain calm. Do not cast about so! I assure you, help is on the way!"

Cassidy dropped to her knees, touched the man's shoulders to steady him, then cradled his head in her lap.

"I must speak with . . . Chief Inspector Dreyfus," the man wheezed. "It's a matter . . . of life . . . and death."

Clouseau shifted a coy gaze toward the ceiling. "I am sorry. I know of no one by that name."

"Good gravy, Clouseau!" Cassidy cried. "This man obviously knows the score. Cut the crap and talk to him!"

"Fine!" Clouseau leaned back over the stabbed man.

"Chief Inspector Dreyfus is inside the arena kitchen. We cannot interrupt him. The cooking contest is about to start."

The stabbed man's eyes widened. "Then he is in . . . great danger . . . De Salivon!"

"Oui, oui," Clouseau said impatiently. "We *know* De Salivon is the assassin's target—"

"No!" the man rasped, trying to sit up. "De Salivon *is* the assassin!"

The outburst seemed to drain the wounded man of much of his strength. He lay back again, against Cassidy. When he opened his eyes again, they focused on Clouseau.

"You . . . you are the famous Pink Panther detective?"

Clouseau raised his chin. *"Oui.* That is so."

"I remember you . . ." said the man with great difficulty. "I was among the guests . . . in the audience . . . when you received . . . the Star of Valor . . ."

Clouseau chuckled and nodded. "Good times, eh?"

"My name is . . . Virgil St. Ivey," he wheezed. "I am the . . . mental health minister . . . of France."

"Minister St. Ivey! *Mon dieu,* I never met you, sir, but I recognize your name. What are you doing in America?"

"I stumbled upon a . . . plot . . . a shameful conspiracy . . . to imprison an innocent man . . . because of his controversial . . . culinary beliefs," St. Ivey said. "That man is . . . the Marquis Marcel De Salivon!"

"But surely De Salivon is retired. Living in Auckland," Clouseau insisted. "Trade Minister Marmiche assured us—"

"Not true!" St. Ivey gasped. "Until several months ago . . . De Salivon was imprisoned . . . in an insane asylum . . . but I just learned this week . . . he broke out . . . and I know that he is the one . . . who is killing our French chefs . . ."

Suddenly, the doors burst open and a medical team hurried into the kitchen, pushing a wheeled gurney ahead of them. A paramedic knelt down next to Virgil St. Ivey. Immediately the man opened the fallen man's jacket to check the wound—and found that the knife blade had penetrated the man's wallet before hitting flesh. The wound was painful and deep, but not fatal.

"Let's get him to the hospital, boys," the paramedic commanded.

As they wheeled Virgil St. Ivey out the door, the minister called to Clouseau. "You must stop De Salivon before he slaughters the entire French team. He is close—close enough to attack me, so no one is safe. Unmask him, Inspector Clouseau! But beware! Trust no one!"

The man's warning still echoing in his ear, Clouseau faced Cassidy. "At least we know the identity of the killer. That's something we can work with—"

"If St. Ivey can be believed," Cass replied. "Can he?"

"I think so, mademoiselle, although he said to trust no one. Perhaps he meant himself as well. But for our purposes, it really does not matter."

"Why not?"

"Whoever our assassin is, whether he is De Salivon or not, he is a master of disguise, remember? That means he could still be just about anyone in the Grand Garden Arena. And that, mademoiselle, is a lot of suspects."

TWENTY-EIGHT

Gauntlet of Doom

"**W**elcome back to the most prestigious event of the World Food Expo, Desserts in the Desert!" Chazz Eiderdown announced.

The competition was more than halfway through, and Eiderdown's high-energy delivery had only increased during the course of the live broadcast.

"Let me tell you, ladies and gentlemen, the situation here at the MGM Grand Hotel in Las Vegas has truly become hot! Hot! *Hot*!"

With a packed house looking on, and millions of viewers watching the event from the comfort of their homes, Dreyfus and Xavier Izard draped a final coating of spun sugar on a six-foot replica of the Eiffel Tower. The delicate structure was formed out of more than fifty pounds of dark, milk, and white chocolate.

Gauntlet of Doom

Babette Beauford and Arnaud Germaine were in front of the cameras, too, because every remaining member of the French team had one more task to perform before the curtain closed.

Unfortunately, only the chefs themselves were permitted inside the television kitchen stage for this grueling final event. Team managers, sous-chefs, and corporate sponsors were barred. Ponton, along with Clouseau and Cassidy Caldwell, were forced to watch the proceedings from a small private cubicle in the broadcast area, called the dugout.

Along with a brace of vintners, exporters, and corporate executives, Clouseau was not surprised to see Trade Minister Marmiche lounging in a plush leather chair, like a king holding court.

Clouseau frowned. St. Ivey's words had stayed with him. *Trust no one.*

The inspector had already begun to wonder whether Trade Minister Marmiche knew about De Salivon's commitment to a madhouse. Had Marmiche been lying about De Salivon's retiring to Auckland all along? Clouseau wondered. Or had he been duped, too? And if he had been lying, why had he done so?

Clouseau still wasn't clear how St. Ivey had discovered the truth about De Salivon's mental state. Or his reasons for murdering France's greatest chefs. Certainly, St. Ivey's sudden appearance, as well as his claims posed more questions than answers.

Meanwhile, on the high-definition monitor in the dugout, Chazz Edierdown was providing commentary on a slow-motion replay from the previous segment.

"The German team constructed a massive replica of the

Brandenburg Gate formed out of sixty-seven pounds of freshly baked gingerbread," Eiderdown reminded the audience. "When the buzzer sounded, the galloping German chefs got out of the gauntlet's starting gate with *their* gate intact! Then they deftly negotiated the wobbly tables, and even made it up the stairs without incident. Unfortunately, Chef Horst Kunckle slipped on the ramp and they lost a little time. The wily Germans knew they had to make up for those lost seconds in the final sprint . . ."

Clouseau watched again in slow-mo as four of the German chefs balanced the gingerbread Brandenburg Gate on their shoulders. Once settled, they moved forward in a quick walk.

"The trouble came in this final burst of speed. The chefs managed to dodge the rolling cart, but look what that sudden lurch did to their masterpiece . . ."

Clouseau again felt the team's agony in the replay as the hollow confection simultaneously slid off its metal tray while it caved in on itself, the delicate gingerbread folding like a house of cards. The prolonged look of stunned disbelief, then horror, on the faces of the German team prompted a howl of laughter from Chazz Eiderdown.

"Ouch, folks. That's gotta hurt!" Eiderdown exclaimed. "The Germans haven't been whupped like that since the Russkies paid a visit to Berlin in 1945!"

Ponton leaned toward Clouseau. "Do you have a suspect yet, inspector?" he asked. "Behind what mask is the real De Salivon hiding?"

Clouseau studied the faces all around him. There were hundreds of them. Cameramen, technicians, grips. Any one of them could be De Salivon, which meant that everyone was a suspect.

Gauntlet of Doom

"Here they come," Trade Minister Marmiche said, leaning forward in his chair to gaze at the monitor.

Hand-held cameras followed the French team as they moved to the starting gate. Inspector Clouseau marveled at the intricacy of the dessert sculpture. Milk and dark chocolate formed the basic structure, white chocolate was used sparingly, to suggest a dusting of snow. The spun sugar was swirled around the spire from top to bottom. When a concealed light was activated inside the Eiffel Tower, the sugar crystals reflected the glow, creating the illusion that the monument was swathed in twinkling Christmas lights.

"That's a winning dessert, right there," Chazz Eiderdown gushed, "if the French team can rise to the challenge and carry it safely through the gauntlet."

Clouseau examined the obstacle course the team would soon negotiate. The infamous gauntlet was a twenty-five-foot corridor running between tall steel fences—a design mimicking a cattle chute at a rodeo. The entry gate was on one end, a large stainless steel table where the dessert was to be delivered on the other.

Above it all, on a podium towering fifteen feet over the gauntlet, head judge Gary Kehoe watched the proceedings impassively, his robes fluttering in the air.

When the buzzer sounded, the team would have four minutes to make it through the gauntlet and deliver their dessert to the presentation table. Along the way, they would encounter a half-dozen wobbly tables to trip them up, a flight of ascending stairs, a narrow platform at the top, then a ramp that led back down into the gauntlet again.

The final ten feet was a straight run right up to the presentation table. But it wasn't without peril. One, two, or even three wheeled carts would fire out of hidden trapdoors at high speed. Dodging them was difficult. Getting struck by one could bring down the entire team. It had been at this difficult point that the German team fell to defeat.

"Ladies and gentlemen, all the French team has to do to win this competition—and the championship title—is deliver their dessert intact to the presentation table," Chazz Eiderdown told the audience. "But can they do it?"

Clouseau watched the French team carefully. Babette Beauford was clearly nervous. Arnaud Germaine offered her words of encouragement and a surprisingly warm embrace. Xavier Izard was positioned next to the woman, his expression tense, nervous, eager. Dreyfus, in the middle, appeared convincing enough as De Salivon—calm, imperious, confident.

"I fear for the chief inspector's safety," Clouseau whispered to Ponton.

"Remember what Captain Titus assured us, Inspector. The Grand Garden Arena is packed with police officers. She said that every exit is covered, and that no one is getting in or out of here without the police knowing about it. That gauntlet is probably the safest place in the world for the French team to be."

"Unless," Cassidy considered aloud.

Ponton and Clouseau gazed down at the little American.

"Unless what?" asked Clouseau.

"Unless the Marquis De Salivon is already somewhere on stage with them," she whispered, "waiting for his moment to strike."

There she is, Sal Minucci thought with a rush of triumph. *I'd recognize that Raggedy Ann carrot mop anywhere.*

The mobster had used his backstage pass to gain entry to the event. He had been lurking in wait for what seemed like hours. When Cassidy didn't show her face for the first half of the contest, he decided he had to get even closer to the French team than his backstage pass would allow.

So while security was busy hunting for a masked man in black, Sal Minucci slipped into the broadcast employees' lounge, beat a cameraman unconscious, and stole his overalls and plastic name badge. After stuffing his victim into a closet, Minucci entered the broadcast area with no problem. Dressed like everyone else, he blended with the horde of cameramen, sound technicians, and grips swirling behind the scenes.

Now, unnoticed by his intended victim, the mobster watched Cassidy Caldwell from a discreet distance. Reaching into his overall's deep pocket, he fingered the gun that rested there, its silencer already in place. Now it was simply a matter of watching and waiting for the opportune moment.

In just a short while, the Caldwell bitch will be dead and I'll be at the craps tables, he mused with a little smile. *Just another MGM Grand guest throwing dice . . . Oh, yeah, life is good!*

TWENTY-NINE

The Villain Unmasked

The buzzer sounded and the gate opened. The audience jumped to its feet and filled the auditorium with cheers.

"And they're off!" Chazz Eiderdown yelled, cuing the track of canned music. A cheesy rendition of the *William Tell* Overture began blasting through the speakers of the Grand Arena.

Deaf to everything but the blaring music, Dreyfus and his team moved speechlessly as one, deftly balancing the towering dessert on their shoulders. As they walked among a series of metal dining tables, the tables themselves began to sway back and forth on wobbly bases.

The entire event was filmed by three cameramen moving back and forth along a pair of catwalks above the action. The narrow planks ran along both sides of the dessert gauntlet, ending at the head judge's podium itself.

The Villain Unmasked

Watching the monitor, Inspector Clouseau saw Babette Beauford bump her thigh against one of the gauntlet's wobbly metal tables. To his surprise, he noticed a burst of blue lightning. The woman yelped in pain, clutched her leg, and nearly went to her knees. Arnaud Germaine managed to shoulder her burden until the woman recovered, but the jolt may have caused cracks in their chocolate Eiffel Tower.

Trade Minister Marmiche leaped out of his seat. "What was that blue lightning?" he demanded. "Babette Beauford was nearly electrocuted. There has clearly been a malfunction!"

Just then, a strange voice came over the speakers in the French team's dugout.

"You are correct, Trade Minister Marmiche," the electronically altered voice began. "Babette Beauford very nearly perished just now, and she is still in danger. You see, each time a member of the team bumps into an obstacle, the voltage rises. There is enough energy crackling inside that gauntlet to kill a thousand French chefs—though these four will be sufficient for my purposes."

Marmiche frantically searched for the source of the voice. "Who are you?" he demanded in a tone of practiced indignation.

"Your worst nightmare, Trade Minister," the voice replied. "I am the Marquis De Salivon!"

Marmiche's eyes seemed to bulge. "Impossible!" he sputtered.

"Then it's true!" Clouseau exclaimed. "I have learned from Virgil St. Ivey that De Salivon was not, in fact, retired in New Zealand. That he was imprisoned in an insane asylum in France. But he escaped that prison and began killing his fellow French chefs—"

"And I will murder these four," the voice interrupted. "Before the eyes of the world!"

"He can hear us!" Marmiche cried.

Ponton turned away from the HDTV monitor. "But our countrymen trapped in that gauntlet are not so fortunate. They don't have a clue what is happening to them!"

The French team had just made it to the top of the staircase obstacle. They crossed the narrow platform at the pinnacle. Cameramen continued moving along the catwalks above them, recording their every move. At the top of the ramp, Xavier Izard let go of the tray for a moment. He grabbed the handrail to steady himself. An arc of electricity leaped from the steel rail to his hand. Izard cried out, jerked spasmodically. Finally, he stiffened, then toppled off the platform.

Dreyfus, Germaine, and Babette saw Izard fall, but they had no idea he'd been electrocuted. Like the audience, they simply assumed he'd taken an unfortunate misstep. They were all concentrating so hard on continuing to balance the tray among them, none noticed Izard lying in a crumpled heap at the bottom of the ramp.

"One down, three to go, Trade Minister," the disembodied voice promised.

"We must cut off the power," Marmiche said, wringing his hands. "Get our team out of there."

"I'm afraid that won't be possible," the voice replied. "Once activated, I engineered the death trap to run on its own. It will only be deactivated when the French team's dessert is placed on the presentation table—"

"Then they will be free?" Clouseau asked.

"No, then they will all die. But the electrical system will burn itself out, so that the authorities may enter to collect the bodies."

The Villain Unmasked

Marmiche's eyes were tormented. "Then, no matter what happens, the French team dies?"

"I am their judge, their jury, and their executioner, Trade Minister. And you get to have a *front seat* for the show."

Marmiche was frantic now. "What do we do! What do we do! Clouseau, you fool! Why are you just standing there, staring at the television screen! No wonder they call it an idiot box!"

Clouseau ignored Marmiche. His eyes never left the monitor. He leaned as close as he could to study a certain image.

"Idiot box indeed," the voice repeated with a chuckle.

"There, I see it!" Clouseau tapped the screen. "Judge Gary Kehoe is the Marquis De Salivon! His lips are moving each time we hear the voice in the dugout!"

"You can see that?" Ponton asked.

Clouseau shrugged. "These high-definition televisions are truly amazing."

"Very good, Inspector Clouseau," the electronic voice purred. "I knew one of you would be clever enough to pierce my disguise. I am honored it was the Pink Panther detective. Unfortunately for you, and for France, it is too late to stop me now."

Clouseau disagreed. "Ponton, you alert security at once."

Ponton was out of the dugout in seconds.

"Cassidy, remember that whistle of yours? The one you used on me and Ponton the other night?"

"When we were chasing Elvis?"

"*Oui*, go out there and use it now. Get their attention over that ridiculous background music. Stop the team from moving! I'll go after De Salivon—the real one."

"Thank goodness somebody is going to do something!" the trade minister huffed. Then he collapsed back into his leather armchair. Suddenly the dugout crackled with energy as the chair exploded with sparks. The trade minister howled once, and then lay still. The electrified chair crackled and smoked. The choking stench of scorched flesh quickly cleared the dugout.

Screaming, Cassidy ran across the set. Inside the gauntlet, the three surviving members of the French team were still struggling under the weight of their teetering tower of chocolate. When they reached the bottom of the ramp, a door opened and an electrified cart flew toward them. They barely dodged it.

Cass reached a ladder and began to climb up to the catwalk, where three cameramen in overalls were filming the action. She peered down into the gauntlet. To her surprise, Chef Izard was stirring.

"You're alive!" she cried.

He looked up at her with a dazed expression.

"Stay down, Xavier," she warned him. "Don't move."

Cass put her fingers in her mouth and blew as hard as she could. Babette Beauford and Arnaud Germaine looked up, hearing the piercing noise above the blare of the show's musical track. But Dreyfus, on the other side of the huge tower of chocolate, remained oblivious.

"Stop moving!" Cass cried down to the two chefs. "Everything metal is electrified. Don't touch anything! And do not complete this gauntlet!"

Cass kept moving across the narrow catwalk, trying to get closer to the French team so that Dreyfus could hear her, too. Suddenly, another wheeled metal cart rumbled toward the team below. Germaine saw the object rushing toward Babette. He quickly swung around so the cart struck him instead.

The Villain Unmasked

Chef Germaine grunted under the impact and felt the sting of the electric volt. He was down a moment later.

"Arnaud!" Babette screamed. She let go of the tray, dropping to tend to her ex-lover. Dreyfus stood teetering with the tower all by himself, balancing the heavy tray and the delicate sculpture with quickly weakening arms. He was only a few steps away from the presentation table—and certain death. But he hadn't heard Cassidy and he didn't yet know it!

"No!" Cassidy called, moving to get closer to Dreyfus. She passed by an assistant cameraman in overalls, standing on the catwalk—and suddenly felt his hands grab her. His powerful arm wrapped around her throat, silencing any protests.

"Not so fast, Caldwell," he hissed in her ear

Sal Minucci! Cass realized, as the pressure on her throat increased.

She felt the barrel of a gun jab her spine. "Just wanted you to know that I'm gonna drill a little hole—"

I have no time for this! Cass thought. Then she exploded like a little orange time bomb. Before Minucci had time to pull the trigger, she'd slipped out of his grip. Both hands firmly grasping the mobster's wrist, Cass heard the snap of bone, saw the gun fall from limp fingers. Moving with the speed of wildfire, Cass stepped to one side and executed a perfect judo flip.

"Hiiii-Yah!" she cried.

Howling, Sal Minucci flew over the railing. He plunged in a graceful arc, to land in the middle of the electrified presentation table. A powerful burst of lightning and a shower of sparks filled the gauntlet. There was so much voltage flowing through the table, and into the flopping form of Sal Minucci,

The Pink Panther's Just Desserts

that the lights throughout the auditorium dimmed for a moment.

Dreyfus, stumbling blindly amid the burning chaos, ended up setting the tray down next to the sizzling corpse. Blinking against the smoke and heat, he stepped back.

Behind him, Babette Beauford was helping a stunned Arnaud Germaine to his feet. Together they watched the dessert sculpture teeter for an instant, then settle into an upright and intact position. With a backdrop of crackling electricity and the burning corpse of the dead mobster, the miniature Eiffel Tower looked like it was framed by Bastille Day fireworks.

"We have a winner!" Chazz Eiderdown screamed. "Whatever the heck happened down there, it's fairly clear that the French team has scored the gold!"

Cass felt a hand on her shoulder. She whirled, ready to flip a new foe.

"My little doll, are you hurt?" Ponton asked.

"Oh, Gilbert!" Cass cried, moving into his open arms.

"Hello! *Excusez-moi* . . . But can I have a little help here, *s'il vous plaît?*"

The couple turned to find Clouseau on the judges' podium, locked in a desperate struggle with Judge Kehoe—the real De Salivon.

"You will never take me alive!" De Salivon shouted through foam-flecked lips. "I will die a martyr, and my name will become a rallying cry in the war against the Old Cuisine."

His powerful hands fastened around Clouseau's throat, De Salivon throttled the helpless inspector with the supernatural strength of a madman.

"Please . . . H-Help . . . m-me!" Clouseau gasped.

"Here!" Cass cried, tossing the inspector a small cylinder

she'd pulled out of her pocket. The Inspector caught the object, aimed, and squirted.

A chemical blast hit De Salivon full in the face. He howled as if he'd been shot. Screaming hysterically, De Salivon clutched his burning eyes—releasing Clouseau. The inspector stepped back, raised his fist, and smashed him in the jaw.

Like a broken toy, the chef tumbled backward, off the podium. The audience screamed in horror when the unconscious judge smashed the chocolate Eiffel Tower.

Clouseau held up the atomizer. "Chemical mace?" he asked.

Cass shook her orange head. "Antibacterial soap, with a little bleach and some carbolic acid tossed in for good measure. That stuff will knock out any germ!"

The inspector glanced down at the unconscious De Salivon. "Apparently so," he agreed.

Outside the gauntlet, an army of MGM security guards and uniformed Las Vegas Metro police were now gathered. Clouseau stepped to the edge of the catwalk to address them.

"Arrest De Salivon at once!" he cried, pointing to the man. "De Salivon is the murderer, and a very dangerous man, too. Use all necessary force!"

Misunderstanding Clouseau's meaning, the officers quickly jumped on Charles Dreyfus. Dazed from his ordeal, the chief inspector, the highest-ranking officer in the Police *Nationale*, suddenly found himself in an unexpected position—at the bottom of a pile of uniformed police.

"Mon dieu!" Clouseau moaned. "Perhaps I should have better clarified my instructions."

Epilogue

"**S**tart at the beginning, Minister St. Ivey," Clouseau said a few hours later. "Tell us everything you know."

Inspector Clouseau, Detective Ponton, Cassidy Caldwell, and Captain Emma Titus were gathered in Virgil St. Ivey's hospital room. The man was finally well enough to talk at length, and everyone, including Charles Drefyus, who had been brought in by wheelchair from his own nearby hospital room, was eager to hear what he had to say.

The minister took a deep breath and launched into his tale. "I was new to my position, just weeks into my job, when the call came from Chief Inspector Dreyfus. He asked me to grant the Sûreté permission to use De Salivon's name. Dreyfus said it was a matter of top-secret state security, so naturally I complied . . ."

"Naturally," Clouseau murmured, narrowing his eyes on

the chief inspector. Clearly, the man had known all along that De Salivon was not in retirement but locked-up in an asylum, or so Dreyfus obviously thought.

"But that very day, I wondered how a great chef like the Marquis De Salivon could become a ward of the state?" St. Ivey confessed. "How did such an amazing, accomplished talent end up a prisoner in one of France's most secure mental-health facilities? Alas for me, I set out to discover the truth . . ."

"And what did you learn?" Clouseau asked, again glancing over his shoulder at Dreyfus, still half-drugged on pain killers.

"I knew that before he left for his final quest in search of new culinary discoveries, De Salivon was the foremost proponent of French cuisine in all the world. But when he returned from America two years later, he had been *transformed.*"

"What do you mean, 'transformed?'" asked Ponton.

"He was no longer a believer in French culinary tradition. De Salivon had discovered the ease, convenience, and satisfaction of American fast food, of the so-called TV dinner, and the cooking of prepared foods in a microwave oven—"

"Mon dieu!" Clouseau held his head.

"His change was almost . . . spiritual. In disguise, De Salivon plumbed the darkest depths of American cooking—"

Clouseau paled. "You mean?"

"Yes! He worked in a high school cafeteria. There De Salivon learned the art of simple foods. Fish sticks. Canned ravioli. Macaroni and cheese. Pizza bagels. Tater Tots. Jell-O and something Americans call the Sloppy Joseph. And after that—"

"Sacré bleu, there's more?" Clouseau cried.

"Much more. Assuming false identities, the Marquis De Salivon worked in other food service industries—a hospital kitchen in Pittsburgh, a diner in Peoria, a food bank in Seattle where he learned to cook with something called . . . government cheese. When he returned to France, De Salivon was talking crazy—he spoke insultingly of the time the French people wasted preparing food, which is then eaten and quickly forgotten. He lauded the benefits of flash-frozen and prepared foods . . . The efficient delights of the thirty-minute meal."

Ponton gasped. "But this is pure heresy!"

Clouseau shook his head. "The man was obviously unhinged by his debased experiences in the culinary underground."

"It . . . . It was too much for our nation's traditional establishments to bear," St. Ivey explained. "French culinary customs had already been eroded by the introduction of Pan-Asian cuisine, by the proliferation of Italian, Chinese, Japanese, and Middle Eastern restaurants springing up all over Europe—even in France! There was a negative economic impact as well. Imports were down. The trade minister became involved—"

"Marmiche?!" Clouseau exclaimed. "So he *did* know of all this?"

"Trade Minister Marmiche was one of the architects of De Salivon's destruction. With the marquis spouting heresy and advocating a dietary revolution that would end French hegemony forever, a secret congress of culinary traditionalists, corporate executives, French food producers, and exporters was convened by Trade Minister Marmiche himself. During that conclave, it was decided that De Salivon would be silenced. And so he was seized by the authorities, and incarcerated in Charenton asylum. To hide the truth, the government concocted a phony story about De Salivon's retirement in Auckland, New Zealand!"

"Why this is a conspiracy of Oliver Stonian proportions!" Clouseau delcared.

"Wait just a minute!" Cass protested. "How did De Salivon get out of the madhouse in the first place?"

"After I learned the truth, I visited the asylum myself, on the outskirts of Paris," St. Ivey informed her. "I was greeted warmly by the head of the institution, a Dr. Tarré. I dined with the board of physicians, headed by the esteemed psychiatrist, Bernard Le Fethier. Only gradually did I conclude, through observation and repeated conversations, that my hosts were not the staff of the insane asylum at all, but its inmates."

Clouseau frowned. "What are you saying, man?"

"Somehow, within months of arriving at Charenton, the Marquis De Salivon led some kind of coup. He wrested control of the mental-health institute from its directors, who were then imprisoned. In the days that followed, De Salivon cunningly placed inmates in key positions, maniacs and psychopaths selected for their ability to dupe the unsuspecting."

"Non!"

"Oui. For months, these crazy men and women fooled bureaucrats and visitors alike into believing that *they* were the staff. While all this time, the real mental-health specialists had been drugged and imprisoned in the cells meant for the maniacs. Only after the plot was exposed did we learn that the Marquis De Salivon did all this to hide the fact that he had escaped!"

"Clever." Clouseau raised an eyebrow. "Diabolically so."

"Last week, French authorities swept in and quietly restored order at the asylum. In De Salivon's cell, a diary was discovered. In it, De Salivon vowed to take revenge on the French culinary establishment by killing the great chefs of France, one after the other, until they were all dead and the very notion of French cuisine exterminated! The government immediately hushed up the affair. Only through great risk to my own safety, career, and reputation did I travel here, to tell you the truth of it . . ."

"The Marquis Marcel De Salivon truly was our killer all along," Clouseau pronounced. "A master of disguise, an engineer, a trainer of animals like that killer peeg—it seems De Salivon, the perfect chef, was also the perfect killer."

Emma Titus shook her head. "We began our search last night for the real Gary Kehoe."

"Any word?" Ponton asked.

Titus nodded. "We found him locked up in the basement of his suburban ranch house. Apparently, De Salivon had drugged him and imprisoned him there a week ago."

"Early enough to report to the World Food Expo under his assumed identity," Clouseau surmised.

"Well, congratulations, Inspector," Emma Titus said, rising and extending her hand. "You have solved another case."

"Thank you, Captain," Clouseau replied, shaking hands with the American officer. "Do you hear that, Chief Inspector?"

Dreyfus, slumped in his wheelchair, lifted his drug-glazed eyes to Clouseau.

"We can return to France now!" the inspector loudly told him. "The crime is solved. It was De Salivon all along. Do you understand, sir? The murderer was De Salivon!"

Dreyfus's head lolled, then he opened his mouth. "If you repeat that name to me . . . . ever again," he murmured, his right hand making an awkward chopping motion. "I shall put your neck in a guillotine."

Clouseau chuckled nervously. "Pay him no mind, Captain Titus. It's the meds talking, you know?"

With the case solved and the World Food Expo concluded at last, the day for departing Las Vegas had finally arrived. Clouseau finished his packing early in the morning and went directly to his junior partner's hotel room.

Their flight was not scheduled to leave until late afternoon, and seeing as they were already in a casino, Clouseau thought a few hours of gambling with the remainder of their official traveling stipend would be a pleasant pastime for them both.

After all, we are still in Sin City, he thought, *and Ponton's hard work on this investigation deserves a reward. If nothing else, the man has certainly earned a few hours of diverting activity!*

But Clouseau did not find Ponton in his room.

"What's this?" The inspector murmured when he discovered the man's door unlocked, his clothes and suitcase missing. The only sign of his recent presence was a half-empty bottle of cologne and two completely empty bottles of champagne.

"I do not understand it," Clouseau muttered as he exited the room and wandered down the hallway. "Ponton knows we are not catching our plane until very late this afternoon. Yet he has disappeared without so much as a call or a message . . . . *Mon dieu*, that is not like him at all. Could he have met with foul play?"

"*Bonjour*, Inspector!"

Clouseau looked up to find two familiar faces arm in arm: Arnaud Germaine and Babette Beauford.

"Bonjour," Clouseau called as they approached from down the hall. "How are you both this morning?"

"Married!" Germaine declared with a grin.

"What?!" Clouseau cried.

The brawny man waved his left hand to show off his band of gold. The slender Babette, her hair down, her expression flushed and cheerful, showed off her ring as well.

"It's true," she said. "After that terrible ordeal, we realized how much we meant to each other."

Germaine hugged his bride tightly to him. "So after we got up this morning, we tied the knot in the chapel downstairs."

"Congratulations, indeed!" Clouseau exclaimed.

"We will see you on the plane later, eh, Inspector?" Germaine called, eagerly pulling his new bride toward his room. "We have some . . . shall we say . . . unfinished business to attend to."

"Oui, oui, of course. But wait! Before you go, have you seen Detective Ponton this morning?"

Germaine and Babette shook their heads. "Sorry!" they called before quickly disappearing into Germaine's suite.

Suddenly, Clouseau stopped. He thought he heard Ponton's deep voice behind another hotel room door—

"Ponton?" he whispered, tapping the door lightly. "Are you in there? Are you all right?"

Clouseau heard a woman giggling inside the room, and he pressed his ear to the door. His brows knitted as he heard Ponton's voice saying "little doll" over and over again in French.

"Little doll?" Clouseau murmured. "What could this mean? A code perhaps?"

Just then, a series of hard taps came down upon Clouseau's shoulder. He wheeled to find the floor maid staring at him.

"*Oui*, madame?"

The matronly woman shook her finger at him. With a scolding smile, she pointed to the sign, hanging on the door-knob.

"*Do not disturb*," Clouseau read. "Ah, *oui*, I see!"

The maid toddled off and Clouseau heard more giggling. It was then he realized this was Mademoiselle Caldwell's room!

Happy for his protégé, Clouseau grinned. "I guess you can take the Frenchman out of France, but you cannot take France out of the Frenchman, eh, Ponton!" he called through the door as he shook with fits of laughter, his fist pounding the wood with each new wave. Then, suddenly, he stopped.

"What's that?" Clouseau called. "Are you saying something, Ponton? Speak up! I cannot understand you?"

"Go Away!"

"Ah, *oui*. That I understood."